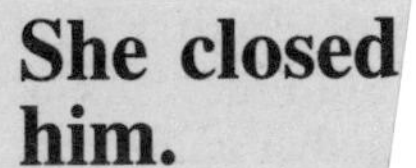

She closed [illegible] him.

Dickon was a man to rely on, a [illegible] y women must have known—and loved—

She shied from the thought. Such a man was not made to marry. Any woman trusting enough to love him could soon find her heart broken when she became a widow. No, whatever her father wished, she would not allow herself to become fond of Richard Allard. She must dismiss all tender thoughts of him from her mind and concentrate on acquitting herself well at Court and—possibly—finding herself a wealthy and steady suitor who was as desirous of achieving preferment and a comfortable existence as she was herself.

Joanna Makepeace taught as head of English in a comprehensive school before leaving full-time work to write. She lives in Leicester with her mother and a Jack Russell terrier called Jeffrey, and has written over thirty books under different pseudonyms. She loves the old romantic historical films, which she finds more exciting and relaxing than the newer ones.

Recent titles by the same author:

THE BARON'S BRIDE
STOLEN HEIRESS
KING'S PAWN
THE DEVIL'S MARK
CROWN HOSTAGE

DRAGON'S COURT

Joanna Makepeace

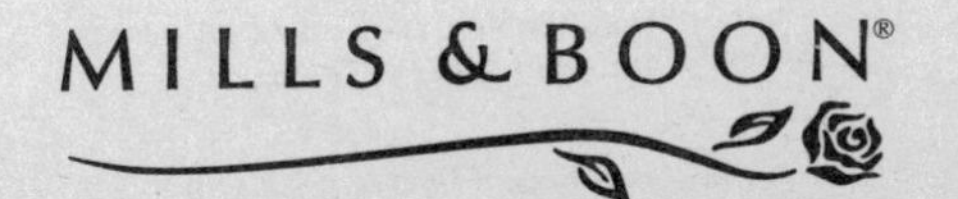

First published in Great Britain 1998
Harlequin Mills & Boon Limited,
Eton House, 18-24 Paradise Road, Richmond, Surrey TW9 1SR

ISBN 0 263 81237 5

Set in Times Roman 10½ on 12 pt.
04-9811-84013 C1

Printed and bound in Great Britain
by Caledonian International Book Manufacturing Ltd, Glasgow

Chapter One

1499

Anne would have managed the rescue of the kitten without any need for assistance had not the hem of her gown caught on a branch of the apple tree she was climbing and caused her to lose balance and, for a dizzying moment, hang almost head down in space. She caught desperately at a lower branch and managed to pull herself to safety again and stayed for a while, winded, clutching at the rough bark of the tree's stout trunk for dear life.

She regained her wits and her courage again eventually and saw she was safely ensconced on a stalwart branch about halfway up. The trouble was that her hem was still caught and, as she looked down, annoyed, and began to tug at it viciously, she discovered that her efforts were decidedly endangering the steadiness of her refuge.

She slithered until she was half-crouched, half-seated, and surveyed the terrain around her. The kitten remained on the topmost branch where it had retreated from the threat of Ned's dog. It mewed pitifully and Anne shook her head at it regretfully.

'I'm sorry, Kitty,' she murmured, 'but, for the present, you'll either have to manage to descend by yourself or stay where you are.'

Frowning, she peered round to discover that Ned and the dog were no where in sight. Her thirteen-year-old brother had declared his intention of fishing in the Nene and the hound pup had given up the chase, abandoned the kitten and run off in the direction of his young master's whistle to heel.

Fortunately this part of the manor orchard was close to the path leading up to the house. Someone, Anne thought grimly, would be sure to come along soon and it had never been her way throughout her sixteen years of life to give way to uncontrolled panic. Still, her position here was not only precarious but uncomfortable.

The weather was fine and bright this September morning of 1499 but it was growing much colder than it had been earlier this morning and she shivered and blew on her fingers. Her back was securely placed against the supporting trunk but she dared not wriggle too hard lest the branch she was actually seated on gave way. She was, she judged, probably more than six feet from the ground.

Only yesterday her lady mother had organised the household servants into the picking of the orchard fruit and most of them even now were engaged in sorting and laying the apples and pears out carefully in attic and barn to keep throughout the autumn and early winter months ahead.

Anne was warmly wrapped in hooded cloak and thick stockings and petticoats beneath her warm russet gown but the chill wind was beginning to permeate the frieze cloth of her cloak and she wished a groom or Ned, returning, would come soon now and release her from her uncomfortable perch. She prayed, though, it would not be her father.

Recently she had displeased him on more than one or two occasions and her mother had warned her many times about hoydenish behaviour. Scrambling up the apple tree would be considered so, she thought, and gave a heavy sigh.

If she came under her father's disapproving eye again it could mean a sore back and she would have only herself to blame. She had been irritable and difficult for weeks now and Ned had castigated her scathingly for causing her father's anger to fall not only on her head but on his as well. It had been to get out of the way of the disagreeable atmosphere of the house that he had taken himself off to the river.

She bit her lip thoughtfully. Her discontent had made itself felt only since Dionysia Gresham, their neighbour's daughter and Anne's closest friend, had been conducted to her place in the Countess of Chester's household where she would wait upon that lady and, in time, be found a suitable husband.

That should not be too long, Anne mused, for Dionysia was pretty enough and gentle and good tempered to boot. Anne missed her friend and envied her her good fortune, and bitterly resented the fact that her own father had made it very plain that such a life amongst the great ones of the realm could never be hers.

A sound beneath her caused her to break off her reverie and glance cautiously downwards.

A man was peering up at her, shading his eyes from the glitter of the low September sun. She could not move sufficiently to have a clear view of his face but she could see he was wearing a brown hooded frieze cloak over a leather jack, stout brown woollen hose and that his leathern boots were mired with dust. His hood had fallen back and she saw he had a thick crop of untamed brown hair.

'Mistress Eve,' he called gaily, 'are you willing to offer me the apple of temptation?'

He had been carrying a canvas pack of some sort which he had deposited at the foot of the tree as he stood, hands on hips, regarding her. He was possibly a travelling chapman, she decided. She did not know him and if he could be persuaded to rescue her before anyone came who did, she would be at a greater advantage when explaining to her mother about the tear in her gown.

She said tartly, 'You can see surely, fellow, that all the apples are picked. My hem is caught on that branch. Please free me.'

He looked round for the offending branch and made a sign.

'I see it. Stay where you are, quite still. That branch you are resting on looks somewhat too frail to hold your weight much longer. Hang on to the trunk.'

Did he think her a fool? she thought dourly. Of course she intended hanging on for grim life. Once he started to shake that lower branch it could unseat her.

She saw now, with some trepidation as he approached the tree, that he was a big man, powerfully built, and she prayed he would not use too much effort in disentangling her hem and cause the bough to shake further and dislodge her. In actual fact, he proved to be surprisingly gentle and dextrous. He was tall enough to reach up and free the hem without needing to climb and Anne was surprised when he called up to her that the material was now free.

'You should manage to climb down, mistress, unless you are scared to do so. If so, I'll come up and fetch you.'

'Certainly not,' she snapped. 'I can manage. I've been climbing trees all my life.'

'Indeed?' The voice sounded amused and she noted that it was not a peasant's voice, but deep pitched and without obvious dialect. Certainly he did not come from Northamptonshire, she determined. Possibly if he were a travelling chapman he would have lost his own dialect and adopted others as he moved around from place to place.

Now that she was free to descend she would rather have done so in privacy. She peered down uncertainly as the newcomer stood slightly away from the tree trunk now, hands on hips, regarding her. There was no help for it, she must climb down under his amused gaze. She could hardly dismiss him, as she would have done had he been one of the Rushton men.

It was more difficult than she had thought, for she had stiffened during the uncomfortable moments she had spent on her precarious perch. She almost fell the last few feet. The stranger stepped immediately close and, putting his arms around her waist, drew her gently to the ground.

She stood for a moment with her back to him, leaning against the trunk, then breathlessly swung round to thank him.

'That was well done,' she said grudgingly. 'You can let go of me now. I am quite safe.'

Grinning, he did as she requested and made to move back to his pack.

'I suppose you can climb well?' she demanded and he turned, eyebrows raised to regard her again.

'Tolerably well, mistress. Like you I have been climbing trees for most of my life though not, I must say, so much recently.'

She chose to ignore his pithy though oblique reference to her youth. She pointed upwards to the topmost branch.

'Can you get up and rescue the kitten?'

He shaded his eyes again then distinguished the animal shaded by the leaves now turning from green to golden brown.

'I suppose so,' he said and she noted again the tinge of amusement in his tone, 'but in my experience cats usually manage to descend without help if you leave them alone. He managed to get up there by himself, he'll come down by himself.'

She drew in a sharp breath of annoyance. 'Why do you think *I* went up there, if not to fetch the kitten? He is very young and frightened. He ran up when my brother's dog barked at him.'

'Ah, in that case—' He grinned and, throwing back his cloak and hood, approached the tree again and began to climb steadily.

She stepped back to watch him, a little alarmed now for his safety. He was no youth and might well not be so agile as Ned. Perhaps she should not have ordered him to climb. He seemed skilful enough, swinging easily from branch to branch after first testing to check whether each would stand his weight, which was considerable. The kitten seemed reluctant to trust him at first and retreated along the top branch, mewing pitifully.

Anne heard him utter a quick curse then he leaned closer to the frightened animal and began to murmur to it beneath his breath. After one or two moments the kitten allowed itself to be lifted up and he thrust it into the opening of his leathern jack and began to descend nimbly. Landing gracefully for so big a man, he handed the quivering bundle of black fur to her with a little bow.

'Safe and sound if still a little alarmed. Is he yours? You must keep your brother's dog under control.'

Her tone was haughty as she replied, 'He is one of our courtyard cat's litter. Cato only wanted to play. He's little more than a puppy himself.'

The man was looking at her appraisingly and she flushed darkly. How dared he stare so insolently? Obviously she was not looking her best for she could feel that the wind had caught tendrils of her hair and pulled them clear of her white linen cap and her gown and cloak had not been improved by close contact with the tree trunk. Impatiently she pushed back her hair and pulled her hood into place.

He had a broad, open countenance, dark skinned as one would expect of a man who had stayed long out of doors, particularly during the summer months. His forehead was high and broad and his nose beaklike, a little craggy. His most attractive features were his wide-spaced grey eyes and a full, generous mouth, surprising in that very masculine face. The chin was firm and well chiselled and bore a decided cleft. It was an interesting face, she decided, and tried to guess his age. There were little laughter lines around the eyes and deep clefts from nostrils to the corners of his mouth. He was well past his twentieth birthday, she thought, but he was not old, not even middle aged.

For his part he was in no doubt about her age. She must be sixteen now or almost so. The last time he had seen her she had been still a child, clinging to her mother's skirts; now true womanhood was almost upon her. Like her lady mother, she was dark. The thick masses of her hair streaming below her cap well past her waist had not been braided and the autumn sun glinted on the waving tresses, touching the blue-black gloss with touches of gold.

She had her mother's creamy complexion, too, and a lovely oval-shaped face with strongly marked but fine features and her father's startlingly blue eyes. She stood uncertainly, holding the kitten which was wriggling and scratching in her too-tight hold, at the same time trying to clutch the billowing folds of her brown frieze cloak about her slender form.

He had expected her to be tall and slim, for both her parents, Sir Guy Jarvis and Mistress Margaret, her mother, were tall and he could see that her young breasts, despite her efforts to hold her cloak close and hide her form from him, were taut and firm, pushing against the stuff of her russet gown. They would soon be looking for a husband for her, he thought, and sighed a little, inwardly. That would be no easy task for Sir Guy, under the present prevailing circumstances.

She moved a trifle uncertainly as if she was not sure how to dismiss him.

'You have come far, sir?'

White teeth gleamed in an answering smile in that dark complexioned face. 'From the north,' he said evasively.

She hesitated. 'My father is Sir Guy Jarvis and my home, Rushton Manor, only a short distance from here. You have done me a service. If you come to the manor I am sure our servants can provide you with a meal. You must be hungry.'

He gave her that little odd bow in answer which was in no way servile.

'Thank you, Mistress Jarvis.'

He shouldered his bag and moved beside her down the path until they reached the gatehouse and passed into the courtyard of Rushton. The house faced them, half-timbered, the undercroft of mellow Northamptonshire stone. The kitten scratched Anne deeply and ungratefully, sprang from her arms and shot off in the direction of the stables. She gave a startled cry. Her companion turned at once to see what had caused her distress and she sucked at the wound on her hand.

'Little beast,' she remarked ruefully, as he bent to examine the hurt.

'Cat scratches can be nasty,' he warned. 'You must ask your lady mother for some tansy salve.'

She nodded. His large hand was holding her slender

small one very gently and she felt suddenly uncomfortable in his presence. This stranger had a way of making her aware of her own childish folly in attempting to rescue the kitten without uttering one word of disapproval—yet why should she heed a passing stranger, an inferior to boot? She was about to point out the way to the back door into the kitchen quarters and quickly rid herself of his disturbing presence when her father's voice came from the top of the steps leading up to the hall.

'Anne, where have you been? Your mother has sent out more than one woman to find you—' He broke off abruptly, staring at the two of them across the courtyard; then, with that grace of movement Anne always associated with her handsome father, he leaped easily down the steps and covered the distance between them quickly.

'Dickon? Dickon Allard, is it really you?'

The newcomer laughed. 'Indeed it is, Sir Guy. It seems a long time since I came to Rushton Manor.'

Anne watched in dawning horror as her father took the stranger's strong brown hands into his own grasp and squeezed them affectionately, then he pulled the man close and clasped him to his heart.

'You are welcome as always, Dickon, you know that. Margaret will be delighted to see you. Come in immediately and get warm near the hall fire. We must order food for you at once. How far did you travel today?' He stepped back apace, frowning, somewhat puzzled. 'Where is your horse, man?'

Again Anne heard that deep-throated chuckle. 'My mare cast a shoe about a mile and a half back, so I led her to the nearest village smithy. The smith said it would be quite a long job so I thought I'd come on here and fetch her later. I was stiff in the saddle, have ridden from Leicester this morning; the walk has loosened me up.'

Anne could not meet the man's eyes. Richard Allard, the son of her father's friend, Sir Dominick Allard, the man whom Sir Guy Jarvis had served for years as squire—and she had treated him like a servant! Her blue eyes flashed dangerous fire. He must have known well enough who she was.

Why hadn't he announced himself immediately and not left her to jump to so unfortunate a conclusion? How was she to know? The man had arrived on foot, plainly dressed, if not shabbily, and carrying his own valise like a pedlar his pack. Could she be blamed for treating him so condescendingly?

Her father was regarding her and she flushed under his critical scrutiny.

'I see you and my Anne have met already. I trust she made you welcome?'

Anne waited in dread for the visitor's reply. He was facing her now, his grey eyes dancing with amusement, doubtless at her discomfiture.

'Mistress Anne greeted me very warmly, Sir Guy, and, like you, was very anxious to assure my comfort. She instantly thought how hungry I must be feeling.' He turned to his host as a servant hastened up to relieve him of his valise. 'In truth, I am not hungry, just saddle sore, as I said, but I broke my fast at the village inn where I waited for the smith's verdict about my mare. I can certainly wait until supper, but I would welcome an opportunity to bathe.'

'Of course, of course. Come first and greet Margaret. How are your parents? I trust your father's old wound does not still trouble him?'

'He still limps, sir. I'm afraid he will carry that reminder of the final charge at Redmoor until his dying day but in himself he keeps well and my mother is blooming, as ever. To me she is the epitome of the Nut Brown Maid of the ballad. Each time I come home to Wensleydale from my travels I expect to see her changed, or, at least, some traces of grey in her hair, for my father's temples are as grey as a badger's these days, but she is as lovely as I remember her when I left.'

Anne was aware that both her father and Sir Dominick Allard had served in the household of the late King Richard and had fought side by side in his last fatal battle and defeat at Redmoor near the little market town of Bosworth in Leicestershire in 1485.

Sir Dominick had taken a severe wound to his thigh in the charge in which his King had met his death, a wound that still troubled him, one that had kept him from fighting in Lord Lovell's attempt the following year at East Stoke near Newark to place the pretender Lambert Simnel on the throne. That battle had proved as ill fated as Redmoor and King Henry had triumphed again. Anne had heard it whispered about the manor that her father had taken part in it, but had managed to return home in secret without his treason being discovered.

'I'm delighted to hear they keep well and hope, one day soon, to see them both again.'

Sir Guy linked arms with Richard Allard and led the way up the steps into the manor hall, Anne trailing behind. She looked anxiously round for Ned to join them but he was still remaining out of the way near the river. Sweet Virgin, her mother would demand an account of her meeting with their visitor, especially in view of the condition of Anne's torn gown and her green-stained cloak. What could she say, how explain her boorish behaviour?

So far Richard Allard had kept the circumstances of their encounter to himself. Would he continue to do so? She did not deserve so much consideration. Now that she thought about it, his very manner and bearing, as well as his speech and mode of address, should have established him in her mind as a man of standing. How could she have been so crass?

Her beloved father appeared almost slight and spare beside this bear of a man. Sir Guy's fair hair, as ever, was dressed elegantly and his handsome features were alight with pure pleasure at Richard Allard's arrival. He led him swiftly to the comfort of the blazing fire in the hall's fine heraldically decorated fireplace and summoned a servant to bring ale and wine and take the visitor's cloak.

'Anne, go at once to the solar and inform your mother that Dickon Allard is here. She will issue orders for the preparation of a chamber. Where is Ned? He should be here too to greet our honoured guest.'

'Fishing in the Nene,' she said promptly and, meeting Dickon Allard's smiling eyes, made him her first quick curtsy. Then, grateful to be out of his presence for a while, she sped off to the solar to break the news to her mother. With her hand on the door knob she reflected that perhaps it would have been better had her father allowed her to remain in the hall. At least she would have heard what Richard Allard said to him.

Margaret Jarvis looked up hastily as her daughter entered. She was sewing at the dark blue velvet of a new-fashioned French hood and was alone. Her dark brows rose in interrogation as Anne swept in, her cloak billowing behind her.

'There you are. I have been looking for you. I wished to try this on you for size. Goodness, child, what have you been doing to your clothes? You know your father's means are limited these days. You should take more care. It is bad enough that Ned tears his hose, but you should know better.'

'I'm sorry, Mother, but a kitten got caught up a tree and

just would not come down. I had to climb. There was no one else nearby. He is safe now.'

The child was breathless and evidently excited. Margaret was surprised. Just lately nothing had excited Anne or pleased her. Indeed, Margaret reflected, had she behaved so badly as her daughter had done recently, her own father would have taken a switch to her. Guy had held his hand and Margaret had admired his patience with the girl. Her own had been fast running out.

The whole of the trouble lay in the fact that Dionysia Gresham had left their neighbouring manor to enter the Countess of Chester's household and would, most likely, attend her mistress at court at Westminster. Anne sorely missed her friend's company but there was more to it than that. Although the reasons for her own ineligibility to attend a noble household had been explained to her often enough, Anne had never really accepted them.

'We have a visitor,' Anne announced breathlessly. 'Richard Allard, from Yorkshire, isn't it?'

Like her father's, Anne's mother's face expressed immediate pleasure at the news.

'Richard, here? Oh, how good it is to have him. I shall have news of Dominick and Aleyne. It is far too long since we heard from them.' She rose at once, laying aside the unfinished hood. 'Your father has been informed?'

'Oh, yes. He is with him in hall. He sent me to fetch you. Father says a room must be prepared for him.'

Again Margaret Jarvis's dark brows rose. 'I did not hear a horse enter the courtyard.'

'No, he is on foot. Apparently his mare cast a shoe. Father will send a groom to fetch her from the smithy later.'

Margaret was moving unhurriedly towards the door of the solar. Anne admired her stately passage in her dark burgundy velvet gown. It suited her well, though the tight-fitting sleeve cuffs were somewhat rubbed and Lady Jarvis still affected the old style of headdress: small cap, hennin and veil.

Though Anne was aware of the latest changes in fashion through Dionysia who took careful note of all news from Court since tidings of her impending term of service in the Earl of Chester's household, she was aware that her mother remained as lovely as her father had declared her to have been when he had wed her at Westminster, more than sixteen years ago, in the late King Richard's time, and in his very presence.

Anne was fully aware that it was this very allegiance to the late King's household and her father's continued stubborn loyalty to the Plantagenet cause that had resulted in their present impecunious state here at Rushton.

Sir Guy Jarvis had been pardoned after Redmoor, for King Henry had shrewdly declared the beginning of his reign the day before the battle, thereby making all those who had fought for their King technically traitors. Anne's father had survived the pursuit following the battle and managed to reach the comparative safety of Rushton, but the King's officers had levied a swingeing fine from which the manor had never truly recovered financially.

The number of household servants and dependents had had to be cut to the bone and for eleven years Sir Guy was aware that his every move was watched by agents of the Tudor now living in Northamptonshire. Anne sighed resentfully as she faced the need for economy in her own dress allowance, which denied her new-fashioned garments like the ones her friend Dionysia had obtained in which to travel to her new household.

She would not have minded that so much if she had not to face the prospect of life here at Rushton, familiar and dear, but irritatingly dull. Anne had listened open-mouthed to her mother's tales of life at Court and the intrigues and adventures that had befallen her there and wished that such a fascinating and exciting life could be hers.

The arrival of Richard Allard brought home further the need for all of them to guard their tongues and behaviour. The Allards, too, made little secret of their contempt for the Tudor's claims and Anne wondered doubtfully what was the reason which had brought Richard here. Could it be to embroil her father into yet another secret plot against the King? She paled at the thought.

Only recently the arrest of the second pretender to the King's claim, the man they called Perkin Warbeck, had caused fear and despondency to spread through those families who still doggedly supported the Plantagenets and Anne knew her mother constantly feared for her father's safety.

How could she constantly live like that? Anne wondered. *She* could not. She wanted a settled, peaceful life, if not at Westminster, at least secure on her own small manor with her husband and children safe by her side. Yet she knew well that the neighbouring gentry would be wary of allying themselves in marriage with the disgraced Sir Guy, that her father would not find it easy to find her a husband.

She put to rights her appearance and joined her parents with their visitor in the hall to find that Ned had now come home and was seated near Richard Allard, listening intently to the tales of his recent travels. Anne experienced a momentary feeling of irritation that her brother should greet this stranger in so admiring a manner and regretted, more than ever, that she had had to appear before him in her old russet gown which had had to be pinned at the torn hem by her maid, Mary Scroggins.

Anne's worst suspicions were confirmed as it was obvious from the line the conversation was taking that

Richard Allard's loyalties were cast in the same mould as her father's.

Sir Guy was speaking as she entered and, at a signal from her mother, Anne seated herself on a stool by Lady Jarvis's side.

'In Leicester did you manage to visit the Friary?'

Richard Allard took a pull at his wine cup and nodded. 'Aye, I see the Tudor has not kept his word and had the promised memorial put on the tomb, but the King lies safe and snug and I paid for masses to be said for his soul.'

Anne had heard that King Richard's body had been shamefully treated following the battle at Redmoor and had been brought back into Leicester town half-naked, across the neck of his own destrier, White Surrey, wearing a felon's halter around his neck. His body had been exhibited for public view in the church of St Mary the Lesser, outside Leicester's castle and finally buried by the Grey Friars within their enclosure.

On his rare visits to Leicester Anne's father had visited the tomb, but had never once taken Anne to see it. She knew his visits there were viewed with disapproval by some of his neighbours, yet another mark against him for his commitment to the former dynasty.

King Richard III had been dead now for fourteen years. Surely, Anne thought angrily, her father and this man could allow him to rest in peace and not continue to antagonise the present occupant of the throne even in secret. If Sir Guy were to accept the situation without complaint it would be more likely that she, Anne, would be allowed to mix with her neighbours' daughters and the prospect of a suitable marriage would be made possible.

It was all very well for Ned to talk boastfully of what amounted to treason, but he was still a boy and his life was unlikely to be blighted by his youthful opinions which, undoubtedly, would mellow with time. She glared at him as he pressed Richard Allard for more news of the world at large.

Richard Allard had clearly been recently from the realm but he was discreet and somewhat vague as to his wanderings. Anne was in little doubt that more than likely he had been at the Court of King Henry's greatest avowed enemy, the late King's sister, Margaret of Burgundy, at Malines.

From time to time Richard Allard's eyes passed over her as she sat demurely and she read amusement in them. Her father had passed no comment on her recent behaviour, so she gathered that her treatment of his friend's son had not been divulged and she sank back on her stool somewhat relieved.

Supper was served and their visitor continued to regale them with news of other men her father had known and loved in the past. Watching Sir Guy, Anne saw that his handsome face was alight with avid interest, a state she had not seen revealed in him for many a month.

Afterwards, her father announced his intention to visit the stables to check that Master Allard's horse had been brought back to Rushton and was being bedded down comfortably. Ned rose at once, eager to accompany him.

Sir Guy smiled at his visitor. 'No need for you to come, Dickon. We will see everything is done for your horse's comfort. Make further acquaintance with my daughter.' He smiled at Anne genially and moved to the screen doors. Lady Jarvis had left earlier, murmuring that she must ensure that the sheets in Master Allard's chamber had been aired and the warming pan brought into use. Anne nervously found herself alone with their visitor.

'Sir,' she said hesitantly, 'I am grateful that you have made no reference to my boorish behaviour in the orchard. My father would have been gravely displeased.'

He shrugged lightly. 'You were not to know who I was.'

'No,' she stammered awkwardly, 'but—but I am enjoined to be courteous to everyone I meet.'

'Indeed? And are you?'

'Yes, no—most of the time,' she added lamely. 'You caught me when—when my spirits were low.'

'You must have been vastly uncomfortable up that tree, possibly frightened.'

'Oh, not frightened.' She found herself laughing as his grey eyes twinkled and she realised he was teasing her gently. 'Well, I was just beginning to panic, just a little, and Ned seemed completely out of range of my calling, but—but it was not that.'

'Oh? You are not happy here at Rushton?'

'Yes, of course I am—but sometimes I long to go further afield as you have done.'

'From necessity, Mistress Anne, I assure you. Often I would prefer to be living in tolerable comfort with my family in Wensleydale.'

'Then why do you not remain there?' she said impulsively and immediately blushed with shame as she realised her question was impertinent in the extreme.

He looked grave for a moment and said quietly, 'Duty calls me from home more than I would wish. My father's old injuries necessitate him remaining at home and we have duties—elsewhere.'

'And you are on your way south?' she enquired diffidently.

'Yes, I journey to London on business but I hope to return home for Christmas. My younger sister, Anne, is expecting her second child then and I am anxious to attend the christening.'

'Your sister is wed to a local gentleman?'

'Yes, she is very happily wed to Sir Thomas Squire

whose manor is near Bolton. She already has a healthy brat of a five-year-old-son, Frank, whom we all love dearly. I am hoping she will bear a daughter this time, for me to cosset.'

Anne was silent for a moment, considering. How fortunate Anne Allard had been to marry a man who loved her and to bear his children, but how could she endure the dull life in the wilds of Yorkshire?

'Is—is Sir Thomas of—your persuasion?' she enquired cautiously.

Richard Allard's grey eyes opened very wide and, again, his expression grew grave.

'Yes,' he replied, a trifle shortly, 'as most gentlemen of Yorkshire are, but he is circumspect and does not pursue his views too actively.'

She knew the unspoken rider to that was 'as I and my father and your father do.'

Her lips trembled as a little tingle of fear ran through her.

When her mother returned and said meaningfully that it was getting late and the ladies should retire Anne was almost relieved to obey. She rose and curtsied and met her father on his way in through the screen doors as she left in her mother's wake.

Sir Guy poured more wine for his guest when they were left alone together.

'How long can you stay this time, Dickon?'

'No more than two days then I must be on my way again.'

'To London?' The finely arched brows rose interrogatively.

Richard Allard nodded and drained his wine cup. 'Yes. You will have heard that Warbeck was rearrested in June after some attempt to escape and now is confined in the Tower—with the Earl of Warwick?'

Sir Guy drew his chair closer. His son, Ned, had already been dispatched to bed and he had given his servants instructions not to disturb him further tonight. Even so he was careful to keep his voice low when talking of such inherently treasonable matters with his friend's son.

'You think he may be too close?'

Richard Allard sighed. Sir Guy had again refilled his wine cup and he swirled it slowly, moodily, watching the firelight glow in the bloodlike depths.

'It would be preferable, for both their sakes, if they were kept strictly apart.'

'Surely Henry will be aware of that and take steps to see that that is done?'

'Yet, if there is danger in such contact with Warbeck, that might prove profitable for Henry.'

Sir Guy sat bolt upright. 'You mean he would have an excuse to rid himself of the Earl? Over the years he must have longed to do so. The late King's nephew has so clear a claim to the throne that it must be a constant thorn to Henry's peace of mind.'

'Precisely.' Richard stared down at his boots and stirred his feet restlessly.

'I go to keep an eye on things, nothing more. If it proves necessary to try to extricate the Earl…' He shrugged. 'I pray heaven there is no such need.'

'You are known at Court?'

'I have never attended since I served King Richard as a page before Redmoor but, like you, as my father's son, I need to remain discreet. I intend to be back in Yorkshire at Christmas. My sister Anne will be delivered then. You know she miscarried a child two years ago and was very ill. She is now recovered and happy about the impending birth but, naturally, we are all anxious for her.'

'Your mother in particular.' Sir Guy nodded. He hesitated. 'You are still unwed, Dickon?'

Richard inclined his head smilingly.

'No romantic entanglements?'

'Oh, plenty.' The young man laughed. 'I have thought myself in love many times, particularly when I was young but—I have never deemed it politic to offer marriage to any woman and I am still heart whole.'

Sir Guy supped his wine. 'I imagine your mother has pressed you to take a wife—for the succession if nothing else.'

'My father understands well my reasons. Like you, we find managing the desmesne is difficult under straitened circumstances. What have I to offer a maid?'

'Strength, youth, good health and you are not uncomely.'

Richard Allard laughed heartily. 'I am no longer so young, sir.'

'How old are you, Dickon, now, twenty-five, -six?'

'Twenty-seven,' the other replied with a rueful shrug.

'I was almost your age when I wed my Margaret.'

'An arranged marriage?'

'We had been betrothed five years earlier but her father broke off the arrangement. He wished her to marry one of Dorset's gentlemen but the fellow died. She was about to enter into a new betrothal when King Edward died and her father's fortunes were altered. King Richard saw to it that I was given my bride.'

'Against her will?'

Sir Guy pursed his lips thoughtfully. 'Perhaps so, at first, but afterwards we realised our love for each other. Our marriage, like your father's, has been totally successful. Margaret has given me her complete support. Her love and loyalty have never faltered, despite our difficulties over the years since Redmoor.' He paused and then said deliberately, 'At one time your father and I considered a contract between you and my Anne.'

Richard Allard turned bright grey eyes upon his host. 'Aye, I know, and—and I would be very honoured, yet I am old for the lass. She must be sixteen or nearabouts.'

'In a few weeks, and mature for her age.' Sir Guy frowned. 'Lately she has been restless, fretting against her exile from what she considers the hub of events. Of course, I am relieved that she is—only, I also know she will soon be ripe for the marriage bed and I am anxious to see her settled.' He shrugged. 'After all, who knows what the future will bring to any of us?'

'I said I would be honoured, sir, but…'

'You do not find Anne attractive?'

The grey eyes lit up. 'I find her enchanting. She has her mother's beauty and a combination of yours and Lady Jarvis's sprightly make-up. It is just that—my duty leads me into dubious business. Were I free to consider marriage I would request her hand.' He broke off, staring into the fire's bright heart. 'You must know, Sir Guy, how deeply our womenfolk suffer when we are engaged in dangerous work. I would not risk either the security or the happiness of Mistress Anne while I am committed elsewhere than in Wensleydale.'

Sir Guy sighed again regretfully and nodded in agreement.

He decided to change a subject which could be embarrassing for his guest. He said quietly, 'You saw this Warbeck at close quarters—often?'

'Not often.' Richard Allard's tone was wary as if he guessed at the other's next question. 'You are about to ask if I believe that his pretensions are genuine?'

'Yes.'

Richard shook his head. 'I wish I could answer that squarely. I just do not know. I saw him quite close once or twice. Certainly he resembles both the late King Edward and Queen Elizabeth, his wife. That likeness is quite uncanny. Were it otherwise I would have dismissed his claims out of hand for, to be frank, sir, he does not appear to have that about his character that would make me accept him as a son of King Edward, for all my father has told me about that man, or a nephew of King Richard. He is charming, courtly, but without that steel core which was their inner strength. Of course, his life has been unfortunate and without that training which would have prepared him for intrigue and war...'

'His confession?'

Richard Allard's grey eyes met those of his host quizzically. 'If you or I had been in the hands of Henry's officials, would we not have confessed to anything? I think we can dismiss the confession from our considerations.'

'You have met with the Duchess Margaret?'

'No. I have been in contact with Wroxeter, of course. He is her trusted man, as you know, and has been in attendance at Malines since Redmoor. He gave me no direct opinion on the man's identity, only, naturally, that he was of use to Margaret in putting a burr beneath the Tudor's saddle cloth. I know only that that slur on the late King's reputation, regarding the murder of his nephews, is slanderous.

'The boys survived Redmoor, as you know only too well. Where they are now, I cannot tell. It is just as well I do not know. Were I to fall into Henry's hands it could be disastrous to their well being if I were to be questioned on such matters. I cannot be certain I would be able to hold out against divulging the facts were I subjected to torture.'

Richard's father had made him aware that, following

King Richard's coronation, Sir Guy Jarvis had escorted the elder of the young sons of King Edward IV north to Castle Barnard, while the younger prince, Richard, had been taken abroad, presumably to Burgundy. He did not know if Sir Guy was aware of the whereabouts of his former charge. It was clear from his question that he was as unsure as all of them were about the true identity of the latest pretender to claim King Henry's throne.

Was the man who now lay in the Tower the very prince who had been escorted to his Aunt Margaret's palace in Burgundy? The man had confessed that he was an imposter, the son of a merchant named Warbeck who had been carefully groomed for his role but, as he himself had said to Sir Guy, who could be sure that such a confession had not been extracted under torture or even the threat of torture? Richard was well aware that such pressures on even the bravest of men could not always be overcome.

Sir Guy appeared to have fallen into a reverie from which he drew himself up abruptly.

'It is getting late, my friend. You must be wearied. You've been travelling some days. I'll escort you to your chamber.'

Richard rose willingly enough. At the door to the inner rooms of the house he stopped for a moment and looked directly at his host.

'Sir, as I have said, I do not expect my business in London to engage me for too long a time, neither do I anticipate any particular—difficulties. When I complete the handling of my father's affairs and—any other problem I might encounter, I would be grateful if I could break my return journey here at Rushton.'

'You know you will be very welcome, Richard.'

The other hesitated for only a moment then he said deliberately, 'Should all go well, I will then request the hand of your daughter, Anne, in marriage, sir.'

Sir Guy gave a faint hiss of breath and his blue eyes shone with an excited gleam.

'That request will be received favourably, you can be assured of that, Dickon. However...' He paused and his lips curved a trifle sardonically '...though you will encounter no opposition from me, you may do so from the lady herself.'

A crease appeared between Richard Allard's brows. 'You would not wish to force her hand?'

Sir Guy looked away from him. He sighed heavily. 'I would not wish to do so, but I am anxious to ensure her safety and happiness. Married to a man who would not hold my views, let us say, she could endanger the security not only of herself but of all of us. Ned's future needs to be safeguarded. I do not wish to have to hold a discreet silence within the bounds of my own family. Anne is by no means docile nor easily silenced from stating her own candid views on such uncompromising matters as the running of a household, fashion—and more volatile subjects.

'She would be safe from the pressures of State affairs in Yorkshire, and I know your lady mother would receive her joyfully.' His smile broadened. 'I can recall your mother, Richard, when she and your father first met and I served him as squire.

'I trod a difficult balancing act between them, unwilling to anger him but anxious not to upset your mother, who held different opinions then from his and those she holds now. She was then, as she is now, a very gracious and courageous lady. I would be happy to think of my child in her care. I know she would neither overcosset nor browbeat her.'

Richard Allard's lips curved into an answering smile. He

could well imagine the situation. Much of the tale of his parents' stormy courtship and marriage had been told to him but, knowing his mother as he did, he was aware that there must have been many a skirmish between them before the state of wedded bliss had been established.

'The only bar to a proposition of marriage being offered today, sir, is the fear that I may be unable to offer Mistress Anne the security you are so anxious to gain for her. I could wish for no more suitable bride or future mistress for my Yorkshire estates than Mistress Anne.'

Sir Guy clapped him heartily upon the shoulder.

'God go with you, Richard. I shall pray for you constantly. Yet swear to me that you will take every care.'

Richard Allard threw back his head and laughed. 'I am used to taking great care of my skin, sir. I shall not cease to do so when such a prize is there for me when this game is played through to its conclusion.'

Chapter Two

Anne found Richard Allard in the stables early next morning examining his horse's new shoe. She stopped abruptly as he swung round to face her.

'Good morning, Master Allard.' She sounded a trifle breathless as if she had been running. 'I trust you slept well.'

He was dressed as he had been yesterday in leather jack, warm hose and riding boots. She glanced at him hastily. 'Are you planning to leave us this morning?'

His grey eyes twinkled as he surveyed her. She was looking fresh and sparkling in a plain blue woollen gown, linen coif as yesterday, pattens for crossing the littered courtyard and warm cloak. She flushed under his scrutiny, as if realising she had been rude to question her father's guest on the matter of his departure, and made to pass by him towards the back corner where the stable cat was energetically licking her kittens. He blocked her way.

'Are you anxious to see me go, Mistress Anne?'

The flush became darker and she stammered, 'Of course not, sir. It was just that I saw you dressed for riding and thought....'

'No, your father offered me his hospitality freely and I told him I would most probably leave tomorrow.'

'Oh,' she said a little lamely. 'He will be glad to have you stay longer and hear in more detail about your home and parents. Ned will be delighted. He longs to travel as you have done and will hang on your every word.'

'You do not find my conversation interesting?'

'Of course I do.' She looked flustered. 'But it is unlikely that I will ever have the opportunity to travel.'

'You would like to do so?'

Her blue eyes grew dreamy. 'I would like to see more of the world than Rushton, certainly, though,' she added hastily, 'I love the manor dearly.'

'You would like to go to Court as your mother did?'

'Yes,' she said, then defensively, 'I know my father would never wish to see either Ned or I in the service of the King but…'

'You think that foolish?'

'My parents are—they have had *their* chances,' she murmured, her cheeks burning. 'It is only natural that I would wish to see London town, see the Queen and, yes, the King also.'

'And the severed heads on Tower Bridge,' he added drily and her blue eyes grew huge and concerned.

'I had not thought…'

'Mistress Anne, you must know it would be unwise, even dangerous, for your father to go near to Westminster considering his former loyalties.'

'But other men have…'

'Changed their coats? Yes, that is certainly so and to good advantage for many of them, but it is not your father's way.' There was utter contempt in his voice and she stepped back apace as if she feared he might strike her.

'But all that is so long ago,' she protested. 'I never knew

King Richard and Ned and I have to suffer for something which took place when I was just a babe in arms.'

'But I *did* know the King,' he returned evenly, 'and so you must excuse my own partiality.'

'You knew King Richard?' Her eyes were huge again now, rounding in wonder.

'Indeed I did, I served him as page and was honoured to do so.'

'You—liked him—in spite of what they say of him?'

'I do not know to whom you have been speaking, Mistress Anne, but no one who knew the King well in the old days, except the traitors who deserted him, would say much to his discredit, certainly not to those who served formerly in his household.'

'But they say,' her voice sank to a whisper, 'that he murdered his nephews.'

'Have you made such an accusation to your father?'

Her face whitened. 'Oh, no, I would not dare. You will not…'

'No, I will not tell him, Mistress Anne,' he returned grimly. 'But do me the courtesy of never referring to such slanderous filth again.'

This time she did withdraw from the rank fury in his tone.

'I must go,' she said hurriedly.

'Why did you come?'

'I came to see the kittens.' She glanced beyond him into the darker recesses of the stables. 'And see that the one which you rescued is—' She broke off abruptly and tilted her chin. 'No, actually, I saw you come in here and wanted to see if you were going to leave.'

'Ah, then you *are* anxious to speed my departure?'

'Yes.' Her lips trembled a little. 'I think your presence here is disturbing my father's peace.'

'You fear I might lead him into treason?'

'I think you could do so.'

'I swear to you I will do nothing to endanger him, for all your sakes.'

She gave a little relieved swallow.

They were about to leave the stable together when they heard the sounds of approaching horses and Ned breezed in and grinned at sight of Richard Allard.

'I'm glad to see you, sir. I was wondering if you would like to take a ride with me. We could go over the desmesne lands and down to the Nene, even go as far as Fotheringhay.'

Richard nodded and held up his hand for a moment's silence then said very quietly, 'Who was riding in such haste into the courtyard?'

'I don't know.' Ned started to answer quite loudly, then, seeing their guest's expression, immediately lowered his voice. 'I didn't wait to see...probably some boring acquaintance of my father, but I...'

He moved towards the entrance to the stable as if to ascertain the identity of the new arrivals, for it was clear from the noise and the flurry of grooms from another stable that there were at least two men who were even now dismounting. Quickly Richard Allard moved to prevent him and, as Anne, too, hastened towards the entrance he hissed in her ear fiercely, 'Please stay within the stable, both of you.'

Anne was outraged by his vehemence and the hard grip upon her arm which halted her in her tracks. How dared the man impose his will upon her and in her own stable! Ned, more amenable, merely opened his blue eyes, so like his sister's, and raised fair eyebrows at their guest in bewilderment.

Shadowed by the stable doorway, Anne and Richard

Allard were able to observe the new arrivals without being seen. Instinctively she knew Richard Allard would take steps to prevent her making any sound, even to putting his other hand across her mouth. Though she gave a little surprised hiss at the sight of her father's visitors, she made no other comment. Ned was content to remain behind them until they were able to enlighten him.

The two men handed their sweating mounts into the care of the Jarvis grooms and moved towards the manor house entrance. Still Richard Allard kept his hold on Anne's arm until they had disappeared into the hall, then he led her firmly back into the recesses of the stable and pulled neatly close the door. Ned blinked at him in the gloom.

'They are the King's men,' Anne said wonderingly, 'wearing the royal device of the portcullis.'

'Aye,' Richard Allard said grimly. 'So I noticed, Mistress Anne. I'll ask you to remain here for a while until we have some idea of the reason for their visit.'

Ned sank obediently down upon a bundle of hay. 'You don't fear harm to my father, sir? If so, surely…'

'He's more likely to fear harm for himself,' Anne returned contemptuously. 'Isn't that so, sir? You do not wish either my brother or I to speak of your presence here at Rushton.'

'That is so, Mistress Anne,' he said suavely. To Ned he added, 'It is unlikely these men intend to arrest your father. Had there been such an intent there would have been a larger escort. It would seem these two are messengers or, possibly, they have arrived to question him on some matter which has come to the notice of the King's council. However,' he soothed, noting Ned's rising alarm, 'it cannot pose real danger otherwise he would be arrested and carted off to London without delay.'

Ned said shrewdly, 'You think they are here to question

him about you? If so, my father could unwittingly speak of your presence here, surely.'

Richard Allard shook his head decisively. 'Your father would not be so unwise as to fall into that mistake. No, neither he nor your mother will mention my arrival yesterday.'

'Are you wanted by the King's men?' Anne demanded bluntly.

'Not that I am aware of. It is just that I have learned to be cautious when calling on any man whose loyalty to King Henry is held in doubt, with good reason or not, by the King's officials. I would never compromise them. So, if you please, we will wait until they take their departure. I cannot think that will be long delayed. I heard one give instructions to the groom to rub down and water their mounts but have them in readiness to depart again within the hour.'

Sulkily Anne sank down beside her brother while Richard Allard took up a watchful position near the partially opened stable door.

Ned was still looking puzzled. He said softly, 'You don't fear that Master Allard and Father are engaged in anything…'

'Treasonable? I should think that very possible,' Anne replied coolly, 'and I blame Father for it. He should have more consideration for Mother.'

'Mother is of father's persuasion,' Ned said equably, 'and when I am of age…'

'You will use more circumspection, I hope,' Anne said cuttingly.

Richard Allard moved away from the door.

'They appear to be leaving already.'

Anne could hear the men talking, but not their words. They did not sound in the least angry or put out, however, so she guessed they had been courteously received at the manor house. She waited impatiently until their horses were led out, the men mounted and she heard the clatter of their horses' hooves upon the cobbles of the courtyard again.

'Well, Master Allard,' she snapped. 'I trust we can now be released from our imprisonment.'

Ned laughed outright and waited until Richard Allard smilingly nodded his permission.

'Oh, come, Anne,' he reproved his sister. 'Master Allard was only ensuring that neither of us said anything untoward in the presence of those King's men. After all, that could have endangered Father.'

Anne knew he was right, but she only gave an angry shrug as Richard Allard opened the stable door now for them all to pass out.

Her relief at the men's departure was short lived, however, when, entering the hall, she perceived her father was in one of his rare, uncontrollable furies. He was waving a parchment at her mother who was seated patiently by the hearth. His other hand pounded the trestle near to him.

'I will not do it,' Sir Guy shouted. 'I cannot be forced to do it. I'll not place Anne in a humiliating position. I'll defy that usurper. He has no right…'

Lady Jarvis cautioned her husband to be circumspect when she saw Anne start anxiously at the sound of her name uttered with such an explosion of fury.

'Anne,' she said quietly, 'we were wondering where you had hidden yourself, and Ned, I see you have found Master Allard.'

Sir Guy controlled his temper with difficulty and nodded to his friend.

'Ah, Dickon, I wasn't sure where you were and also unsure whether you wished me to keep your presence here secret. Did you note our visitors from Westminster?'

'I did indeed, sir,' Richard said quietly. 'I hope they brought you no disturbing news.'

'Disturbing enough.' Sir Guy indicated the parchment in his hand with disgust. 'I am ordered, if you please, to present my daughter, Anne, to the Court at Westminster.'

'The letter is from the Queen, in actual fact,' Lady Jarvis interposed. 'And it is more a request than a command, though, of course, it must be considered as such. She asks that Anne should come to Westminster to be a companion to Lady Philippa Telford, Lord Wroxeter's daughter, who is to come from Burgundy to serve Her Majesty.

'Knowing Sir Guy's past friendship with Lord Wroxeter, she thinks it would be desirable that the two girls share accommodation and duties at Court. Philippa, as you are no doubt aware, is only thirteen years old and Anne would act as a friend and chaperon.'

Sir Guy let out a pent-up gasp of pure fury.

'How can I believe this farrago of nonsense? Richard, can you believe that Wroxeter, the Tudor's most bitter enemy, would consider the prospect of sending his daughter to Henry's Court where she would be what amounted to a hostage to ensure Martyn Telford's acceptance of Henry's usurpation without further assistance to the Duchess Margaret's attempts to unseat him?'

Richard Allard perched on a corner of the trestle. 'Can I see the letter, sir?'

Sir Guy thrust it at him as if it were encrusted with filth.

Anne had been listening incredulously to this account of the contents of the letter and burst out, 'But, Mother, you cannot refuse me this wonderful chance to...'

'Be silent, girl, while your betters are considering,' her father snapped. Ned shrugged uneasily and took himself some distance away out of reach of his father should an incautious word from him bring down on his head the full extent of his sire's wrath.

Richard Allard pursed his lips and, while reading, ran his other hand through his thick brown hair in a gesture which Anne, watching, thought was probably habitual.

'It does appear strange, I grant you,' he said at last, 'but reads genuine in tone. If I recall, my mother once said that Lady Wroxeter and the Queen had been close companions during the time of Queen Anne's last illness. It could mean that Queen Elizabeth has now recollected that past friendship and wishes to offer her friend's daughter a place at Court and the opportunity of a fair match.

'I hear Wroxeter was ailing the last time I was at Malines. They lost their second child, you know, a boy, so Lady Wroxeter must have had a hard time recently. If Wroxeter were to die, the Countess would be in straitened circumstances. Since Redmoor, Wroxeter's lands were sequestered and their fortunes have been greatly strained as all of ours have been.

'Wroxeter may well have come to the conclusion that this offer would be in his daughter's best interest as,' he added meaningly, 'this invitation to you to send Mistress Anne to Court could be in hers.'

Sir Guy blew out his lips and, turning from them, began to pace the hall restlessly. Anne watched uneasily. She knew only too well that the haughty stride and proud, rigid set of the shoulders indicated that he was by no means satisfied with Richard Allard's final assessment of the situation. Lady Jarvis caught their visitor's eye and shrugged helplessly.

Anne, knowing it unwise, ventured an opinion though her mother shot her an angry glance.

'Father, I want to go. You cannot deny me this chance.'

He shot round instantly and stood regarding her, feet

astride, hands clasped behind his back, his blue eyes cold with fury.

Richard Allard said quietly, 'As I see it, sir, you have really no choice. The Queen's request is a royal command, couched however kindly.'

'Then I must consent to my daughter becoming a hostage for my own compliant behaviour.'

Blue eyes met grey ones and, finally, Sir Guy's drew away and he turned his back on them again. He gave a slight impotent movement of one hand and at length came back to the hearth and threw himself down in his chair.

He looked apologetically at his Margaret. 'Forgive me, my dear. My feelings got the better of me. I cannot bear to think of Anne within the dragon's lair.'

Anne made a little moue of concern as she recognised her father's contemptuous reference to the King's personal device of the Red Dragon.

Richard nodded in sympathy. 'Mistress Anne is unlikely to be within the King's presence often. She may not even be presented to him. I understand Henry frequents his wife's apartments rarely these days. Not even those closest to the King can avoid acknowledging that he is not demonstrative.'

He gave a little bark of a laugh. 'One of our spies reported that the King's Majesty, as he insists on being referred to these days, appears to bestow his warmest caresses upon his pet monkey which disgusts and angers his councillors. The little beast is destructive, particularly to state documents, I hear.'

Sir Guy did not appear either amused or mollified by the information. He glared at his daughter who stood before him in an attitude of beseeching docility now that she had a glimmer of hope that her wildest dreams might be possible of attainment after all.

He sighed heavily. 'As you say, it would be unwise to give Henry what amounted to an affront, and a refusal to comply with the Queen's request would be received as such.'

Anne waited in an agony of suspense for his decision, her eyes modestly downcast.

'Anne has no suitable garments nor jewellery,' Sir Guy grunted at last, looking to his wife for support.

'We can manage to send her attired fittingly,' Lady Jarvis said slowly, 'though it will come hard on our household purse. It will not be expected that the daughter of the disgraced Sir Guy Jarvis arrive at Court dressed extravagantly and in the height of fashion. The King would be unduly suspicious about the source of such unusual wealth and would, no doubt, manage to find a reason for fining us again, more strictly this time. However, that is not my immediate concern.'

She cast a doubtful glance at her daughter. 'I fear for Anne's safety on the journey. Guy, you should not venture into London and there are still pockets of discontent throughout the realm and some masterless men preying on travellers, many of them unfortunate remnants of the battles of Redmoor and Stoke. I shall worry—and we all know that Anne can be her own worst enemy. She says straight out what she thinks, has no skill in subterfuge and knows nothing of the lies and intrigues which makes all Courts miasmas of fear and hatred.'

'Mother, I swear I will be discreet and docile,' Anne interposed. 'I would not be so foolish as to anger Her Grace the Queen or place Father in a difficult position by unwise references to his former loyalties.'

Lady Jarvis sighed. 'It is not so easy to change or disguise one's nature as you think, my girl, and your promise still does not relieve me of alarm about your journey.'

Sir Guy said doubtfully, 'I trust my men and she would have Mary Scroggins with her. The woman is sensible and reliable. Thank the Virgin she takes after her mother, Kate, rather than that rapscallion, Will, her father.'

'If it would relieve your mind, Lady Jarvis, I, myself, could escort Mistress Anne to London,' Richard offered. 'Sir Guy knows I have business there and could see her safely installed at Court and report to you both about her reception and accommodation there on my way home to Yorkshire.'

Anne could not have been more astonished or dismayed by this announcement and was about to remonstrate when she saw that her parents were considering this offer with considerable favour.

'If you would do that, Dickon, it would certainly relieve me of one source of anxiety,' Sir Guy said. 'Unless it would mean some measure of inconvenience to you or—' his eyes searched the other's carefully '—some element of added danger.'

'No, no, sir,' Richard replied cheerfully. 'I could see Mistress Anne and her maid safely bestowed and take lodgings in London for a few weeks and keep a careful eye on the situation. If I had any cause for concern I could inform you immediately and, if necessary, take steps to remedy the matter.'

'But I would not wish—' Anne stared rebelliously at their visitor whose restricting presence on this fascinating adventure awaiting her was the very last thing she wanted. Then she realised that her father's consent to this journey could only be gained by her willing acceptance of Richard Allard's offer of escort and she finished lamely, 'If Master Allard's business will not be put out by this arrangement, then I shall be glad of his company on my ride south.'

Sir Guy lifted his two hands as if he was helpless to object and Lady Jarvis nodded briskly at her daughter.

'Go up to your chamber, Anne, and ask Mary to come to me in the solar. We cannot insist that she go with you. We must give her the opportunity to refuse if she is so minded though, I admit, I hope she will be willing. I would not wish you to be in any other woman's charge during these next months.'

She rose as Anne did with alacrity. 'The Queen's messenger requested that you set out for Westminster as soon as can be arranged in order to be there when young Lady Philippa arrives. Since that is so there is a great deal to be done in preparation.'

Anne rushed towards her father and planted a kiss upon his cheek. He grinned broadly though pushing her gently aside.

'There, minx, it looks as if you will get your way as usual. Mind, I expect you to be obedient to Master Allard upon the road and give him no cause to be alarmed for your safety or angered by some stupid prank.'

Anne's blue eyes blazed, though she quickly veiled them from her father's gaze. Why must he continually treat her as if she were a naughty child when, within a few weeks, she would have reached marriageable age?

She sank into a little curtsy and, nodding at her mother and laughing in Ned's direction, for he was pulling a comically wry face, she hastened from the hall in search of her maid.

Lady Jarvis bent over her husband's fair head as he sat in the chair. She read defeat in his eyes and gently ruffled his still-bright hair.

'The Queen is Plantagenet, Guy, remember. I do not think she would wish to bring your daughter to any harm nor Lady Philippa. I think we can give Anne into Master

Allard's care readily, knowing she could have no finer mentor. I'll go up now and see what I can to refurbish some of my old Court gowns. The materials are still fine though the style is outdated. Mary will help me. Her skill with the needle is prodigious. I've only recently been fashioning one of the new French hoods for Anne.'

He reached back and squeezed her hand and, as she then withdrew, he raised fair eyebrows in Richard Allard's direction.

'By all the Saints, I hope you are all right in your assessment of this,' he said fervently.

Anne rushed up the stairs to her own chamber, calling imperiously for her maid, Mary Scroggins. The woman appeared soon enough, her sleeves rolled up to her plump elbows, for she had been carefully laundering some of the fine lawn shifts which remained of the better garments Lady Jarvis had retained from the days when coin had been more plentiful in this house. Some had been skilfully darned for none of the newer garments were so soft and delicate and Mary insisted upon dealing with Lady Jarvis's and Anne's garments herself.

'What is all the pother?' she enquired mildly in the familiar tones of the trusted servant. Mary had come into service at Rushton four years ago from Lady Allard's service in Wensleydale where her mother served in attendance upon Sir Dominick and Aleyne.

Anne did not try to reprove her for insolence of tone. She regarded Mary as her trusted companion as well as her attendant.

'Mary, you will never guess…'

'I won't unless you tell me,' the older girl replied. She was nearing nineteen years of age, brown-haired, with bright hazel eyes and plump rosy cheeks.

She had been reluctant at first to leave the only home

she knew in her beloved Yorkshire but she had two other sisters who required places and her mother had insisted upon her going south into a household she knew well, for Kate Scroggins's husband had served both Sir Dominick Allard and Sir Guy Jarvis. Mary had fitted into the household at Rushton very well and had come to love the girl, three years younger than herself, though there were times when she found Anne a handful and made no bones about telling her so.

Anne was breathless from her run upstairs. 'Messengers from Court came and—and, Mary, I have been offered a place in the Queen's household.'

'What?' Mary stared at her blankly. She was well aware of the situation that existed between those at the new King's Court and the loyal followers of the late King Richard. 'And has your father consented, Mistress Anne?'

'Well, of course, he does not wish me to go but he has had to give his consent, hasn't he? It is the Queen's command that I should go,' Anne returned blithely, swirling her skirts as she twisted round in a little jig of triumph. 'Mother says you are to go to her in the solar and she will ask if you will go with me willingly. Mary, you will, won't you? It will be such a grand adventure for both of us.'

'I don't know about that,' Mary said practically. 'My ma says there's lots of disadvantages to waiting on them great ones at Court but if I don't keep an eye on you, Mistress Anne, who else will be there to keep you out of mischief?'

'Well, on the journey, Master Allard,' Anne snapped. 'Father insists he escort me.' She frowned. 'He is so oafish. I do not want him beside me when I arrive in Westminster.'

'Master Richard an oaf?' Mary demanded, scandalized. 'Mistress Anne, I'll thank you to remember my ma and pa have been in service with Master Allard's family for years and I'm telling you now he has excellent manners. His pa would stand for nothing less, even now, when he's long been a grown man and gone travelling so far from home.'

'No, I don't mean he's oafish in behaviour,' Anne said, somewhat chastened, 'but he's wild and woolly in appearance, like a great shaggy dog—or a wolf,' she amended. 'There's nothing elegant about his clothes or his style of address, is there?'

Mary allowed a little secretive smile to linger round her mouth.

'His father was known as "Wolf Allard", from his personal device, you know, but there was many a maid who thought his rugged looks appealing. I've heard many a tale about Master Richard, too. He's had many admirers.'

'But never married,' Anne pressed. 'Why not, do you think, Mary? He's quite old, isn't he?'

'He's no great age for an eligible man,' Mary retorted. 'He's twenty-six or -seven, I think, a good age for deciding to settle down into matrimony, and, Mistress Anne, I'll have you remember that the Allard lands have suffered the same deprivations of those here at Rushton. Master Allard needs to find a good wench who is worthy of him and isn't looking for some fine, elegant young gentleman of means not to be compared to him, and not good enough to tie his points, in my opinion.'

Anne laughed. 'You cannot be said to be impartial, Mary. Can I surmise you've admired him yourself from afar?'

'Indeed I have not,' Mary replied stoutly, 'and even if I did I know my place and wouldn't dare look so high.'

'Perhaps you are right,' Anne conceded slowly. 'I am foolish to look for handsome looks and fine clothes. Oh,' she said irritably, 'I am so tired of being told how necessary it is to economise. Am I pretty, Mary? Do you think some gentleman of court will find me attractive and offer for me even without a large dowry? Would not that be splendid?'

'Handsome is as handsome does,' Mary said darkly with downright Yorkshire common sense which made Anne laugh again as she held her skirts high and tripped daintily around the chamber as she imagined those grand ladies at Court did.

Anne was very concerned about the contents of the travelling chest she would carry with her to Westminster; over the next few days she watched, wrinkling her brow in doubt as her mother and Mary began to prepare those Court gowns she would need. In the end she thought she would have less need for concern for her mother's heavy brocades and velvets were cut and restyled for her in those fashions Lady Jarvis had seen on wealthier ladies encountered in Northampton and Leicester.

She doubted the gowns were in the very latest designs but they would not disgrace Anne either in fit or quality and Anne was delighted when dressed in them and caught glimpses of herself in her mother's travelling Venetian glass mirror. As she had inherited her mother's dark luxuriant locks the colours suited Anne, with the rich hues of gold brocade, crimson velvet and blue samite bringing out the vivid shade of her eyes.

One gown charmed her most with its subtle draping of the overgown to the back, which Dionysia had told her was the very latest fashion. The new dark blue velvet hood trimmed with seed pearls sat well back from her glossy locks and would complement the other colours.

The day before her departure, as her sense of mingled excitement and apprehension rose, her mother sat alone with her within the solar after sending Mary on some small errand. Margaret Jarvis frowned slightly as she observed her daughter's flushed countenance. She bit her underlip and wondered how best to broach the matter in hand.

'Anne,' she said at last, 'I hope you will not pin too much hopes on future happiness at Court. I have been there and I can tell you it can be very lonely and frightening, even surrounded as one is by a veritable press of people.'

Anne eyed her thoughtfully. 'But you were happy there. You loved Queen Anne for you named me after her and—and you met my father and...'

'I did not surrender to my love for your father from the first moment we met,' Lady Jarvis said tartly. 'It took some time for me to learn to trust his motives and to love him truly. I do not want you to fall for the first popinjay who offers you flattery.'

'Do you judge me so foolish?' Anne demanded hotly.

'No, but your head is turned by your longing for this venture and I worry about you. You must learn to be decorous in behaviour, to keep your opinions to yourself, to accept without complaint any demand put upon you. I must also ask you to be particularly kind and protective of Lady Philippa, who is considerably younger than you. Doubtless she will feel very lost at Westminster for she was born in Burgundy and, to my knowledge, has never been to England before. Indeed, her English may not be good and it will be for you to be patient with her.'

'Perhaps she will not like me,' Anne considered, 'or she may be haughty mannered. She is the daughter of an Earl.'

'Both Lord Wroxeter and his Countess are sensible, considerate people. I shall be very surprised indeed if you find their daughter lacking in either of those qualities yet she is little more than a child and you have been chosen to be her friend for specific reasons. Do not lead her into foolishness, Anne, as I know you are prone to do on occasions.'

Anne regarded her mother gravely and read very real anxiety in her eyes.

'I promise I will behave so as never to disgrace you,' she said quietly.

Margaret Jarvis hesitated and Anne turned to her sharply as if she had thought the homily was over, but, no, her mother had something else upon her mind and Anne waited in suspense for what was to come.

'Your father and I are particularly anxious that you should also behave well while under Master Allard's care,' Lady Jarvis said with what Anne considered unusual vehemence.

That would be it, she thought sourly. They have already noted my distaste for the idea of his escort.

'I will give him no trouble, though,' she added tartly, 'to hear Mary sing his praises, he is capable of dealing with any emergency which arises, a veritable paragon, Master Allard.'

'Your father thinks a great deal of Dickon Allard,' her mother said sharply. 'See that you *do* heed him, for…' She hesitated and Anne pounced on that slight hesitation instantly.

'For?' she questioned. 'What were you about to say, Mother?'

Lady Jarvis's troubled eyes met her daughter's challenging ones squarely.

'You might as well be told now. We have high hopes that when he has completed his business in London town Richard Allard will offer for your hand.' There, it was out and she compressed her lips as she saw first bewilderment and then pure fury dawn in her daughter's expression.

'Marry Richard Allard?' she echoed in a high shrill tone. 'You cannot mean it, Mother.'

'Why not? Despite the fines imposed after Redmoor the

Allard lands are quite extensive and it would be a fair match.'

'But he is far too old for me.'

'Nonsense. Your father was almost that age when we were wed. Richard has reached the age of experience and will know how to deal with a high-strung young woman like yourself.'

'I will never consent to marry him,' Anne said through gritted teeth. 'Do you hear me, never.'

Margaret Jarvis looked perplexed, then she gave way to anger.

'You will do as your father wishes, as every girl of your age must do. I cannot for the life of me understand why you are so much against the notion. Some time ago you were complaining that no one would ask for you since you are without dowry and that you wished to settle down soon, marry, have a household of your own and children.

'Richard Allard is an honourable young man. He has not been discourteous to you, at least, not in my hearing. He is tolerably good looking and still young. Neither I nor your father have heard anything to his discredit in the matter of his dealings with women, which is saying a great deal, I can tell you. Many men neglect their wives and some are prone to treat them badly, even beating them. I cannot imagine Richard would treat you so, however you try his patience.'

Slowly Anne articulated, 'I will never, not even if I were to fall in love with him, which is grossly unlikely, agree to marry a man whose loyalty to the Crown is in question. I have seen what such sympathies can do,' she said forcefully.

'You have lived with it for fourteen years, worrying constantly in case Father would involve himself in treasonable business and end up in the Tower, or worse, at Tyburn. I am aware that many men who come here do so to discuss treason. I even doubt Master Allard's motives for travelling to London at this time. I am no fool, Mother. You cannot hope to keep secrets such as these from me now I am of age to understand.

'Even as a young child I was aware of intrigues and anxieties within this house. I will not live like this. Yes, I want to marry and have a family but I want to have a peaceful life, one in which I am not looking over my shoulder every moment in case King Henry's men should ride into my courtyard intent on arresting my husband.'

For moments Lady Jarvis was struck quite dumb in astonishment. Anne, at almost sixteen, had seemed to her still a child who needed constant protection from the knowledge of the anxieties which continually beset her. She had believed that, between them, she and Guy had managed to keep their children unaware of the fears which shadowed their lives. She gave a great shuddering breath.

'We have no evidence that Richard is keen to work against the King's Grace,' she said shakily. 'You must never breathe such matters. Words like those could injure us as well as his family. You are talking nonsense. He goes to London simply to deal with business for his father, business concerning wool sales, I imagine. Dominick Allard keeps many sheep on his land. I have no fear that you will be endangered by Richard's presence on your journey.'

'Of course he will embark on nothing treasonable while I am with him,' Anne said pithily, 'but, nevertheless, his father's loyalties are his, and he would never forsake his work for the Plantagenet cause, whatever the needs of his wife and children.'

'Anne...' Her mother took her gently by the shoulders '...I think I understand now your concerns but marriage is never easy. I did not think you were foolish enough to believe the troubadour tales of romantic love and unalloyed happiness which lasts for ever. I ask you to remember that finding you a suitable husband will not be easy for your father. He is doing his best to provide for you.

'You would not wish to be an unwed dependent on Ned when he brings his wife home to Rushton and, in due time, inherits, would you? This time at Court will widen your horizons. It may well make you think that what is offered is all for the best.

'Do not speak to your father of anything I've said. It was his wish that we wait to tell you of Master Allard's offer but I decided it was high time you were kept informed of our plans for you. The next few months will be crucial to your future welfare. I want you to do nothing to jeopardise that.'

Firmly Anne drew away. Tears glimmered in her blue eyes and she curtsied formally and asked permission to leave the solar. Lady Jarvis sighed heavily and took up another French hood she was embroidering with silver thread and seed pearls for her daughter's travelling chest.

Anne was not aware that she was really crying as she ran across the courtyard towards the stables when Richard Allard's familiar deep tones demanded that she stop and explain her reason for such obvious signs of distress. Apparently he, too, had been to the stables and was now on his way back to the house. She almost cannoned into him.

'Mistress Anne, whatever can be the matter? You are not hurt?'

His tone was genuinely concerned and she stopped and turned her face from him. How could she explain? She simply could not reveal the source of her distress. Her mother had forbidden her to speak of it. She laughed a trifle shakily.

'Oh, Master Allard, I am so sorry I did not see you for a moment. The sun blinded me. I think—think that I have at last realised that I am leaving home and all those I love for the first time. It is just a little—frightening.'

He had a consoling grasp upon her arm, gentle but calming, and she was grateful for his care of her.

'It is silly,' she chided herself. 'I really *do* want to go but now—' she gave a little gulping gasp '—my departure is so near and I am afraid I will not know how to conduct myself and Lady Philippa might not like me and—and everything could go wrong and I shall be so far from home.'

He shook his head, smilingly. 'Even in so short a time I have come to know your worth, Mistress Anne. Of course you will pine for home at first, it will all seem so strange to you, but you will settle after the first nervous hours. I felt just the same and I was much younger and less self-composed than you are. You have been well trained in matters of deportment. The Queen will be delighted with you, I am sure.'

'Yes,' she said, blinking back tears. 'Yes, I have been waiting for this opportunity for so long and now it is here I am frightening myself with foolish notions of failure. Thank you, Master Allard, for your encouraging words.'

For the first time she looked full at him and, in the light of her mother's disclosure, regarded him as a possible suitor.

He was, she thought, after all, ruggedly attractive, if not handsome. He seemed to exude an excess of raw physical power and was just too big to appeal to her, but his features were regular and, what was more important, his expression good humoured and kindly. She saw no trace of cynicism or cruelty about the set of his mouth and the crinkles at the sides of his eyes told her he laughed often.

Had he not been Sir Dominick Allard's son, could she

have come to accept him willingly as a prospective husband? She put the thought firmly aside even when the touch of his strong brown fingers upon her arm sent tingles throughout her trembling body.

What would he be like in the marriage bed? Considerate, gentle, passionate? She thought he might possess all of those qualities and, she considered with a little pang of alarm, he was more than likely adventurous and brave, too much so for his own well-being and the peace of mind of any possible wife.

She moved to free herself, though gently and courteously. 'I am keeping you, Master Allard, from whatever you are about to do.'

'Why so formal, Mistress Anne?' he teased. 'We shall have opportunity to get to know one another better during the next few days of our journey together.' He shaded his eyes against the glare of the bright, low sun. 'It appears the weather should hold good. I hope so. We do not want to be wallowing in mud on the highway.' His lips twitched as he glanced up at her slantingly from beneath his thick brown lashes. 'I hope you are not fearful about our journeying together. Once or twice I have thought you are avoiding me.'

'No, no,' she amended hastily. 'I—we—have been so busy preparing. I am grateful for your offer of escort. Otherwise my father would have been reluctant to let me go.'

'Then you are not afraid I will disgrace you at Westminster? I remember that when we first met you took me for some servant or wandering chapman. Am I so uncouth? I shall merely deliver you at the palace, you know, not force my attendance upon you afterwards. Only, I want you to be aware of the fact that I shall be nearby—lodging in the Chepe, probably. I will let you know where, in case you should have need of my services, just for the first few weeks.'

She drew a heavy breath. Already he was aware of his responsibilities towards her. Walls around her, cabinning, confining, were drawing in close. She would not allow that to be. What she had said to her mother was an expression of her strongest resolve. She would marry no man whose dubious behaviour would threaten her happiness and tranquillity.

'Thank you again, Master Allard. Of course I am not ashamed of your presence. I was very stupid not to recognise your worth that first day. I was, if you recall, too concerned for my own safety to be aware of much else. We should both retire early tonight so as to make an early and invigorated start in the morning.'

She bobbed a curtsy and turned back towards the hall. She must hasten up to her chamber. It would never do to encounter her father while her thoughts were in chaos.

He bowed and stepped back to allow her passage and she turned towards the hall again, all thought of escape abandoned. At the hall door she turned and found him watching her gravely, a slight frown on his normally good-humoured face. Did he guess that she had been made aware of the likelihood of their betrothal and of her reaction against the idea? Guiltily she turned from him to look straight ahead, conscious of the deep blush that was suffusing her cheeks and throat.

Chapter Three

All Anne's good intentions regarding her attitude to Master Allard were put to naught the next day as he set her teeth on edge by his insistence that absolutely everything must be checked before departure. That included the equipment and weapons of the two men her father had deputed to escort her south, the panniers containing food and the travelling chests strapped upon the backs of the two sumpter mules; even the hoofs of the horses and mules were inspected and, last of all, her own saddle.

Anne's pretended anxiety and welling apprehension about the coming leave-taking which had formed her excuse for weeping yesterday when she had encountered Richard Allard in the courtyard, was now, in fact, making itself felt. She dared not look at her parents and Ned lest she burst into a storm of weeping and she was in all haste to ride off quickly, but Richard Allard's stupid and needless precautions were delaying her so that she thought she would scream at him.

He lifted her into the saddle of her palfrey and tightened her saddle straps and checked her girth himself.

He straightened up, smiling. 'We cannot have you falling

from the saddle before we are a mile or so from Rushton,' he commented.

'I assure you, Master Allard, I am a perfectly competent horsewoman,' she retorted irritably.

'I'm sure you are, Mistress Anne, but let us not leave anything to chance. You want to arrive at Westminster in good fettle,' he replied cheerfully. 'You would be little use to attend Her Grace the Queen if you had injured yourself en route and, besides, I am responsible to your father for your well-being.'

Anne gritted her teeth in irritation and forced a smile as her mother and father came to her side to kiss her farewell.

Her mother reminded her softly, 'Remember what I told you. Keep your sharp tongue in check and mind Master Allard on the journey.'

Her father said little. His fine mouth was held in a hard line and she knew he was deliberately holding back further doubts about this journey and its eventual conclusion. He hugged her tightly and nodded at last to Richard Allard to give the order to ride from the courtyard. Anne turned in the saddle and, through a blur of emotional tears, saw her parents and Ned waving her off. Even Ned's dog was barking furiously with excitement. She took a final glimpse at the dear, familiar shape of the manor house and then they were off, riding through the gatehouse.

Mary Scroggins was riding pillion behind the younger of the two men at escort who took the rear of the little company. The other, an older archer who had ridden with her father to Redmoor, near Bosworth—and possibly to East Stoke also—rode slightly ahead while Richard Allard rode close to Anne in the centre. Each of the men led one of the mules.

It was a fine, bright day as Richard had predicted, the sun watery and rather low, lacking in warmth but still gilding the remaining leaves upon the trees and sheening the water on the manor fishpond as they passed.

Once upon the road Anne's spirits lifted and she rode joyfully, gazing around with eager interest at the road ahead and the now-fallow fields stretching out to either side of them. Richard Allard was whistling softly between his teeth and she glanced at him sharply. He was interfering with her pleasure in the peace of their surroundings, for, so far, they had encountered no one else upon the road. He caught her glance and grinned mockingly.

'I am sorry, Mistress Anne, it is a habit of mine.'

'I wish it were not,' she said huffily. 'It is irritating, to say the least.'

He shrugged lightly but desisted. She felt unaccountably ashamed of her churlish mood and said, hesitantly, 'I suppose you have travelled this way many times before.'

'Not so many. Normally I pass along the Great North Road from Yorkshire, but I detoured this time to see your father. It was well I did so for I have the privilege of escorting a lovely lady to her destiny.'

'I wish you would not tease me, sir,' she said uneasily.

His twinkling grey eyes softened. 'I think you are already suffering the onset of homesickness pangs.'

'I'm not a baby, but,' she admitted wryly, 'I hadn't realised quite how hard it would be to leave Rushton for an unspecified period and to part from all my loved ones.'

'I doubt it will be for long,' he consoled her.

'You think I shall not please the Queen?'

'No, no, I am sure you will. It is just that you will soon be formally betrothed and the Queen will not keep you in attendance then, when your proper place will be by your future husband's side.'

Her blue eyes widened and a scarlet flush dyed her

cheeks. 'My father has said that it is for this reason that he has sent me to Court?'

His teasing manner had deserted him as he said, quietly, 'Your father did indicate to me that he hoped soon to see you settled. Enjoy your last months of freedom.'

'Did you ever meet the Queen when you were at Court?' she enquired, anxious to change a subject which was becoming increasingly embarrassing to her.

'No, I did not. The Lady Bessy, as she was then, was living at Sheriff Hutton in Yorkshire with the young Earl of Warwick.'

Anne's blue eyes grew moist with pity. 'The poor young Earl! My father has often spoken of him. All his life seems to have been passed in a state of imprisonment. How he must long for freedom, confined in the Tower.'

'He was not imprisoned at Sheriff Hutton during his uncle's reign,' Richard Allard enlightened her. 'He was living quite happily with others of the royal household and was being educated and prepared for his military training. It has only been since the accession of King Henry that he has been kept under close guard.'

'Do you think it is true what they say of him, that he is slow witted?'

'I can well imagine that perpetual imprisonment will have left his mind blunted against the general experiences and slight blows and disappointments that beset the rest of us.'

She was silent for a while, contemplating the sad truth that it was a misfortune to be born the son or nephew of a King. Uneasily she remembered that it was her own deep desire to sample the excitement of court life which had brought her to this journey; at the end of it, she would come into contact with those lordly beings who intrigued and fought for high places, even to the detriment of their own kinfolk. Her mother had warned her that life there would not be easy.

'Master Allard?' she asked and he turned from his watchful survey of the trees and hedges that bordered the road, mindful that such vegetation could harbour footpads, to face her again, one eyebrow lifted quizzically.

'Mistress Anne, do you wish to stop and rest already?'

'Certainly not,' she snorted. 'I told you I am an experienced horsewoman. No, I just...wanted to know—did you find it difficult at Court? Was the work strenuous or unpleasant and the King hard to please?'

'King Richard could be.' He grinned. 'Usually he was fair and courteous in his demands, but he could be very demanding on occasion and his Plantagenet rage showed itself then.' He smiled down at her. 'Life at Court is tiring. You will find yourself constantly on your feet and at the whim of the monarch at all hours of the day or night but, of course, you are strong and healthy and will expect that.'

'Were you—beaten?' she enquired anxiously.

'Not often—' his grin broadened '—but I, too, can display a temper sometimes and was punished for it. I was very young,' he said dismissively.

'But you liked the King?'

'I loved him,' he said quietly, 'as did my father and your father.'

He looked ahead as they were coming to a crossroad and excused himself to take the lead for a while.

Anne watched his back thoughtfully. How well he rode, not showily but competently and easily, as her father had showed her, so as to be sparing of his own body and easy on his mount. Many women would find him attractive, she thought, as she had many times since her mother had revealed to her her father's wish concerning a future betrothal.

Richard Allard would doubtless make some woman a tolerably reasonable husband, she conceded, capable in running his small demesne, probably patient and undemanding, but he would be seldom home and—how *dull* it would be on that desmesne for a wife left to her own devices much of the year, caring for her children and the household. It was a lot her own mother appeared to find satisfactory but, Anne decided grimly, it was not a fate to which she would submit herself willingly.

She looked about her complacently as they were now on the main road south heading towards Northampton. This was the excitement she craved, the thrill of seeing new places and observing people. Here there were many travellers; all life, it seemed, stretched out before her. Carts rumbled by, loaded with farm produce; a company of liveried retainers passed them at one juncture and Richard Allard ordered his small procession to draw in close to the roadside to allow them passage.

A hedge priest trudged patiently by, his coarse black robe girdled high, smeared with the dust and mud of many journeys, his sandals worn and flapping, offering little protection to dirty and calloused feet. A fat pardoner, attended by a servant, stared curiously at their group but Richard made a small but commanding gesture of his hand, as if ordering the man not to attempt to delay them by offering his wares.

As they passed Anne noted that the man's cloak was ornamented by the shell brooch of St James of Compostela, so the man had made pilgrimages. She had heard tell of adventures on such expeditions. Her father possessed a printed copy of Master Chaucer's tales of the famous pilgrimage to Canterbury and her own mother had visited the shrine at Walsingham. She had longed to go there too and considered that, when she was wed, she would most probably go to the shrine of Our Lady of Walsingham also to pray for a child.

They passed through Northampton without being delayed and it was the first and only time Anne did not wish to linger there to gaze into the booths of the silk merchants.

Simpkin Cooper, the man-at-arms who had been in the van of the little party, suggested they take refreshment at an inn on the southern side of the town.

'It may be some time, Master Allard, before we find anything so suitable for the ladies. The village taverns are very squalid in this district.'

'I defer to your experience, Master Cooper,' Richard Allard said mildly and turned in the saddle to inform Anne of their decision.

'You will certainly become saddle sore if you do not stop and rest soon, however much you insist that you enjoy riding,' he said, 'and the horses will need watering.'

Anne looked up at the sun, low and bright, and thought how the weather was unusually sultry for this time of year.

'Can we not eat outside in the open since it is warm?' she enquired. 'I do not suppose we shall get another such opportunity on this journey. Inns are always so smelly and crowded. I shall feel more refreshed if we stay outside. Surely we can find shelter from the wind, though it is very mild and I doubt we shall need that.'

Richard shrugged. He was accustomed to camping out even in the depths of winter, and she was right: the weather was pleasant for the time of year. He consulted Simpkin as to the whereabouts of some pleasing spinney where they could be away from prying eyes on the road for an hour or two.

'We'll need to find water for the horses,' he reminded the man, who nodded thoughtfully.

'Aye, Master Allard, it is a good notion, today, at any

rate.' He thought for a minute, then scratched his chin and grinned. 'I know one small spinney about a mile and a half further on.' He cast Richard a knowing look. 'It's not more'n a few yards from our way and sheltered by bushes. A small stream runs through it.' His roguish glance confirmed Richard's suspicion that Simpkin had, most likely, done some of his courting in that same spinney.

'Right, man, lead us to it,' he agreed. 'We have cold meats and cheese as well as fresh bread in plenty and good wine and ale too.'

Anne had been listening to the exchange and called to Mary Scroggins, who was riding behind with Wat Glazier. Mary passed no comment. Objections would be useless. She knew, from past experience, that there was no arguing with Mistress Anne when she had one fixed idea in her mind, though, for her part, Mary would have welcomed the opportunity to sample a tavern's hot food and have warmed water and towels for washing at their disposal.

For all her protestations, Anne was glad to be lifted from the saddle of her palfrey when they pulled off the road some half-hour later, following Simpkin's directions into a small spinney bordering open pasture land beyond. Well-matured oaks and beech trees gave ample cover and a bramble hedge offered protection from the wind. Simpkin led the way unerringly to a small clearing from which, in the distance, Anne could hear the faint burbling of a small stream.

'It'll be more'n a mite muddy round the stream bank,' Simpkin advised. 'Better camp here, Master Allard, it'll be more comfortable for the women folk.'

Richard glanced round and nodded approval after first moving off to reconnoitre the ground further on and returning to the clearing.

'This seems fine,' he said. 'Spread horse blankets on the ground for the ladies and Mistress Anne can lean back against my saddle. She'll find the roughness of the tree bole somewhat uncomfortable.'

Mary looked round anxiously and Simpkin reassured her.

'Don't worry, Mary. There's a spot just behind them bushes as you and Mistress Anne can use when you need to, while we keep watch without 'aving to intrude on you, like.'

Mary grunted and Anne gave a little chuckle. It seemed Simpkin was, indeed, very well acquainted with this terrain.

Food was unpacked from one of the panniers and ale and wine poured. It was quiet in the wood and she lay back against the supporting saddle, her hood pushed back, listening to the song birds who had not flown south for the winter and the rustlings of the little wood creatures.

She had often gone fishing near the Nene with her father and Ned and always enjoyed the peace of the countryside, for the manor was rarely quiet, echoing with the sound of voices from kitchens, dairy and buttery as well as calls from the stables and the sounds of hammers in the outbuildings where smiths, carpenters and coopers were going about their various duties on the desmesne.

Anne's mother had kept her employed, learning housewifely skills in the house itself, as well as overseeing the maids in the dairy. Anne enjoyed learning the healing arts in her mother's still room, but she hated the hours in the hall and solar with her embroidery and distaff for Margaret Jarvis had insisted that it was necessary still for every woman to learn to spin.

Richard Allard sat eating and drinking ale but she thought he seemed more than a whit restless, as if impatient to be once more on the road. However, he said little, every now and then glancing in her direction and ensuring she had all her needs provided.

Food always tasted good to Anne eaten out in the open and she revelled in the fresh, clean tang of cheese and new-baked bread and the salty tastiness of crisp, cold bacon. She wondered if she would develop a taste for the rich sauces and extravagant roast peacocks and swans served at Court, though her mother had informed her that often those strange, exotic meats were tough and everything had grown cold before it reached the table, having been carried from kitchens some distance from the eating hall.

The men went off eventually, leading the horses to water them. Mary sat back against a moss-covered rock, seemingly dozing. Anne rubbed at her greasy hands. She had a napkin but would welcome now some water for washing. The men would be at the stream bank, which could not be far away. She would go in the direction of the sound of water and wash her hands. She looked down at Mary then decided not to waken her and, soft-footed, hurried off.

The track appeared well marked as if people had come this way often and she had few problems with overgrowing branches. She walked confidently, humming a little tune she had heard one of the grooms sing. In the distance she could hear the reassuring sound of laughter and jovial voices in banter. The three men were very near and would hear if she cried out.

She reached the stream at last and stood admiring its quaint beauty as it burbled over stones. The summer had been dry but there had been several days of heavy rain about a week back and the stream was quite high. It was very narrow—she could have leaped across very easily—and, obviously, it was not deep, but she approached the bank cautiously. She had no wish to slip on muddy ground and fall into the water, it would ruin her fine new cloak and gown.

There was an area of rock some feet away, overhanging the stream, and she could crouch down there and refresh her hands and face without fear of muddying her gown hem. She moved carefully and managed it quite well, stooping low on solid ground which fortunately was not slippery. The water was cool and clean. She dangled her right hand in for some time, revelling in the chill but silky feel of the water on her flesh, then washed both hands and splashed her lower face gently to remove any surplus bacon grease from around her mouth.

She stood up and was aware now that the sounds of the men had stopped, so they had moved back towards the clearing. She almost stumbled over her cloak hem as she made a little hurried leap towards the relatively dry track with its carpet of fallen leaves. She would be missed. She must hurry. She knew, instinctively, that Master Richard Allard would be angered that she had not woken Mary and had moved alone out of sight of her escort.

To her surprise she discovered there were several well-marked tracks leading away from the stream bed that she had not noticed before. She stood for a moment, uncertain as to which one to follow back to the clearing. She had been so certain that the way was unmistakable that she had taken no particular note of her surroundings and the varieties of certain of the trees in passing.

Finally she decided the wider track must be the correct one; in any case, she could not end up far from the clearing and she was in hailing distance of the others so she set off along that one.

When she heard sounds of movement ahead she thought she had followed the right path and was now close to the clearing. Either the men had returned or Mary had begun to gather up the remains of the meal and the utensils they had used. She was about to call to her when she stopped still suddenly and listened intently.

She could hear muttering, heavy breathing and scrabbling sounds that seemed unmistakable. There were people struggling together ahead of her, fighting. She knew those sounds only too well for wrestling and fighting with the broad sword and dagger were necessary lessons in Ned's military training, undertaken with expert advice from Simpkin Cooper and her own father as tutors. She had watched them often in the courtyard at Rushton.

She remained, for moments, stock still, uncertain how to proceed. These combatants could not be members of her escort. Simpkin Cooper and Wat Glazier were friends and utterly trustworthy. Neither man would fight with the other or attack Master Allard for any reason whatever. She went a trifle cold as it occurred to her that someone might have discovered Mary alone in the clearing and accosted her.

A sense of the enormity of her guilt suffused her. How stupidly crass she had been to leave Mary alone—and yet Mary had been within call of the members of the escort, as she was. Mary Scroggins was perfectly capable of defending herself if necessary, she would not stand by tamely and allow a strange man to approach her without giving tongue.

No, this could not be Mary, nor did Anne think it could be the two men-at-arms. Someone else was in the spinney. She had branched off further from the clearing than she had expected to be and was obviously on the wrong path. She was suddenly frightened. Anne was rarely frightened. Life at Rushton had never allowed her to be.

She had been terrified once when out hawking with her father and a boar had suddenly broken cover and rushed straight at her, but she had been aware of the nearness of her father and had trusted him to come to her rescue which he had done immediately. He had launched his merlin at the creature to frighten it and then rushed it on horseback so that it turned at bay, then, squealing ferociously, run into the undergrowth.

Now she felt totally unguarded and uncertain what to do. The noise of conflict grew louder and more desperate, and even over that Anne could hear the sound of her own frantic fast breathing. She could turn and run, but if she did, would the combatants hear her, cease their fighting and turn on her, or should she stay where she was, quiet, and await the outcome of the conflict?

Suddenly the decision was taken out of her hands when the two men burst on to the track in front of where she stood petrified. They were grappling close, panting hard for mastery and she caught glimpses of sunlight on dagger blades as each struggled to get one crippling or fatal blow at the other. Anne gave a gasp of horror when she saw one of the men was Richard Allard.

That one gasp betrayed her, for Richard's assailant turned to look at her—an erroneous decision, as Richard struck a sudden blow at his arm. He sprang away, clasping it as bright blood dripped to the floor of the forest track. Anne gave a sharp scream of dismay.

She was so startled that she was taken totally by surprise when she was suddenly seized by the stranger and drawn across his thick, muscular body to face his antagonist. Blood from the arm wound dripped on to her cloak. She tried to struggle free but his strong arm held her fast and the other hand lifted his own dagger to her throat. She was effectively held hostage.

She could smell the male sweat of exertion and the sharper, unmistakable musky stink of fear. She stopped struggling then and remained very still in his grasp, looking steadfastly at Richard Allard who stood back a little distance, chest heaving, mouth stretched in the distinctive attitude of utter hatred and the trained warrior's determination to kill. Anne drew in a hard breath and swallowed.

Her captor grated hoarsely, 'Drop your weapon, Allard, or I shall undoubtedly kill this woman. I noticed before in our acquaintance you have a somewhat foolishly gallant attitude to women, even peasant women, that prevents you from harming them or allowing harm to come to them.' His tone was sneering.

Neither man moved. Anne found the dagger was so close she dared not swallow again. The utter shock of events caused her to remain unnaturally calm. She knew she must not scream or cry out to Richard for assistance. She could not imagine what had caused these two men to engage in so desperate a fight or how they had encountered each other here in this wood. Obviously they were old enemies and knew each other's worth in the art of killing.

A deadly numbness assailed her. One of these two would not come out of this alive, she knew, and she prayed silently that it would not be Richard Allard. He must deal with his assailant and she must do nothing now to endanger him further. Her eyes widened in abject terror as she ascertained that Richard had been wounded. She could see ominous markings upon his jerkin and his left sleeve. An ugly scratch marred his right cheek. They had been so close in this struggle it was a miracle that both still remained on their feet. She continued to remain passively still, looked coolly at her protector and waited for him to determine the next step in this game.

It came so swiftly that she had no time to cry out. There was a sudden flash of light as Richard Allard's dagger flew from his hand unerringly and buried itself in her captor's shoulder. He gave a harsh scream and let her fall forward on to her face.

She lay still for moments, scarcely able to breathe; when at least she managed to scramble upright, Richard Allard had sprung once again at the stranger who was now supine on the track with Allard's body full across him. Anne stood back on very wobbly legs as Richard stood up. His back was to her but with trembling lips she saw him retrieve his dagger, stoop to wipe it on the grass and turn to face her.

Her frightened eyes went to the man lying now so still.

She tried to speak but could not, then she swallowed and croaked, 'Is—is he dead?'

Richard smiled at her grimly as he looked down at his enemy, then back at her. 'Very,' he said pithily.

She stumbled back against a nearby tree trunk and he came quickly towards her and pulled her into his supporting arms.

She sobbed against his leather jerkin, clutching at him in an emotional storm of relief from immediate fear and bewilderment. For the moment she could think of nothing but her need for his physical nearness; his comforting arms tightened around her. He bent and kissed the top of her head upon her soft linen coif where her hood had slipped back in her frantic struggle with her captor. Her sobs did not slacken and he whispered softly, 'All is well, Anne. There is nothing more to fear. He cannot hurt you now.'

Her slim form, taut with fear and revulsion against the sight of her dead assailant, pressed even closer and he felt his own loins throb with an anguished response. She was so very young and vulnerable, totally within his power at this moment. During the days he had been in her company he had found himself drawn to her, at first with a sense of tolerant amusement for her lordly ways and complete self-confidence.

He had been stirred by her beauty but there was more to it than that. For years he had steeled himself against commitment, against the giving of his heart, for he knew the main purpose of his life must be everything to him and that very deadly purpose could lead him to disaster and bring danger and sorrow to any woman who loved him, a threat which could cause him to deviate from his sworn oath of loyalty to one who was no longer able to release him from it.

He had amused himself with women, flirted with them, frolicked with them, bedded them—but never had he promised any one of them love. He had known when he first saw this lovely child again that he would be drawn beneath her spell, had thought ruefully that many men would be so, and when her father had asked him if he would want to wed her he had been first disturbed, later willing enough, yet aware that committing himself to the care of such a beguiling creature would place restraints upon his future conduct, restraints that until now he had not contemplated.

He bent his head lower and nuzzled strands of her curling raven black hair straggling free from the displaced cap. The softness of her small, proud breasts tight against his heart stirred his senses and he was forced to take himself in hand and gently put her from him.

She lifted blue eyes swimming with tears to gaze up at him and he smiled reassuringly.

She said softly, 'Are you much hurt? He—he meant to kill you.'

He bowed his head in acquiescence.

'I've taken scratches only, nothing that will not heal or that could prevent me from continuing to escort you to Westminster.'

She sniffed back further tears and stood back a little.

'I am sorry, sir,' she said. 'I should not have—troubled you so—at such a time.'

She turned to look at the body and then averted her eyes,

shuddering. He thought she had probably not seen a man dead from violence. There must have been occasions when she had viewed dead souls, for the manor accommodated many servants of the household, some of them elderly, but that was different, in the way of natural happenings to which she had become accustomed, but the sight of this killing had undoubtedly alarmed her.

She drew fast but deep breaths and then suddenly, it seemed, she had regained her previous composure.

She said quietly, 'Who is he? Why—why did he want you dead? How did you come to meet in this wood?'

He moved to stand beside the body of his enemy and looked down dispassionately. 'I know him only as one Simon Benton. He was a creature of Bishop Morton's and I imagine is now in the service of King Henry's spymaster. I discovered him following me on my last journey but thought I had shaken him off when I returned to England. Then, I thought I caught a glimpse of him as we rode through Northampton and was not surprised to see bushes rustling near the clearing. I was sure he was still on my track. Clearly he was aware of my visit to your father and I had to dispose of him before he endangered both of us.'

Her eyes stretched wide, displayed real horror now.

'You mean you pounced on him deliberately—to kill him.'

Richard Allard shrugged. 'Do not shed tears for him. He has been responsible for the deaths of many good men. He would not have had the slightest qualms about killing you. His one purpose was to obtain evidence of treason against me, fabricated, if necessary, and have me die horribly at Tyburn. It was either him or me—and, of course, as it turned out, you.'

'So you are involved in treason?' she accused him. 'And you have criminally endangered my father.'

'Mistress Anne,' he said coldly, 'I am not prepared to discuss these matters with you. It is needful only to explain that I intend no harm to the King nor to any other soul in this coming visit to Westminster. Rather I go in the hope that I might be instrumental in helping to save one.'

Before she could protest further he bent on one knee and methodically began to search the body of the dead man. Anne looked wildly round in search of the right way now to join Mary Scroggins but it was obvious she had completely missed her way and she dared not set off again alone. She was shivering with cold now, so much so that her teeth were actually chattering.

She could not bear to look at the corpse yet she knew instinctively that Richard Allard was right. The man would have killed both of them had he had opportunity. She had been glad enough for Richard to save her, had counted on him to do so. She understood too that her father could be in danger from the spying activities of this man. Even the suspicion that Richard Allard had come to Rushton to beg for his aid in this new venture would be enough to condemn her beloved father to the terrible death Richard had hinted at.

She murmured fearfully, 'Do you think he could have already sent off an incriminating report about—about you and my father?'

He looked back at her over his shoulder. 'Who knows? We must hope not. That is what I am trying to determine now. He appeared to be on his own when I saw him in Northampton.'

'What will you do about—about the body?' she enquired in a sad little whisper. 'I expect you will not want him to be found—too quickly.'

'Exactly,' Richard said grimly, rising to his feet and

pushing a package wrapped in oilskin within the opening of his jerkin.

'Do you think that is...his report on your activities and...and your visit to Rushton?'

'Most likely. I'll examine the contents later. For the present I'll take you back to the clearing, get Simpkin or Wat to help me put this fellow in a shallow grave beneath the undergrowth somewhere and then we must be off again as soon as possible. I intend to reach the nunnery where you and Mary must sleep tonight before darkness falls and see you both safely disposed.'

He took her elbow and began to push his way through the overhanging branches. Obviously, despite the distractions of the fight, he knew his way, which was more than Anne did. She concluded he was an expert woodsman, had slept out, hidden out, often and was accustomed to finding his way by noting particular stones and trees in passing.

Soon they were on another track and walking was easier.

He said sharply, 'Whatever caused you to leave the clearing without Mary? That was foolish and dangerous behaviour as you've now discovered.'

She was thoroughly miserable now and reaction to the dreadful happening she had taken part in was setting in. She thought she would never feel warm again. The sun had almost disappeared and she realised he was right, they had been unaccountably delayed and could be benighted. She experienced a sudden urge to rush away from this place and blamed herself that she had ever suggested eating out of doors instead of within the protective walls of some inn. The terrible events of the last hour could not have taken place, then—yet she gave a little gulp as she realised the man would still be living and carrying incriminating despatches to Westminster which could harm her family.

Richard Allard was staring down at her, silently demanding an answer to his question and she said miserably, 'I just wanted to wash my hands and face. Mary was asleep. I didn't want to disturb her and I could hear you all splashing away and talking by the stream well within call. I saw no danger.' She gave a little gasp of dismay. 'When I turned from the stream I must have taken the wrong track.'

'Indeed you did. It veered away at an angle,' he said grimly. 'Promise me, Mistress Anne, you will not take yourself off alone again. Your father entrusted your safety to me. He could not imagine you would do anything so foolish.'

'Neither did he think you would be engaged in a fight to the death,' she riposted sharply and he inclined his head in silent acknowledgement of her rebuke. It had been grossly unfortunate that he had encountered Simon Benton on this journey. It had caused him to risk the life of his charge.

They were within earshot of the clearing where they had eaten now and Simpkin Cooper called out to his leader.

'Is that you, Master Allard? Is Mistress Anne with you?' His voice contained a note of real alarm. 'She must have left the clearing while Mary Scroggins slept.'

'Aye, she is safe with me.'

Richard Allard pushed back the last low-lying branch of alder and led Anne into the clearing to the obvious relief of all of the waiting group. Mary rose at once, her face drawn with anxiety.

'Mistress Anne, how could you have...?'

'Explanations later,' Richard snapped. 'We must get ready to go shortly. See all our belongings are packed up. Leave nothing to be discovered. We must carry everything away with us, even our food leavings.'

Simpkin regarded him anxiously while Wat stared at him curiously. Mary was too concerned about the dishevelled state of her mistress to notice anything unusual in the behaviour of the two men.

Simpkin said, 'And that other matter, Master Allard?'

'Has been dealt with but I shall need your assistance to dispose of all signs of it.' He looked round briefly at the little group. 'Simpkin and I will be busied about our own business for perhaps a half-hour. Have everything ready for our departure when we come back to you.' He gave Anne a warning glance, enjoining her to remain silent about what had occurred. She inclined her chin in obedience to his implied command.

She watched while Simpkin Cooper procured a shovel from one of the saddle bags and the two men plunged off together along the track again. Hysterically she wondered if they had all come prepared to bury any inconvenient bodies they found along the way. Mary was scolding her gently but Anne was too distracted to hear what she said. Her brain was furiously considering any possible obstacles which might obstruct them further on this journey. What had seemed an exciting new venture had taken on a much more sinister purpose. She was very close to tears again and dared not give way to them.

The men returned very shortly, indeed, so quickly that Anne wondered how they could possibly have managed the grim task in the time. While Simpkin was replacing the shovel within his saddle bag Richard Allard caught Anne's eye and she looked hurriedly away.

They soon resumed their journey and she was very glad to be away from this clearing, which had now become a place of ill omen.

Some twelve miles south they reached the nunnery of a community of Poor Clares, which readily offered hospitality to Anne and her attendant. The place was small and possessed no real accommodation for male visitors so the men were forced to sleep in a barn outside its walls. As he lifted her down from her palfrey Anne felt Richard's arms tighten around her when he lowered her to the ground.

'Swear to me that you will give the sisters no cause for concern,' he said quietly. 'Stay with Mary the whole time until we leave in the morning.'

'Of course I will,' she retorted, more snappishly than she intended. She had had quite enough of a lesson to remind her not to stray from her escorts again.

She watched him move away from the gate as the sister portress admitted her and Mary. She was suddenly aware that she would miss him during what could prove to be a somewhat long night.

Mary asked no questions once they were left alone together after a frugal supper with the sisters in the refectory. The little cell-like chamber they were allotted possessed sparse comforts but the pallet beds were clean and fragrant with the scents of lavender and rosemary. Anne was thankful that Mary was to sleep beside her; she could not have borne to be alone after her frightening adventure.

At length Anne ventured to give some explanation for her absence from the clearing earlier for she knew she had given Mary a thorough fright and, though Mary had made no complaint, she must have been very curious.

'I—went to wash my hands in the stream,' she explained, 'and—and I must have missed the right track back. Master Allard found me and—' she swallowed '—you must have guessed, Mary, that we were set upon in the wood. Master Allard was forced to—kill the man and…'

Mary inclined her head. 'I gathered as much. Were you physically assaulted? You are unhurt?'

'Oh, yes, the man seized me and—and held me—but Master Allard managed to overcome…' Her eyes were bright with tears. 'It was dreadful, Mary. I had no idea that such terrible things could happen away from home and...'

'And you will keep me in sight in future?'

'I promise.'

'Was Master Allard hurt?'

'He said he sustained merely scratches but—but I was really afraid for him.'

'He is a resourceful young man. You could have no finer protector.'

Anne glanced at her maid sharply. Was Mary aware of her father's desire for a betrothal to Richard Allard? Mary knew, of course, how closely the two families were linked and of their alliances to the Yorkist cause. Had she guessed at the identity of the man who had attacked them? If so, she would not speak of it. Throughout her life her loyalty had been given first to the Allard household and now to the Jarvis one. She would keep very quiet about any possibly treasonable conversation she had ever heard. Mary, Anne was sure, would be delighted if her charge was to wed the young master she so much admired.

As Anne lay beside Mary on the narrow cot, her thoughts went again to the encounter in the wood. She thought she would never forget the terrifying moment when the man's knife had pricked at her throat and she had relied totally on Richard Allard's ability to save her.

She closed her eyes and pictured him, strong, brawny, his tousled brown hair shining with the pale sun behind him at the moment when he had been poised to throw his dagger. How skilful he had been with it; obviously he had had much practice.

She remembered how she had sobbed against his jerkin and how he had reassured her. Even now she could feel the strong beat of his heart against her own. He was a man to rely on, a man many women must have known—and loved—

She shied from the thought. Such a man was not made to marry. Any woman trusting enough to love him could soon find her heart broken when she became a widow. No, whatever her father wished, she could not allow herself to become fond of Richard Allard. Soon this journey would be over and his responsibility for her safety at an end. Then she must dismiss all tender thoughts of him from her mind and concentrate on acquitting herself well at Court and—possibly—finding herself a wealthy and steady suitor who was as desirous of achieving preferment and a comfortable existence as she was herself.

Nevertheless she uttered a silent prayer to the Virgin that she would keep Richard Allard safe and free from any taint of treasonous dealings which might result in his terrible end at Tyburn.

Chapter Four

When she awoke next morning the sun was shining into the little bare cell. Immediately, Anne felt she could put behind her the terrible events of the previous day and was able to smile at Mary Scroggins confidently when she came in with a ewer of warm water for Anne's toilet.

'You managed to sleep at last, Mistress Anne? For the first part of the night you were very restless.'

Anne nodded. 'I was—thinking about that man and how he died—and—and how he might have carried information that could bring grave danger to my father and…'

'He is gone, Mistress Anne,' Mary reassured her. 'Your father has managed to live with greater threats than this, as has Sir Dominick and his lady. You must put those frightening thoughts from you now. Master Richard will know how to protect you. The sun is shining as you can see and we'll make good progress this morning if you hurry up with dressing and break your fast.'

Obediently Anne washed and stood docilely while Mary laced her into her travelling gown. Her thoughts went to her escort who had remained outside the nunnery with the men. A little thrill of pleasure went through her as she pictured Richard Allard waiting for her to emerge. As Mary said, he was a rock of strength and she would be relieved to see him again. She made a hasty breakfast, visited the prioress and made her thanks, called into the chapel to make her devotions and prayed for the soul of the dead Simon Benton and was relieved at last when the portress opened the gate and she saw that Richard Allard stood ready, holding the reins of her palfrey.

He exchanged courtesies with the portress and smiled at Anne encouragingly as she stepped towards him.

'Are you refreshed, Mistress Anne?'

'Yes,' she said a little tremulously. 'It took me a while to get off to sleep but I am perfectly ready to ride.'

He lifted her effortlessly into the saddle and handed her the reins.

She looked down at him. 'Were you very cold in the night?'

'No, no,' he replied cheerfully. 'We bedded down in a barn just outside the enclave. We've fed and watered the animals. All is well.'

She glanced round at the two men-at-arms and nodded. It seemed that everything had been completed early to ensure a prompt start. Mary was helped into her pillion place behind Wat Glazier and they set off once Richard was mounted. Anne turned once, lifting her hand in grateful acknowledgment of hospitality received as the portress closed the gate.

They travelled south, as she expected, by the old Roman road, Watling Street, passing first through Stoney Stratford. Here, Anne knew, the elder of the two lost princes, sons of King Edward IV, had been taken into the charge of their uncle, Richard of Gloucester, all those years ago before they were formally declared illegitimate and he himself mounted the throne.

Richard noted her curious glance as they passed the inn and he nodded grimly.

'I expect you are remembering the imagined fate of the princes.'

'My father was present on that occasion when the Duke quelled the threatened rebellion and arrested Earl Rivers and Sir Richard Grey, the boy's half-brother.' She added gravely, 'Those two men were both executed.'

'Had they not been the peace of the realm would have been instantly shattered,' Richard said coolly. 'My father was also present and saw for himself that the men from Ludlow escorting the prince brought with them carts laden with weapons and armour which was later displayed to the officials in London as proof of their intended treason. It was by a codicil to the late King's will that his brother, Richard, should be Lord Protector of England.'

'You were not with him, then?'

He laughed. 'No, I was still enjoying boyish pleasures on our manor in Yorkshire. I went to Westminster to serve at Court a year later.'

'My mother and father met soon after that incident,' she mused. 'He arrested her on the road and was given custody of her. They were enemies yet, later…' She broke off in some confusion.

'They were wed and fell deeply in love with each other,' he completed, chuckling. 'Something of the kind happened to my mother. Do you know, she was found trying to steal my father's horse, his prized courser, Roland.' He laughed out loud. 'It is a wonder he ever came to forgive her.' He turned merry grey eyes upon her. 'There, we have something else in common, Mistress Anne.'

'It would seem so, sir,' she rejoined stiffly.

She was silent for a while as they continued their ride, then she ventured, 'My father is convinced that King

Richard did not harm the boys. Do you—do you think they can both be alive?'

He too was silent for moments then he said soberly, 'No one can be sure. Of the Lord Edward we can have no idea of his fate. As for the Lord Richard, well, you know rumour has it that he resides now in the Tower.'

'Warbeck?' she mouthed silently and he shook his head.

'Yet, surely he confessed that he was not the prince he had claimed to be and the Queen—she must know whether or no this man is her brother…' Her voice tailed off miserably and she glanced behind at the two following riders as if she feared being overheard even by those two whom she knew were stolidly loyal to her father.

Richard Allard shrugged. 'It is doubtful if Queen Elizabeth has been allowed to speak with Warbeck; even if she had suspicions as to his identity, would she dare to voice them?'

'But the King could not harm her?'

'No?' Richard Allard's expression was very grim indeed. 'He was very quick to thrust her mother into a nunnery where she conveniently died. Apart from that, Elizabeth now has her own children to consider, Prince Arthur and young Henry in line behind him.'

He urged his mount forward a little as if determined not to discuss the matter further and she too spurred her own palfrey to keep up with him. She considered in silence what had been said—and implied. If Richard Allard had business in London, was it really to do with his manor as her mother had declared, or were his motives for being in the capital now more sinister? Did he believe that the prisoner, Perkin Warbeck, was truly the Queen's brother, and, if so, did he intend to involve himself in plots to free the man and try to restore him to what he believed was his rightful place on the throne?

She was relieved to find that when they reached Dunstable Richard Allard had decided that it would be both safe and proper to sleep at a public inn, The Rising Sun, where he had stayed several times before on his road to London. She was glad that this night she would not be separated from her escort.

The chamber she was to share with Mary was no larger nor less spartan than their cell at the nunnery but it was private—she was grateful she had not to sleep with several other women in the inn's main common sleeping chamber. Richard Allard himself insisted on seeing and approving the room personally and chivvying the young chambermaid to bring a warming pan to air the sheets and to provide them with warm water for their toilet. Anne could not help noticing the admiring glance the girl gave him as she scurried past, giggling, and trying to avoid his good-natured slap on her rump. Tartly Anne thought he certainly was attractive to women of that sort.

Supper was served to her in the bedchamber and, hearing the rowdiness below, she was glad of it. The men would be bedded down in the stable and Richard assured her that he would be comfortable enough in the second common chamber given over to male patrons.

After supper, however, when Mary had gone below to request a posset to assure her charge's restful sleep, she ventured to descend to the taproom where she thought she would find Richard, to bid him goodnight and thank him again for his assiduous care of her during the day, and his good offices that had seen to it that she and Mary would be comfortable here.

She was ridiculously glad to know he would be much nearer to her tonight than during the previous one and found herself wishing to see his ruggedly charming face again.

No one accosted her on the stair and she found the door to the taproom simply enough. A curious serving wench passed her, brows raised at sight of a lady of quality, and Anne drew a relieved breath, noting that there would be at least one other woman in the taproom.

She pushed the door further open and then looked hurriedly round for Richard.

There he was, seated on the far side of the fireplace, his back to her, but she could not fail to know the set of those massively broad shoulders or the confident way he carried his head. She was about to advance towards him when she saw that he was in close conversation with a man facing him across the stained table. He was lifting a tankard of ale but his head was inclined towards the other and he was obviously listening intently to what his companion had to say.

Anne paused, a little bewildered. Had Richard so soon made the acquaintance of this fellow traveller, or perhaps the man lived in Dunstable? She had somehow not expected him to so casually converse with strangers. Something about their nearness, their intimacy, told her they knew one another—and very well.

She bit her lip uncertainly. Had they met by chance or was this inn a place of assignation? She could not dismiss from her mind the constant nagging dread that Richard was engaged in questionable activities—yet, surely, had her father suspected that, he would never have entrusted her to Richard Allard's charge.

Richard's companion looked up and bowed his head in courteous acknowledgement of her presence. She saw now that he was much shorter than Richard Allard, soberly though well dressed in some style and quality, obviously a gentleman. His face was long and thin, his expression melancholy. His hair, she thought, was dark though most of it was concealed beneath his broad-brimmed velvet hat. Richard turned as he saw his companion's attentions shift and he rose instantly to greet her.

'Mistress Anne, is something wrong? You should have sent Mary down and I would have come upstairs instantly to deal with the matter.'

She approached a little hesitantly and took the stool he drew back for her to seat herself, nodding a trifle self-consciously at the stranger who had also risen to his feet.

'No, sir. Is it not proper for a lady to come into the taproom?'

'No, it is certainly acceptable at an inn so well respected as this is,' Richard assured her. 'I just thought you need not have troubled yourself. You must be very tired. Our journey today has been long.' He looked towards his companion. 'Allow me to present a friend of long standing who lives near here, Master Roger Needham. Roger, my betrothed, Mistress Anne Jarvis.'

She stiffened immediately, her lips tightening at his presumption, but made no comment.

She only half-heard Master Needham's courteous and flattering congratulation. She was seething with anger. She had not thought her father's intentions had yet been made formal and certainly she had given no consent—nor would she be likely to do so.

Richard was speaking. 'Mistress Jarvis is to spend a short time at Court to attend on the Queen's Grace at her request, so unfortunately we shall be parted for some months, though for a short while I intend to stay in the city and make certain all is well with her during these first bewildering weeks at Court.'

Roger Needham was smiling. 'You are fortunate, Mistress Jarvis, to have the good will of Her Grace the Queen who is a very gentle mistress.'

Anne was startled. 'You have met the Queen, sir?'

He smiled a little sadly. 'Yes, when I was very much younger.'

She judged him to be about Richard's age or perhaps a little older. So he had seen the Queen at her uncle's Court. Was he, like Richard, banished from the new one?

Richard ordered mulled ale for her and she remained with them for a little while, though she was conscious that her cheeks were stained red with indignation and she was lost for the words she had originally intended to say to Richard Allard. The men talked now of mundane affairs, how the weather had affected their demesnes, the possible price of wool in London and the south and east coastal ports. Anne knew none of this had been what they were discussing before she arrived.

Master Needham chatted with her courteously, asking after the health and well-being of her parents. She was not sure if he was acquainted with her father. When she rose at last, asking to be excused, the two sprang to their feet, Roger Needham murmuring his good wishes for her stay at court.

Richard said quickly, 'Excuse me, Roger. I will escort Mistress Anne to her chamber. I will return to you soon.'

So their business was not concluded. She had interrupted them.

She said a trifle frostily, 'There is no need, sir, to leave your friend so precipitously. It is but a step to my chamber and Mary will be waiting there.'

He remained firm. 'I will go with you to the door. There may be some rude fellow to accost you in the corridor or on the stair.' He stared into her furious blue eyes. 'Your father entrusted you to me, remember.'

If anything those eyes grew stormier and more alight with snapping lights. She turned from him.

'I bid you goodnight, Master Needham. Thank you for your good wishes. We may meet again, since you are friendly with my—with Master Allard,' she concluded lamely.

Richard could not be unaware of her anger as he moved close to her rigid young body as they climbed the stair. At her door she turned on him furiously.

'How dare you tell that man that I am your betrothed.'

His grey eyes continued to stare back at her but mildly. There was no anger or irritation in his gaze.

'But you are,' he returned reasonably.

'I most certainly am not.'

His lips curved into a smile. 'Your father has promised you to me. It is concluded, though we are not formally betrothed before a priest. I consider myself betrothed to you and shall continue to consider myself bound to you as you, I hope, will be equally careful in your association with courtiers at Westminster.'

There was no trace of command in his voice. She could have wished there had been so she, in her turn, might have turned upon him again roundly. He merely reminded her gravely that she was his promised bride and she must conduct herself as such during the next months when they would be parted.

'I have not the slightest intention of entering into a betrothal with you,' she snapped. 'My father knows my mind and...'

'Is amused that you are hoping to ensnare an earl or marquis, or even a duke,' he said, smiling.

Anger made even more hectic spots on her fine cheekbones.

'You make me sound as if I intend to tout my goods at market.'

'Isn't that what you imply, that I am not good enough for you?'

His shot had gone home and for the first time she saw clearly how her avowed intention to wed only a man loyal to the crown would look to someone like Richard Allard.

'That is not it,' she said hastily, the tone of her voice higher than she would wish and she tried hard to lower it and calm her rising temper. 'You do not understand. I am not out to obtain a wealthy husband. Indeed I do not flatter myself that I have anything to offer such a man but—but—' she floundered, 'I cannot and will not marry you, Master Allard, however much my father is in favour of the match.'

'You find me repulsive?'

'Of course not.'

'I am too old for you, too ugly, too poor, is that it?'

'Certainly you are not ugly,' she countered weakly. 'In fact—in fact—you are attractive, or would be to some women.'

'Like inn wenches and servant girls.'

'Do not be foolish,' she retorted. 'Though, doubtless some of them will find you attractive as you do them.'

'Some of them,' he agreed smiling.

She turned from him, unwilling to meet his gaze. He was unsettling her with his even, quiet tone, his ability to meet her temper with calm.

'I must have a husband who is—' she struggled for words to explain '—who is not bound to the lost Yorkist cause, who will not leave me constantly to worry that he has been taken for treason, tortured and executed, his lands and goods attainted…'

'Ah.'

She turned back to him, reading his total understanding of the situation in his single syllable.

'You must see my point. All her life my mother has been

subject to these pressures and anxieties, yours too, I don't doubt. I keep trying to get people to understand that it is not gold I seek in a husband, but security.'

He was regarding her so intently and gravely now that she felt decidedly uncomfortable. He was so close to her, his breath fanning her cheek. All day she had been aware of the fact that she had gloried in his presence on the journey, had been relieved that they had not been parted as at the nunnery, that she was growing more and more conscious of his rugged good looks and the overpowering masculinity of him.

She had come down, just now, in search of him. His nearness set her pulses racing. This must not be allowed to go on. Deliberately she moved further from him.

'Even were I to love you, sir,' she whispered, 'and I assure you, I do not, I could not consent to wed you. It would be—unwise.'

He gave a faint sigh and, stooping, raised her unwilling hand to his lips. 'We shall see,' he said gently. 'Do not upset yourself. I ask you to be merely—cautious—in your dealings with others at Court, as I am sure your father has exhorted you to be.'

'You are not in love with me,' she said hastily. 'This is an arrangement between our parents. It cannot be humiliating for you or disappointing.'

His smile had not diminished. 'I think you underestimate both your beauty and your spirited nature, Mistress Anne. It will not be difficult for any man to fall in love with you in a very short time, indeed, find it very hard to resist your charms. That is why I am anxious to ensure that you should not be disappointed or your reputation dishonoured at Court.'

She was bewildered, searched his expression for the full meaning of his flattering words. She had been petulant in her dealings with him. Despite herself she knew she had behaved childishly when she had been most anxious to act in a mature, sensible fashion. He *could* not be in love with her. She was not dealing him so harsh a blow in her refusal of him.

He leaned forward suddenly and, before she could protest, kissed her lightly upon the cheek, then bowed and set off down the stair again.

She stood staring after him, her hand to the spot where his lips had rested, so featherlight in touch and yet she felt the burn of the hasty caress. She gave a little half-sob and, lifting the latch, hurried into her chamber.

Next morning she breakfasted with him downstairs in a room set aside for the convenience of travellers. He made no mention of their exchange the night before and she was both grateful and embarrassed. It was still early and, as yet, there were few travellers at tables near them. At length she put down her spoon and said softly, 'Did you meet Master Needham last night by intent? Is that the reason why you chose this inn for our stay?'

He shook his head, his attention given to carving the leg of cold beef set before him. 'No, I did not.'

'Then how did he know you were here?' she demanded accusingly.

He considered. 'I don't know. I imagine he heard word from someone who knows me and saw us on the road that I had passed this way and he came to enquire for me here. We have stayed here together on several occasions.'

He turned towards her and his eyes were steely this morning. 'I did not come here to discuss treasonous matters with Roger Needham as you appear to imply. I promised your father I would take great care of you. Do you think I would be foolish enough to involve you in questionable matters?'

She gave a little intake of breath. She knew that her fears had been groundless, that he was speaking the truth. He would not, willingly, endanger her but—she could not help but be suspicious.

He said deliberately, 'He asked me for news of those companions we hold in common, especially those who no longer live here in England. I was able to tell him of some, reassure him about the fates of others. We talked of nothing else that could incriminate either of us.'

'Yet had that man Benton seen you together, he might not have thought the meeting innocent,' she said slowly.

His grey eyes were still wary as he regarded her. 'No, probably not. Roger was unwise to enquire for me and I told him so. He is, as you guessed, known to be a Yorkist sympathiser though, as yet, nothing has been proved against him. He did not realise I was travelling with my betrothed or he might not have approached me so openly.'

She opened her lips to refute his claim and then closed them again. When she looked up at him he was smiling once more.

They continued their journey by way of St Albans and Barnet, neither commenting upon the battles which had taken place there, so poignant with the remembrance of former Yorkist victories, and, eventually, entered London, passing through Temple Bar and the fine newer houses of the Strand on their way to Westminster.

Anne was fascinated by the memorial cross at Charing which a grieving King Edward I had had erected for his dead Queen and recalled how her father and mother had spoken of King Richard's terrible grief on the loss of his beloved Anne and how that grief had been compounded by rumours that he intended to wed his niece, the present Queen Elizabeth. He had stoutly refuted those vile rumours and relegated his niece to the northern castle of Sheriff Hutton.

Anne thought Elizabeth must have been humiliated and distressed by such treatment and wondered afresh why, knowing Anne's father's allegiance to King Richard, she had invited Anne to attend her. The reason given had been to befriend Lady Philippa Telford, yet Philippa, too, was the child of a man known to be devoted to the late King.

Anne could not but be uncertain about the Queen's motives for summoning them both to Court. Now that they were drawing nearer and nearer to the palace of Westminster she was beginning to have more and more misgivings. She glanced covertly at Richard Allard, riding beside her, and her lips compressed. Despite her irritation at his claim on her, she could not help wishing that they need not part so soon and that he would be by her side over the next few frightening days.

She was disappointed by the squalor of the buildings which they were now approaching and that Richard told her were the dwellings adjacent to Westminster palace itself. The afternoon was damp and somewhat misty and she detected a rank odour, most probably emanating from the nearby River Thames. She knew that most visitors to the palace travelled by river barge from London Bridge, but mounted and with the sumpters carrying her baggage, it had been necessary for her party to go by road.

They were soon embroiled in a slow procession of market carts delivering provisions to the palace kitchens. Richard drew closer to her as they were jostled by the carters and pushed to the edge of the road. He called imperatively to one such impatient carter to give his lady room and was answered by a bawled obscenity. Richard rode up to the man and appeared to issue a challenge. Again the driver leaned from his perch and mockingly replied.

Richard dismounted, his horse remaining obediently still despite the distractions around it, for Anne's palfrey was moving restlessly, unused to such noise and confusion, and he simply climbed on to the cart wheel, seized the driver by the throat and shook him as a terrier shakes a rat. Adjacent drivers and those on foot cheered loudly, whether in support of the carter or, goodhumouredly, his attacker, Anne could not be sure.

She felt she should intervene and call Richard back, but she was uncertain how to respond to this brawling. Her two men-at-arms with Mary drew even closer to her protectively, and Simpkin Cooper cautioned her to remain silent and patiently wait the outcome. This, apparently, was how experienced men dealt with impertinent tradesmen in the capital. But then, Anne thought ruefully, she had never before known peasant folk or tradesmen in Leicester or Northampton treat her father with anything but profound respect.

The man sullenly slunk back on his driving seat as Richard strode arrogantly back to his little company. The nearby carts drew aside as he mounted and led them forward towards the main entrance to the palace courtyard.

Anne felt herself trembling with excitement, both from the alarm of the incident and for the moment of arrival.

It was then that she saw their progress must be further checked. Another cart in the very gateway had lost a wheel and the sweating carter, whose vehicle was swaying ominously and about to lose its load of farm produce, cabbages and winter salads, butter and wooden pails of milk, was climbing unwillingly and angrily down from his seat to the jeers and loudly voiced complaints of those behind him. This, then, was the cause of all the impatience and irritation experienced by those around her. Anne looked towards Richard as they neared the entrance and were unable to pass.

'Perhaps,' she called anxiously to him over the noise of raised voices shouting angry advice and exhortations to the poor man to move his cart out of the way, 'there is another entrance, if we can manage to extricate ourselves from this crowd.'

He looked back to assess the situation but they were well and truly hemmed in and he realised, with some annoyance, that it would take some time, possibly an hour, to persuade this rabble to co-operate with the unfortunate carter and help him clear the way. Meanwhile his charge was at the mercy of the importunate rudeness of this crowd.

There was a sudden shout behind him and he turned back again, to see a little knot of mounted men-at-arms forcing their way through the assembled tradesmen. At their head was a fashionably dressed young man in black velvet doublet, slashed to show an abundance of white silk beneath, tight black hose and, over all, one of the smart, long gowns in tawney velvet, sleeves turned back and bordered, like the front opening, with black velvet to match the doublet beneath. His broad-brimmed beaver hat was also black, set at a jaunty angle and adorned with golden dyed feathers.

He drew apace and immediately took in the sight of the little party attempting to gain access to the palace yard. He was tall in the saddle and Richard saw he wore his fair hair long and curling beneath his beaver. He saluted Anne courteously and his light blue eyes surveyed the problem. He bowed in the saddle.

'I bid you good afternoon, mistress. I take it you are endeavouring to enter the palace. Can I be of assistance?'

Anne looked anxiously at Richard for guidance but he merely shrugged his shoulders.

The young sprig had dismounted and came to her side. 'Allow me to introduce myself. I am John Hilyard, squire to the body of His Majesty. I do not think we have met before.'

She shook her head, nervously taking in his fashionable splendour.

'I have just arrived,' she explained. 'I am come to serve Her Grace the Queen at her request. I am Anne Jarvis from Northamptonshire and this—this is my escort and my maid.' She indicated the two men, Mary and Richard. 'We are just wondering how to get inside the gate...'

The newcomer's arrogant stare encountered that of Richard Allard and took in his sober and somewhat shabby attire.

Before she could prevent herself Anne heard herself saying, 'This is Dickon Allsop, my father's under steward. He—he comes with me to see me safe and established before he returns to report to my father. His services have proved indispensible on the journey.'

She saw Richard's eyes widen, his cheeks redden and heard him give the slightest hiss of breath. Mary Scroggins did more than that. She gave a distinctive gasp. Neither of her two men uttered a word.

John Hilyard issued a swift word of command to his own attendant soldiers who dismounted and, without ceremony, cleared their way through the crowd, impatiently using their riding whips to facilitate progress. Hilyard watched, light eyes narrowed, while the damaged cart was unceremoniously pushed aside and the way made clear for Anne's party to ride through the gate.

John Hilyard mounted and took his place beside her while Richard obsequiously fell in behind as expected in his role of servant.

Defiantly Anne averted her head so that he might not see

she was troubled by the sudden impulse that had made her acknowledge him as her servant. She only half-listened to her new companion who was openly appraising her as her hood slipped back and he had a clearer impression of her smooth cheeks, dark-fringed blue eyes and glossy dark locks. That he liked what he saw, he made very plain.

Haughtily he ordered the grooms and servants, who appeared as if by magic at their sides near the imposing main doors to the palace, to take charge of Mistress Jarvis's horses and baggage and to see to it that her men were taken first to the stables and then to the head groom to be afforded suitable accommodation. He dismounted and lifted her down and, taking her chilled hand, began to lead her inside. She tried to turn to look anxiously after Richard's progress, but it was obvious that Master John Hilyard was accustomed to being instantly obeyed and of taking charge of situations and she was forced to go with him docilely.

She was escorted down innumerable corridors, dark and lit by flaming brands, Mary scrambling after them. Anne was totally bewildered and thought she would never be able to find her way, once left to herself in this bewildering array of corridors opening off other larger chambers, each with doors leading off to other offices and guardrooms, from which she caught a glimpse of dark-clad officials and clerics busy on the King's business as she was hurried past.

Men-at-arms, armed with long pikes, wearing the Tudor rose and the familiar portcullis device of the King upon their tunics, guarded the entrances to all halls and chambers. Master Hilyard was clearly well known, for he was not once challenged and strode forward confidently. Anne peered about her doubtfully and tried to concentrate on the words he was saying to her.

He led her at last into a small chamber off what appeared to be a presence chamber, for she had a glimpse of fine

Turkey rugs upon the stone floor and carved and cushioned chairs over which hung a cloth of estate. An elderly man, tall, stooping, and with a curly beard, rose respectfully at their entrance and bowed. He was clad in a black open-fronted gown and wore a small close-fitting brimmed black felt hat ornamented with a gold brooch in the shape of a dragon rampant.

'Master steward,' John Hilyard announced imperiously, 'this is Mistress Anne Jarvis. I understand she has been summoned to attend on her Grace and is expected. Will you see to it that she is shown to the chamber appointed and the Queen informed of her arrival as soon as it is convenient.'

The older man bowed low and took from the side of his chair where it had been left a long white wand of office. He came immediately from behind his desk to greet Anne.

'You are, indeed, expected, mistress,' he intoned in a deep funereal voice. 'I have been instructed to see to your accommodation, and it has been made ready for you these two days past. I will conduct you there and her Majesty will, no doubt, send a page to inform you when she will receive you in audience.'

He was so splendid, both in his authoritative stance and manner, that Anne almost dropped him a curtsy. Then she caught the amusement in Master Hilyard's light sparkling blue eyes and remembered who she was and the respect which must be afforded her from all the royal servants.

'Thank you,' she said a trifle huskily and turned to offer her gloved hand to Master Hilyard gratefully. 'And thank you, sir, for quickly coming to my rescue outside the gate and kindly going out of your way to bring me here.'

He bowed and kissed her fingers. 'I am delighted I was opportunely there to give my assistance, mistress. I am sure we shall meet again soon when we both wait upon their Majesties and, of course, in the great hall at meal times.'

Anne felt that everything was coming so fast she could hardly catch her breath. The imposing steward was already almost impatiently showing signs that he was waiting to conduct her to her chamber. Hurriedly she made Master Hilyard a curtsy and, turning to see that Mary was close behind her, set off after her new guide.

She was shown to a small apartment of two rooms which the steward informed her she was to share with Lady Philippa Telford. The smaller room leading off the bed-chamber was to accommodate their two maids.

She glanced round the room, sparsely furnished and small, but she was grateful that she had not to sleep in a dormitory of ladies-in-waiting, as her mother informed her many new attendants did. Especially the younger ones, it being thought necessary for the Mistress of the Wardrobe to keep her charges well within her sight, particularly during the hours of darkness when there could be the temptation to misbehave.

There was a bed large enough for two, its linen and coverlet of excellent quality, a chest on which stood a ewer of water and bowl, two stools, a prie-dieu and a small cupboard on which stood candlesticks, tinder and flint, and two prickets.

She said briskly, 'This will do very well, thank you. Would you be so kind as to inform my escort, Master Allsop, where I am lodged, so that he can attend me here and see to the disposal of my baggage.'

The steward bowed. 'Certainly, Mistress Jarvis. Should you need anything, be pleased to summon one of the pages on duty outside in the corridor. He will do your bidding and escort you where you wish in the palace. Her Majesty is closeted with her chaplain at the moment but will be informed of your arrival directly he leaves her. She has asked to be told the moment you arrive here. Lady Philippa is expected tomorrow, but, of course should there be rough seas, she may be delayed.'

'I understand.'

Anne nervously waited while the man bowed his way out of her chamber. She had seen the two young boys outside, scarcely less youthful than she was, richly clad, their silken tunics bearing the royal device. She thought they looked most haughty in manner and that she would feel somewhat in awe of them, yet she must assert herself if she was to remain here and assume the exalted position of lady-in-waiting to the Queen.

Not for the first time she wondered about the personality of her companion and if they would be able to live in amity together in these rather cramped quarters.

Left to themselves, Mary took stock of the room's appointments and went to see her own quarters. At the door she said somewhat tartly, 'I hope you have decided exactly what you are going to say to Master Allard when he arrives. I doubt he will be pleased by the way events have shaped themselves.'

When the peremptory tap came on her door Anne felt a little shiver run down her spine. She called a command to enter, knowing her voice to be a trifle shrill with excited apprehension. Richard Allard walked in carrying the smaller of her two travelling chests and followed by Wat Glazier with the other. Silently Richard signalled for Wat to put down the chest and leave them. He glanced significantly round to see where Mary was.

'She is in that room next door. There are a couple of truckle beds in there for her and Lady Philippa's maid,' Anne said hesitantly.

He walked to the door and called, 'Leave us for a while, Mary.'

Then he returned to face Anne, who was standing a little defiantly, her back against the bed. She had removed her cloak and hood and was glancing longingly at the one small brazier which warmed the room, standing beneath the unglazed but shuttered window. A candle had already been lighted, though it was not yet full dark.

'I know you must be very angry,' she said defensively before he could speak. 'I—I had to think very quickly when Master Hilyard appeared. I—I was not sure if there could be anything known against—against Master Richard Allard and—' she drew a hard breath '—anyway, I—I did not want you to leave me here alone—not yet.' The last words were uttered in a sudden rush.

'Ah.' He used that significant single syllable again.

She said petulantly, 'You seem overfond of that word, sir.' Then, pleadingly, she added, 'Say something to me, Richard. I—I know I should not have introduced you as a servant but…'

'I seem to remember you thought something similar when we first met.'

'I—I was not sure. Your clothes…' She broke off, horrified that she was making the situation more humiliating each time she opened her mouth. 'It is but a ruse to allow you to remain near me and—and you will get free accommodation,' she added. 'It will save you from seeking lodgings within the city.'

'I fear you have not seen my accommodation,' he said, his lips twisting wryly. 'It is much less commodious than this, or indeed, what I was expecting in the Chepe, but, there, it will do for a while.' He frowned thoughtfully. 'You are not feeling frightened, are you? I thought Master

Hilyard had put himself so immediately at your service that you could not help but feel graciously welcomed to Court.'

She coloured. 'He is rather—overdressed,' she confided with a little impish grin. 'But, oh Richard, is he not handsome?'

Richard's heavy brows rose and he shrugged. 'Yes, Master Hilyard appears to be a fine figure of a man.'

'I thought,' she ventured, 'that you would not find it inconvenient to be here—close to the King and Court. You would hear things and—and that could prove useful to you.'

'I shall also be under close scrutiny of the higher servants,' he said brusquely, 'which could prove most inconvenient.'

'I shall be sure to grant you leave to absent yourself so that you can run errands for me in the city,' she offered. 'My mother indicated you had business there, to enquire after the price of wool from your manor, she thought.'

'I do have business in the city,' he said, but without offering her any further information. 'Well, you appear to be comfortable here. Lodgings in palaces can be most uncomfortable, you know. This indicates the Queen wishes you well and you will have a pleasing companion in Lady Philippa.'

'You know her?' Anne asked eagerly. 'You have not said so before.'

Again he shrugged. 'I do not think the subject came up. I saw her when she was just a little girl. I am acquainted with her father, the Earl.'

'Is she very grand?'

'She may have changed and become so, but I doubt that. She was never proud or haughty when I met her.'

Anne gave a little sigh of relief. 'I shall feel so out of my depth here if she proves so.'

'I thought Court life was what you have been longing for all these months.'

'Yes, of course, I am gratified by the summons but somewhat overwhelmed by it all as well. That is why...' she looked at him shyly '...that is why I wanted you near me. You are truly not angry with me for my deception?'

He gave a wintry smile. 'Naturally it pleases me that I shall have my betrothed well within my sight, especially as she appears to have made so soon a very strong effect upon the susceptibility of Master Hilyard.'

'You know, Dickon,' she stressed the servant's name she had bestowed on him deliberately, 'that I do not acknowledge your prior claim on me. I have not given my consent, whatever my father's wishes in this matter and—and I feel myself free to encourage Master Hilyard or whoever else I shall meet at Court, should I wish to do so.'

'Dickon?' he remarked wryly. 'It was Richard a moment ago when I was so flattered that you so wished to hold me near you.'

'I thought you would be proud to answer to that name. Was not your beloved King known by it?'

'Only to his intimates and never spoken by any of his humble pages,' he returned grimly. 'However, I am not averse to its use. Both my parents call me Dickon.'

'Then I shall continue to do so.'

'You must *remember* to do so,' he reminded her grimly. He made her a little mocking bow. 'Now, Mistress, am I dismissed and at what time do you wish me to wait upon you tomorrow?'

She bit her lip thoughtfully. 'I do not know what my duties will be until I am summoned before the Queen and given in charge of the Mistress of the Wardrobe. Perhaps you can come up during the morning and speak with Mary? She will tell you when we can meet.'

He nodded his head and then moved to the door. As he reached it and had one hand on the latch she said quickly, 'Richard…Dickon, you will be very careful now—now that you are in the Court of—of your enemy, won't you?'

He put his head slightly upon one side. 'Concern for me, my love? That attitude shows promise.'

She retorted tartly, 'You know very well it is a concern I would feel for any man, especially a friend of my father's.'

Once more he bowed obsequiously, so that she flushed darkly and when he had left, pulling the door closed behind him, she gave a heavy sigh, partly of regret at losing sight of him and partly of the need to keep him so firmly at a distance.

She was not at all sure that she had acted wisely in keeping him here at Westminster. He could be in very real danger. Despite her determination to continue to reject his claim on her, she held Richard Allard in very high regard. She went suddenly cold at the thought of what his fate might be, should he be taken and tried for treason.

In passing, one of her men, Simpkin, she thought, had commented dourly on the shrivelled heads which adorned London Bridge. She must be very careful in her dealings with Richard and try to keep him continually near her in attendance. That way he would have little opportunity to meet other malcontents within the capital.

Chapter Five

Anne thought she would have been too excited to sleep but she must have been totally exhausted by the journey for she woke to find Mary leaning over to waken her. It was still early but Anne knew she might be summoned to attend the Queen at any time so she rose quickly, made her toilet and dressed hurriedly with Mary's help.

A page, dispatched by Mary, brought breakfast to her chamber: cold meats, manchet bread with butter and honey. Anne was not hungry, filled as she was with apprehensive excitement, but Mary reminded her that waiting on royalty was an exhausting business and she would need her strength, so she swallowed some food to please her maid.

The vessels were cleared and still no summons reached them, so Anne sat down again, knowing she would need to be patient. She could hear the chattering of pages outside her door and what she thought was the chink of dice within the cup as the boys whiled away the long hours waiting attendance.

There was no message from Richard. Mary sat opposite her mistress, her hands folded in her lap, for once idle, since there was no immediate stitching to occupy her. She had already taken out Anne's clothing from the travelling chests and saddle bags, shaken out the creases, hung the gowns and cloaks within the press in the small garde robe adjoining their chamber and carefully folded the undergarments, sprinkled with dried lavender, within one of the chests provided.

Anne thought fleetingly of Master John Hilyard and her lips curved into a little secret smile. Would he acknowledge her when they met again? Perhaps not. Since he was squire of the body to the King himself he must be considered an important personage at Court. Richard had been decidedly piqued by his attentions to her, but Anne was determined that Richard's opinions would carry no weight with her on that score. Master Hilyard had been kind and courteous and certainly she did not intend to keep him at arm's length because Richard Allard objected to the man's interest in her.

When a youthful page knocked and announced that Master Allsop was seeking to visit his mistress, she bade the boy admit him.

Richard entered, closed the chamber door and leaned his back against it. He saw that Anne's expression revealed both frustration and anxiety and he smiled broadly.

'I take it you have not yet been summoned to the presence. That is not unusual. People have been kept waiting for days at a time within the palace antechambers. You must learn to be patient, mistress.' He stressed the word mockingly. 'As I must, waiting attendance upon you.'

She bit her lip uncertainly. 'Is all well with you and the other men? Have you really been dreadfully uncomfortable?'

He laughed. 'Well, I've had more comfortable lodgings, to be sure, and less comfortable ones also. I shall do well enough for the moment. The head groom has had me grooming mounts in one of the stables where our horses are quartered or I should have been here before this. It's clear the man has found in me someone to put upon. Mind you—' his grey eyes glinted with amusement '—he will soon find he is mistaken and to his cost, too. Since you cannot ride out today until you have been received by Her Grace, I take it you have no special need for my services and I can go off and amuse myself?'

She longed to insist that he remain within call in the palace but knew that would be churlish.

She said very deliberately, 'Do you go into the city?'

He shrugged. 'I am not sure. First I will re-acquaint myself with the palace environs, particularly the ways in—and out.'

As she nodded to dismiss him she said again, as she had yesterday, 'Richard—Dickon—be careful.'

The summons did not come until after dinner. Unwilling to present herself in the great hall before she had been officially received, Anne asked Mary to procure food for them once more within their chamber and one of the pages obliged. Though his manner was curious and somewhat perky he was not overtly insolent and Anne was glad she had not had to assert herself in order to make the boy respect her.

She had hardly completed the simple repast before another, older boy knocked and informed her that her presence was required immediately in the Queen's presence chamber.

Heart fluttering wildly, Anne rose at once to follow him.

The Queen's apartments proved to be quite near and, carefully, Anne took note of their route so that she might not get lost the next time she was needed and appear foolish. Two liveried billmen stood aside from the door, their weapons raised, to allow her to enter the presence chamber with her page guide.

The room was pleasantly warm though large, possessing an imposing oriel window which looked out on to the river terrace. Anne's eyes were immediately directed to a cushioned armchair drawn up to the great fireplace where a woman was seated, a tall, angular lady standing behind her. Anne sank at once into a deep curtsy as the page was dismissed.

A pleasant, low-pitched voice bade her rise and come to the chair.

'Welcome to Court, Mistress Jarvis. Come into the light so I might see you properly.'

Anne found herself under the scrutiny of light blue eyes which appeared somewhat faded though kindly. The Queen was dressed in a gown of heavy cut blue velvet, trimmed at the hem and cuffs of the tight-fitting sleeves with ermine. She wore the fashionable gable hood with its high, pointed wired framework, the long lappets of matching blue velvet, ornamented with strips of gold braid falling on to her shoulders. Even seated as she was, Anne perceived that, like her companion, the Queen was tall for a woman and remembered that her father, King Edward IV, the famed Rose of Rouen for his personal beauty, had been well over six feet in height.

The Queen's features were pleasant and regular and her complexion good though rather florid. The golden hair Anne had heard spoken of was hidden beneath the confines of her white coif under the elaborate headdress. Her mother, Elizabeth Woodville, had been renowned for her pale, almost silver-gilded locks, Anne's mother had said. Elizabeth of York had inherited her father's stature and once, Anne thought, she had been truly pretty, but now that she had borne the King several children, that glow of youth had faded and her whole demeanour was one of kindly tolerance rather than the flashing intelligent enthusiasm Anne had expected.

Even so the Queen's mouth parted in a welcoming smile and Anne felt warmed by the sincerity of her greeting.

'Sit down, child. I am truly glad to see you here. Lady Philippa is expected soon and then I shall have two children of my old friends near me. Tell me, how is your mother, Anne? You resemble her greatly and yes, I see in you the fine sculptured features of that handsome father of yours.'

She indicated a footstool near her and turning, smiled up at the lady behind her.

'Lady Hartley, you will be in charge of my two newest ladies and instruct them in their duties.'

Turning back to Anne she asked, 'Tell me, do you read, child?'

'Yes, Your Grace.'

'Good. I shall enjoy having you read to me from the old troubadour romances. Sometimes my eyes tire quickly, these days. Do you embroider?'

Anne hung her head. 'Yes, Your Grace, I have been instructed by my mother who is very skilled. I fear I am not very proficient and she has scolded me often and made me undo my work.'

The Queen smiled and made no comment, then she asked, 'And are you musical?'

Again Anne's expression was rueful. 'I play the lute, Your Grace, though with no special ability, but my father insists that I have a very pleasant singing voice. I sing to my own accompaniment in the evenings to entertain my parents and my brother.'

'Ah, I had forgotten to ask after your brother. He is younger than you, I believe. What is he called?'

'Ned is thirteen, Your Grace.'

The Queen was silent for a moment then she said softly, 'Named for my own father, Edward.' Then more briskly, 'You appear to possess talents enough, child, and your duties will not be arduous, mainly to amuse me, and I am most anxious that you and Lady Philippa will be very good friends. I ask that you make that your first responsibility. She is so very young and will feel homesick at first, I'm sure. I do not know yet how good is her English so she will need a special friend.'

Anne believed she was about to speak more of her special friendship with Philippa's mother when the door was abruptly thrown open and a tall, rather stooped individual, dressed soberly in a scholar's black stuff overgown, strode in without ceremony.

Instantly the Queen rose and Lady Hartley sank into a deep curtsy. Bewildered, Anne stared blankly at them both then, realising that the visitor who had arrived unannounced was the King himself, blushing with shame at her tardiness, Anne, too, sank into the deepest of curtsies.

He waved a hand almost testily. 'Rise, ladies, please,' then without giving them more attention he approached his wife's chair waving a sheaf of parchment.

'These accounts,' he said querulously. 'I have been examining them this last hour and the expenses for the servants' clothing this year are much too high. We must do something about it quickly. The exchequer cannot…' He broke off impatiently as Lady Hartley bustled forward with a chair, and, before seating himself, he turned and regarded Anne curiously.

'Who is this? I do not think I know this child.'

'This is Mistress Anne Jarvis, Your Grace. You remember you agreed that I could add her to my personal attendants. Lady Joan is about to be married and…'

'Yes,' he said, raising one white womanish hand as if to

silence her, 'I do recall something of the sort. Jarvis,' he mused. 'Your father is a Midlander, I recall.'

Again, nervously, Anne curtsied. 'Our manor is in Northamptonshire, Your Grace.'

He was seated now and Anne saw that he was younger than she had first supposed. She recalled that he must now be about forty years old, with a thin, somewhat long face, the chin pointed, the features sharp, particularly the nose, though the pale eyes showed great intelligence and shrewdness. His hair beneath the black velvet cap, adorned with the badge of the Welsh Dragon picked out in gold and rubies, was thin and lacklustre, brown in colour threaded with grey, and reached, uncurled, just above the shoulders of his black gown.

'Ah, yes.' He nodded, then turned his attention to the parchment again. 'Elizabeth, perhaps we could discuss this...'

Lady Hartley hastened to the chamber door and signalled for Anne to join her. It was clear that they were dismissed. Both women bowed themselves out backwards, though the King appeared to give the courtesy no heed.

However, he did call in his rather thin, high-pitched, womanish voice, 'John, see that our latest arrival at Court is escorted back to her chamber.'

The door closed and Anne found herself gazing into the light blue eyes of John Hilyard who stood waiting attendance on his sovereign just outside.

'Oh,' she said, a trifle inadequately, as the elegant young squire smiled disarmingly and bowed to the elderly Lady Hartley, who nodded coolly and walked off along the corridor, a page scampering in her wake. Anne stared after her helplessly while John Hilyard smiled down at her.

She said breathlessly, 'I—I wish she had told me when I shall be required—and—'

'You will be sent for, never fear. The pages on duty bring messages and do not dare delay. Allow me to escort you to your chamber. Do you know which direction?'

'Yes, but I—would not wish to give you any trouble…' Her voice trailed off uncertainly. It had all happened too fast. She had been nervous under the Queen's questioning, then the King had entered so suddenly and now, once again, she was left alone, apart from the impassive gaze of the two billman on duty, with this young man who made no secret of his flattering interest in her.

'We must not disobey the King, who gave me the specific task of escorting you,' he reminded her. 'Not that,' he added, with a twinkle, 'I needed any prompting, let alone a command to do what is pleasurable in the extreme.'

She said, hastily, 'You must not imagine that because I am a country mouse just arrived at Court I do not recognise outrageous flattery when I hear it, sir.'

He laughed heartily. 'Then I think your chamber cannot have been equipped with a mirror, Mistress Anne.'

She could not resist a little amused smile in reply.

They walked together, his hand upon her elbow, gently guiding her around bends in the darkened corridors. She was unable to watch his expression as she was too intent on finding her way and was relieved at last to find they had reached what she was sure was the corridor off which her own small chamber led.

She was made more than a trifle uncomfortable by his attentions and looked at the pages to see if they, in their turn, were amused by his behaviour but, apart from looking up hurriedly from the dice game to see if their services were needed, they looked just as quickly down again and resumed, ignoring the presence of the two new arrivals on the scene.

She moved to lift the latch on her chamber door but he forestalled her and took her hand.

'I trust you have been made comfortable here?' he enquired.

'Oh, yes, sir, thank you, very comfortable. I am expecting my bed mate to arrive shortly, Lady Philippa Telford.'

'Ah, I perceive you will be well chaperoned.'

She glanced at him sharply from under sooty lashes. 'At all events I have my attendant with me, Mary Scroggins.'

'Who guards you like a veritable dragon.'

'Mary is entrusted with my care and Master Allsop—'

'Yes, Master Allsop. I saw what tender care he had for you.'

Anne lowered her gaze in embarrassment. 'He, too, is trusted highly by my father…'

'Sir Guy Jarvis. Was he not in high favour with the late King?'

The tone was polite but Anne, sensitive to any nuance which might betoken distrust of her family, said, defensively, 'My father was in the late King Richard's household when he was Duke of Gloucester and served him loyally on the Scottish border…'

'And fought just as loyally for him at Redmoor?'

'That, too.' Her teeth bit a little savagely upon her nether lip. 'He paid his fines and has accepted the present dynasty, sir, I can assure you. You will find no disloyalty in him nor in my own deep desire to serve Her Grace, the Queen.'

'Of course not,' he said sincerely. 'Believe me, I mean you well, Mistress Anne, but I must warn you that you may well face some hostility from the other ladies regarding your family's past allegiances. There is jealousy at Court even amongst the Queen's ladies and you have been chosen specially, I am informed, which will not please those of them who have been in attendance some time and anxious to find preferment for their relations. Be forearmed and meet their snide comments with the courage and tact which I am sure you possess to the full.'

She drew a hard little breath and smiled back at him. 'Thank you, sir, for your consideration and for your—warning. I had considered my position carefully before I even left Northamptonshire.'

He bent and touched her palm with his lips. 'Trust me, mistress, to be your champion at Court should you have need of me.'

Her hand trembled within his grasp and then she withdrew it firmly, inclined her head in a little gracious nod of gratitude and turned once more to her own door.

The door was thick, smothering sound, and until she had entered she received no indication from within that someone was laughing, an enchanting sound like water in summer tinkling down the weir on the Nene near home, and, echoing the sound, was a man's deep, amused chuckle. Anne paused on the threshold to stand in wonderment at the sight which met her eyes.

A slip of a girl stood near the bed, a slight, elfin form, tiny, but regal, head thrown back in laughter, so that Anne could see the movement of muscles in her lovely throat as she reacted to something which was said to her by Richard Allard who was facing her, hands upon his hips. It appeared he had just put down at her feet a small leather-covered travelling chest, probably containing jewels or smaller articles used for the lady's toilet. He stood up smiling as Anne made her presence known.

Anne could not but stare at the child who was, obviously, Lady Philippa Telford. She was small and slight certainly, but so overwhelmingly lovely that Anne could not resist swallowing back a little gasp of pure envy. Philippa was wearing a drab travelling cloak and the hood had slipped back displaying a wealth of golden hair which rippled to below her waist from beneath the confines of a simple linen cap.

She had the ethereal beauty of a fairy and that hair—it could hardly even be called golden, for the red tints which shone in it from the light which streamed through the unshuttered window gave it a glory Anne had never seen in another.

The newcomer turned to face Anne and revealed a small, heart-shaped face with a finely sculptured nose and a deliciously curving mouth of which the under lip betrayed, even in extreme youth, a sensual curve. The eyes, under straight fair brows, were slightly heavy lidded and, when opened fully as they did now to scrutinise Anne, were seen to be an unusual blue green, almost aquamarine.

Anne remembered that her mother had once commented on Lady Telford's exquisite beauty though she had seen her only once, and Anne saw that her daughter had certainly inherited that famed perfection. The eyes narrowed a trifle as they met Anne's deep blue ones and instantly the woman became a true child. The lips parted almost beseechingly and she held out her arms wide.

'You are Anne—Anne Jarvis? Oh, I have so longed to reach here and see you. My father has told me so much of his friendship with yours that—oh, Anne, you will be my true friend, will you not?' Impulsively she threw herself forward, hurling herself into Anne's arms.

She spoke with the faintest of accents and the voice itself was a trifle husky, the intonation somewhat sing-song, musical, as if nothing this child could do could be less than perfect, for all men at Court would find it fascinating, Anne felt sure. Yet there was no trace of hesitation or doubt concerning her reception as she drew back a little to peer delightfully trustingly up into Anne's face.

That moment of jealousy faded as quickly as it had been aroused. Anne glanced hastily from Richard, who stood grinning inanely, to the rapturous face of this happy child and, bending, gave her a welcoming hug.

'Yes, Lady Philippa, I am Anne Jarvis and delighted to see you have arrived safely.' She glanced again at Richard and said a trifle waspishly, 'I see my servant, Dickon Allsop, has made himself useful.'

'Oh, but, Anne, you must not call me Lady Philippa. If we are to be friends I am Pippa, as I am to my maman and papa. Indeed he has. He was here when the page brought me up to this chamber. This is such an enormous palace. Malines, the dowager Duchess of Burgundy's house, is nothing like so big and grand,' the girl rattled on. 'I thought we would never find my *apartement*.' She pronounced the word in the French fashion. 'And then Master Dickon—' the pronunciation of his name was a trifle unusual too '—he came to my rescue and then went down with the page to help bring up my baggage.'

'I'm glad,' Anne said slowly, looking round for sight of the girl's maid. 'My own attendant, Mary, seems to be missing. She must have gone down to the kitchens for something. Where is your maid?'

'Alas…' the girl made a moue '…Louise did not come farther than Damme harbour—she took one look at the sea, it was grey and dark and very rough. I felt afraid too,' she confessed, 'though it calmed when we set sail, but Louise had been ill on the journey and I thought it best to leave her in a nunnery in Bruges.' She shrugged. 'I shall not miss her services. She would have become more of a nuisance than a help, you understand? She was always weeping and saying how homesick she would become.'

Anne nodded dumbly. This child appeared already to have grasped realities and could quickly sum up the abilities of people. How quickly she would mature! Certainly, Anne thought, with a momentary return of the sourness of envy she had experienced at first sight of Richard laughing joyously with the new arrival, it would not be difficult to find her a husband, and very soon too, despite her youth.

'Perhaps you are right,' she conceded. 'I'm sure my maid, Mary Scroggins, will be only too glad to attend you too.'

Again there came that faint Gallic shrug. 'I can manage to dress myself and tire my hair, if you will consent to help with my back lacing.' Her aquamarine eyes danced. 'Though my papa is an earl, we have been very poor, you know, since my papa was forced into exile after Redmoor, dependent upon the good graces of the dowager Duchess Margaret. But,' she added ingenuously, 'she has been most generous for she values greatly the worth of my papa—only he has not been well these last months and Maman has been worried for him.' Her lips trembled a little. 'I did not wish to leave Malines at this time but—but Maman, she insisted.'

Anne recognised the true note of childish terror at this parting from those she so loved and her heart went out instantly to this enchanting creature and all her doubts about their friendship vanished as if they had never existed.

The door opened and Mary Scroggins hastened into the room, then stood staring almost rudely at their fair visitor.

'I am sorry, Mistress Anne, I thought you would be longer with the Queen and was down in the kitchens. Then one of the pages came for a mulled drink for Lady Hartley and said you were dismissed to your own chamber...'

She broke off as Philippa Telford turned her lovely eyes on the maid and smilingly asked, 'Is this your maid? Marie, is it? Will you consent to help me when I need you?'

Anne could see at once that Mary was instantly captivated by the girl's simple question and her lack of haughtiness.

She said quickly, 'Lady Philippa, Mary, has only this last hour arrived. Her own maid was taken ill and remained in Bruges so she will need some help with unpacking.'

Mary was clearly bewildered but nodded at once and curtsied, as Anne signalled to Richard that she wished to talk to him outside. As she drew the door closed behind the two of them, she could hear Philippa's light voice chattering away as Mary bent to the travelling cases to begin unpacking.

Anne glanced briefly back. 'Surely she did not arrive without an escort? Her father, the Earl, would never have allowed that. Are her men quartered with you and will they stay here with her as escorts when she rides out?'

Richard shrugged. 'She arrived with one servant from a convent in the city. It appears that her father was away on the Duchess Margaret's affairs.' He looked at Anne keenly as he said this and she frowned doubtfully. 'I heard he has not been well recently—an affliction of the lungs, it was intimated. The business must have been urgent or he would not have been sent. However, Lady Telford had only one young man-at-arms to send and it appears he was taken with the maid, so, when the girl was left behind in Bruges…'

'He abandoned his young mistress?' Anne said, scandalized.

'So it seems. Two of the sisters where the girl was left were on a visit to the mother house in Bruges from London and readily agreed that Lady Philippa should travel with them when they returned home, so she was well chaperoned. They sent her with their servant on to Westminster when they reached their own convent in Aldgate and I happened to be in the yard when she arrived with all her baggage. Naturally I believed you would expect me to offer assistance.'

'Of course.' Anne sighed. 'Then she is here, friendless, and totally unattended.'

Again he shrugged. 'I do not think she will remain friendless for long. She has quite a way with her, wouldn't you say?'

'Yes,' Anne replied a trifle pithily and he turned quickly to glance at her sharply, then he gave a broad smile. Angered by what she was sure he believed was passing through her mind she reddened, then sighed again.

'Poor child, she must have been very frightened by the time she arrived in Bruges and everything began to go wrong for her. She is obviously homesick already and very fond of her father and anxious about him.'

He nodded. 'If she has anything of the qualities of Martyn Telford in her make-up, she will be tough enough to withstand unkind fortunes, but she is vulnerable and will need our help.'

'I understand you have met her parents—in Burgundy. She did not recognise you?'

'No-o,' he said slowly. 'Not at once, but, of course, she may do later and my posing as your servant could be deemed suspicious if she blurts out the truth.'

Anne nodded, pursing her lips thoughtfully. 'I will sound her out, but carefully. At present it might be wiser for her to go on believing that you are my servant. She is inclined to chatter,' she said doubtfully.

'I met her once some years ago when she was still just a young child at her mother's knee. It is doubtful that she would remember me from so long back. Children rarely notice their parents' visitors keenly.'

Anne was by no means so sure of that. 'Do you think…' She paused, glancing round to see none of the pages were in earshot. As it happened, the corridor was deserted at that moment. 'Do you think she is aware that her father may be in treasonous correspondence with King Henry's enemies?'

Richard rubbed his nose thoughtfully. 'That would be hard to say, though, living at Malines at the Duchess's Court as she has been, she must know some of it. The place is a hotbed of intrigue and most of it levelled at Henry Tudor.'

'Yes.' Anne's blue eyes grew clouded as she pondered over the mystery of it. 'Which makes me think it stranger and stranger than ever that the Queen has sent for us both to wait upon her.'

Again Richard shot her an alarmed glance, then nodded abruptly. 'It behoves all of us to act with circumspection over the next few weeks. What worries me is not so much what the Queen wanted but—why the King consented.'

His grey eyes met her darkening blue ones, then he made her a hasty bow as a page came running towards them on some urgent errand, and, turning, hurried off to his own quarters.

Anne dispatched a page to the Queen's apartments to inform Her Grace that Lady Philippa Telford had arrived. As it was now getting late and her new friend's face was showing signs of exhaustion, Anne made arrangements for them to eat together in her chamber and, afterwards, Mary saw to it that the two of them retired early.

Anne had not slept with another person since she had left the care of her nurse and wondered how she would fare with a bedfellow but, lying later with the sleeping child curled up beside her, she could only smile tenderly. Philippa Telford brought out a latent maternal streak in her, as she was sure she had in both Mary and Richard and, as she gazed down at the curling fair lashes and heard the soft sound of her breathing, she reached out, blew out the candle and turned to sleep contentedly herself.

As Anne had expected, Lady Philippa was summoned into the royal presence quite early next day and clearly exerted the same charming influence on Queen Elizabeth as she had on the rest of them. Even Lady Hartley's grave expression softened at sight of the child's obvious delight in the warmth of her reception. The Queen dismissed both girls graciously to make themselves cognisant of the palace and its environs and to entertain themselves fittingly until the following day.

She smiled at Lady Philippa graciously. 'You will have been wearied by your long journey and the misadventures along the way and you should not begin your duties today. Report, both of you, to Lady Hartley early tomorrow and she will instruct you. I will see to it that both your parents are informed as to your safe arrival here and how pleased I am to receive you.'

Outside in the corridor their page escort stopped suddenly in his tracks as the King passed by with John Hilyard and several officials in attendance. Both girls swept low curtsies and Anne was wryly amused to note that John could not resist turning back to stare after the lovely newcomer.

Philippa gave a delightful gurgle of a laugh. 'And who is that, pray, *ma chère* Anne?'

'That was the King, goose,' Anne said, a trifle breathlessly.

'I know that, *ma chérie*,' the other girl laughed. 'I meant the very handsome and overdressed young courtier with him.'

'That was Master John Hilyard, squire of the body to His

Grace.' Anne could not help but notice the tartness of her own response.

Philippa was not abashed. 'He has eyes only for you, *ma chère* Anne.'

'Nonsense,' Anne said even more sharply. 'He was merely curious about you.'

They returned to their chamber and began to sort through their gowns. Anne noticed that, indeed, Philippa's wardrobe was as sadly depleted as she had thought her own would be before her mother had made various sacrifices from the manor accounts to provide her with at least several gowns which would not shame her at Court. Clearly Philippa's beauty would not be dimmed by the shabbiness of her attire but other ladies would undoubtedly find fault, if only behind her back, concerning her lack of fashionable garments.

Philippa shook her head at them sadly. 'As I told you, Papa's fortunes are not good and I must make the best of these, but I see they are further behind the present fashion than I had thought. The English Court is ahead of that of Burgundy. The Duchess is a dowager and no longer young and her ladies do not seek to outdo her in the finery they wear.'

Though Anne's wardrobe was small she would willingly have shared those gowns she had with her new friend, but Philippa was so petite she would have been buried in Anne's gowns. She smiled brightly.

'I am sure no one will notice,' she said, somewhat untruthfully. At any rate, she thought, if they did they would be unlikely to pass any derogatory comments in the Queen's presence.

Philippa's blue-green eyes twinkled. 'When my mother fled England to join my father in exile after the battle near Market Bosworth, she took with her a quantity of jewels, but they have all been sold these many years past to make ends meet.'

Anne said quietly, 'My father also fought for King Richard and our own manor has been constantly impoverished since that battle. He was forced to pay very heavy fines in order to receive a pardon.'

Philippa looked admiringly at the rose brocade gown Anne was wearing and compared it with her own saffron rubbed velvet. 'Then your maman must be very clever with her needle, *ma chère* Anne.'

'Yes, she is good at making things do. Many of my Court gowns have been cut down and altered from those my own mother wore when she was at Court long ago.'

As Mary entered the chamber at that moment, one of Philippa's cloaks over her arm which she had been cleaning and pressing after yesterday's journey, she exchanged glances with Anne and said briskly, 'I think, my lady, we could find the funds to make some alterations, perhaps the addition of some gold braid and a little fur, if you will allow me to try.'

Impulsively Philippa rose and hugged her. Scandalised, Mary stepped back, red-faced, and Anne laughed.

'What an excellent idea, Mary. The Queen has given us leave to spend the day at our own devices. Do you send down a page with a message for Master—Dickon Allsop to join us and he shall take us down river to the Chepe so we can buy ourselves some fripperies that may serve that very purpose.'

Richard arrived very soon afterwards and Anne outlined their needs to him. He grinned broadly and agreed that a visit to the city would be pleasant for all of them.

'I recommend you put on warm cloaks and hoods,

Mistress Anne,' he warned. 'It is fine but cold outside and will be especially so on the river.'

They dressed accordingly and made their way to the King's steps and waited, Mary in attendance, while Richard went off along the quay to procure a ferry boat.

Philippa, it seemed, had been used to travelling by water for, often, she had gone with her parents to Bruges where journeying by river and canal was quite usual. Though Anne had sometimes ventured by boat on the River Nene to places like Fotheringhay and Croyland, she had rarely travelled this way and found the journey on the great thoroughfare of the River Thames from Westminster to London Bridge both exhilarating and fascinating.

She watched the waterman plying his oars with interest and listened, spellbound, as Richard told of the places of interest along both the banks as they passed. Several times they passed large sea-going carracks and the long decorated and elegant river barges of the nobility.

She was so enthralled that she did not feel the chill and damp air and was quite disappointed when their ferryman skilfully plied his craft through the dangerous rapids beneath London Bridge and they disembarked at the water steps. From here they would proceed on foot to the busy district of shops and booths surrounding the principal shopping area around the famous Chepe side.

Anne shivered once more with fear and disgust as they noted the decaying heads upon pikes displayed upon the ramparts of the bridge and was awestruck by the noise and confusion near St Paul's and St Paul's Cross.

When Richard informed them that the great cathedral was indeed a mart for booksellers and purveyors of sundry wares she was somewhat shocked.

'Keep very close to me now, ladies,' Richard warned. 'This district abounds in thieves and beggars. Keep tight hold upon your purses or, better still, hand them to me for safe keeping.'

Anne decided that that would be far the best idea and Philippa readily confided her small one into his keeping along with Anne's.

From time to time Anne looked at her escort's sturdy back as he forged passage for them and was heartily glad to have him near her once more. His manner towards her had been suitably deferential though she noted, on one or two occasions, a wicked glitter in his grey eyes that told her she might well suffer for this deception one day in the future. She bit her lip thoughtfully at the prospect and stole a glance at Philippa to see how she was taking their relationship.

It appeared that the young girl had accepted Richard Allard as the servant he purported to be but, with her habitual kindly courtesy, she treated him as she would any one of her acquaintances. Ruefully Anne thought back upon her previous fears that her new friend would appear haughty and imperious.

Another of Richard's skills, it turned out, was an ability to bargain and the two girls were delighted by how little their purchases of gold braid, ribbons and laces actually cost them, since Anne, at all events, was bewildered and somewhat intimidated by the shouting of the 'prentice lads and the continual pressure to buy launched upon them near the various shopping booths in Drapers' Row.

When they had concluded their purchases, Richard conducted them to an inn on Chepe side, The Golden Cockerel, insisting they must take refreshments and rest after their busy hours on their feet. Anne was not sorry, for her feet were beginning to ache and she looked with interest at the quality of the place when they entered the tap room. Certainly it looked clean and well tended and the floor was freshly relaid with rushes from which came the sweet smell of thyme and rosemary.

A buxom woman, middle-aged though still attractive, neatly dressed in clean homespun kirtle and blouse, overlaid by a spotlessly white apron, her brown hair just speckled with grey confined beneath a white linen cap, looked up as they entered and her broad, homely face broke into a genuine smile of welcome.

'Master Dickon,' she declared, coming hastily forward to greet him, 'how good it is to see you again. Father will be that pleased. Do you stay with us? I can manage a private chamber, small but…'

He shook his head, smiling. 'Thank you, Bess, but I have duties in Westminster with my young mistress. I am accommodated in the servants' quarters at the palace.'

She looked totally bewildered. 'But, Master…'

'Allsop,' he reminded her and Anne noted that her dark eyes grew wider in astonishment.

Obviously Richard was well known to her and under his true name. This, then, was his intended lodging for his planned stay in London.

The woman drew the little party to a table near the inglenook of the fireplace and Anne revelled in the cheery warmth from the blazing fire of sea coal. Philippa was gazing round with her usual avid curiosity for all places and things typically English.

'Food, Bess, of your best, and malmsey,' Richard said smilingly. 'I would like my mistress and her friend with their attendant to stay here for a couple of hours this afternoon.'

The rosy-cheeked woman smiled again. 'Why, certainly, Master Allsop.' So quickly had she accepted his new identity that Anne wondered if he was habitually changing it on his varied visits to this inn. She looked back at him meaningfully.

The woman went on, 'Father is in the parlour. He'll be right glad to see you. Will you come through?'

'Aye, that I will, Bess, as soon as I have seen to the comfort of my party.'

He hooked an extra stool to the table with his foot and looked towards Anne as if requesting permission to seat himself with his betters. That gleam was there in his eyes again and, frostily, she nodded as he sat down. Philippa was throwing back her hood, displaying the glory of her bright hair beneath her linen coif. The taproom had only one other customer as it was still early and he stopped deliberately in his walk to the door to stare at her, then turned away, embarrassed and overcome by his near rudeness in such fine company.

Richard beamed at them all as Mary sat down also, encouraged to do so by Anne who said hastily, 'Do sit, Mary, you must be even tireder than we are since you were on your feet all morning.'

'As you can see, I am well known here,' Richard announced, 'so you will be made very comfortable and provided with the best of everything. Jake Garnet, the innkeeper, must be nearing seventy now but my father knows him and he has served us well in the past. His daughter, Bess Aldred, keeps the inn these days with her husband Joshua and everything is as well run as it has always been, despite Jake's advancing age.'

Anne was somewhat uneasy. Richard had been so well received, indeed, he had been glowingly confident of his welcome, that she wondered if the innkeeper and his family were aware of some of his more nefarious reasons for visiting London so often. However, she looked up hungrily as a young serving wench entered, as nimble and cleanly dressed as her mistress, and began to serve them with malmsey wine and what looked like lentil or bean pottage, promising to bring in the roast meats and pasties later. The food was delicious and the women began to tuck in hungrily.

Richard drank some ale and hurriedly finished his pottage, then rose and prepared to leave them.

'Mistress, you promised to excuse me for a while from my duties if I had business in the city to do for my father. Will you do so now? You will be perfectly safe here until I return.'

Anne was nonplussed but she could not deny Richard and she nodded, crumbling her fresh manchet bread awkwardly. Philippa appeared to be not in the least surprised by his request and as Bess Aldred appeared in the entrance to the kitchen quarters he bowed to them and went to her, asking quietly as to the well-being of her husband and his present whereabouts.

Anne only caught part of the answer as he went back with her into the inner recesses of the inn, ostensibly to speak with her father, the elderly Jake.

'He is on duty this afternoon, Master Dickon, and should be home late this evening, but if you wish to contact him…'

The rest was lost to Anne's straining ears.

He went off soon after and the innkeeper came through into the taproom. Anne had rather expected a doddery old man but Jake Garnet was still very active, a big man, balding, though Anne saw that he had once had a thick crop of carroty red hair for his ample beard still showed traces of that colour in its streaking. Like his daughter, Bess, he had a broad face and homely, jovial features. He was dressed somewhat unfashionably in a leather jerkin over homespun shirt and thick brown hose. He came towards Anne, beaming with pleasure.

'Dickon tells me I have the honour of entertaining Mistress Anne, the daughter of Sir Guy Jarvis, and Lady Philippa Telford.' He bowed to them. 'Your father, the Earl, my lady, sometimes gave me the honour of his patronage.'

Phillipa was delighted and her pearly teeth gleamed as she smiled warmly at the old man.

Anne said quickly, 'Please sit with us, Master Garnet. My man—Dickon has told me that the quality of service here has always been a matter of pride to your family.'

'That it is. The gentlemen of the late King's household, God assoil him—' the old man crossed himself reverently and the two girls followed suit '—often came here and I was proud to serve them to the best of my ability. Now my lass, Bess, takes the greater share of the responsibility off my shoulders, though that's not to say I don't still keep a wary eye on the quality of my cellar.'

Quietly Anne asked, 'I hope your custom has not fallen off in these new times, Master Garnet.'

'No, no, we manage well enough but…' He heaved a heavy sigh '…nothing is the same, but you can't expect it will be.'

His expression was lugubriously melancholy and Anne was sorry for the old man as she was for their former head groom, Jan Rawlins, whose duties at Rushton had been similarly abrogated by his son-in-law. The innkeeper's daughter hurried over with a tankard of ale for her father, and behind his back gave Anne a conspiratorial glance as if she was grateful for her kindness to Jake.

He supped his ale appreciatively and, in answer to Philippa's eager questions of what he remembered of her father's visits to The Golden Cockerel, began to talk of the old days when the young squires and knights of Richard of Gloucester's household had frequented his inn on their visits to London in his train when he came to Westminster to confer with his brother King Edward.

One or two of his stories of their adventures were amusing and Anne began to see her father as he had been then, tall and handsome and popular with the ladies of the town. She wondered if her mother had been aware of just how much in demand Guy Jarvis had been then.

Jake Garnet's tales were interrupted when a gentleman accompanied by two men-at-arms entered the tap room and the young serving wench bustled forward to greet him.

He was about to order when his attention was caught by the little group near the fire and he made a sudden exclamation of recognition and strode over to them instantly.

'Mistress Anne, Lady Philippa, whatever are you doing here in Chepe side?'

Anne turned at once as she recognised the light tones of John Hilyard. He was dressed extravagantly as ever, with a tall beaver hat in the new style decorated with an enormously tall dyed feather, but also warmly cloaked against the autumn chill of the day.

She was startled by his appearance and concerned by the scandalised note in his voice as he scanned the taproom for signs of her escort.

'Master Hilyard, how coincidental that you should come here. Master Garnet has been telling us how he remembers our fathers when they were young and the good times they had here.'

Too late she realised that her opening gambit had been mistaken. Who could tell what construction John Hilyard might put on that remark, considering the former loyalties of both hers and Philippa's sires!

'Surely, Mistress Anne, you have not travelled into the city unescorted. Where are your men-at-arms?'

'No, no,' Anne explained, 'of course not. The Queen graciously allowed us time off duty and my servant, Master Allsop, accompanied us.' Her voice trailed off a little miserably as John Hilyard's fair brows knit together in a deeper frown.

'Indeed? Then where is the fellow?'

'He—' she floundered awkwardly '—he had some business in the city—for—for my father and—and he left us here to await his return, knowing Master Garnet would see to our comfort…'

'Truly,' Jake Garnet's deep tones rumbled, 'the ladies are as safe here at The Golden Cockerel as they would be in their own homes or in the palace of Westminster itself.'

'I am by no means sure of that,' John Hilyard snapped. 'The fellow had no business to leave you unprotected. He needs to be soundly thrashed. How dare he abandon you to go about matters of business, however seemingly important! His first concern should always be for your safety.'

'I'm sure,' Anne began to argue, 'he knew nothing could hurt us here…'

'Well, it will not now,' John Hilyard declared. 'I have been making some purchases for His Grace who has been attending a council meeting at The Tower and is about to return to Westminster in the royal barge in about a half-hour. I know His Grace would not wish me to leave you both here, neither would Her Grace the Queen. Allow me to escort you to the water steps. I shall explain to the King and I am sure he will have no objection to two of his wife's attendants travelling in his barge.'

Philippa looked bewildered and not a little alarmed. Anne struggled to find some reason for remaining here and waiting for Richard's return. She met her friend's worried expression doubtfully, then rose and offered her hand to John. Really, there was nothing she could do. It would be pointless to expostulate further and to stand up for Richard very openly could prove suspicious. The man was merely a servant.

'That is most kind of you, Master Hilyard,' she said quietly, 'but I hope and trust this arrangement will not inconvenience His Grace.'

Helplessly she allowed John Hilyard to adjust both their cloaks and hoods and then she turned to Jake Garnet who was standing back deferentially, his own expression revealing his anxiety for the situation which had arisen so suddenly. Since he knew Richard's true identity, he must also have had some knowledge of his purpose in the city and could not risk making any comment which could further this young gallant's disapproval.

The two girls, Mary trailing miserably behind, allowed themselves to be walked through the streets protected by two somewhat sullen men-at-arms who had expected to take ale in the inn and had been sadly disappointed.

At the water steps near the Bridge was moored the stately royal barge with the royal standard at the prow and an awning over the stern to protect the royal personages who travelled within it from any severity of the elements. The Queen's two youthful attendants with Mary were helped into seats near the prow and sat uncomfortably and silently as the oarsmen sat patiently awaiting the arrival of the King.

He did so very shortly afterwards, guarded by four men-at-arms, and took his seat beneath the awning. He looked up briefly at John's deferential explanation of the presence of the two young attendants and gave a cool nod of acknowledgement. Anne shifted uncomfortably under the scrutiny of those cold grey eyes then, on command, the oarsmen pushed off from the bank and the barge moved into midstream.

Philippa was trailing one hand in the water. She looked perplexed, as both girls felt they dared not talk in such exalted company. Anne gave a heavy sigh. She wondered how Richard would take her abrupt and unexplained departure from the inn but, most of all, she looked back at John Hilyard, as he sat facing his King under the awning, and hoped he would not carry too reprehensible a tale back to Westminster concerning the shortcomings of her servant. Worst of all, she considered, as she bit her lip so hard it gave pain, whether John Hilyard could possibly harbour some suspicion of her true relationship with Richard Allard and of his real business in the city.

Chapter Six

Richard Allard strode into a noisome tavern near the main entrance to The Tower and brusquely ordered ale. While the tapster's back was turned towards the barrel, Richard looked hastily round the crowded room. Unlike The Golden Cockerel, the place was packed with vociferous customers, many grimy and unkempt. The scarred and pitted tables were stained with ale and probably vomit and looked never to have been properly washed down.

The innkeeper, it seemed, did not have to bother to ensure cleanliness in order to invite custom, since the place was popular with the denizens of the nearby squalid streets and even more so with the workers in The Tower itself: servitors, men-at-arms and jailors. Men sat with doxies on their knees, already roaring drunk, singing lustily and banging tankard bottoms upon the table tops, although it was still only more than one hour after noon.

The tapster banged a leather tankard down upon the equally filthy counter and Richard paid him. His eyes were narrowed, still scanning the crowded room for the man he sought. He was taken suddenly by surprise as a touch on his shoulder made him swing round abruptly, alerting him to the presence of his quarry.

'I am here, Master Richard. Shall we sit down over there for a moment, near the window?' The newcomer gave a throaty chuckle. 'We are hardly likely to be observed together by anyone outside since the windows have not been cleaned, I doubt, since the last King reigned and everyone in here is too busied with his own concerns to note our closeness.'

Richard followed the man to the table he indicated. A slatternly girl looked up wearily as they approached from her task of collecting up discarded tankards. She made Richard's guide a half-smile and hurried off, skilfully avoiding clutching hands that reached out to waylay her or smack her bottom, calling bawdy rejoinders to the drunken banter which followed her progress.

Richard's companion sat down and sipped his own ale, watching his visitor thoughtfully over the leather rim of his tankard.

'I came in here during my hour off yesterday, then today since you got the message to me that you'd arrived in the city. Have you been to The Golden Cockerel? We thought you would have stayed with us as usual.'

Richard grinned back at the stocky individual opposite. Like his father-in-law, Josh Aldred was a big man, barrel-chested, already balding, with a huge round face gleaming with sweat and a jovial expression which belied his shrewd and suspicious nature. Bess's husband was a man Richard would trust with his life and on whose advice he could rely in any emergency. He had known the man since his own father had brought him to The Golden Cockerel on their first visit to the capital on very special secret business.

'I hoped you would be here at this time. Bess informed me of your habit.' He swallowed down ale and pushed the tankard aside. 'I cannot stay at The Cockerel. I found myself entrusted with the care of Sir Guy Jarvis's daughter who has been summoned to Court to attend the Queen and the foolish minx, for reasons of her own, announced I was her servant, so I'm forced to stay at Westminster.'

Josh clucked his tongue in sympathy. 'Sweet Virgin, here's a coil. How long do you think you'll be forced to stay there?'

'Not long, I trust.' Richard smiled grimly. 'At all events my task should be finished soon now. You are still working at the Tower as jailor, then?'

'Aye, I was fortunate to get the work when one of the older men fell dead in the street. His friend, one of the head jailors, comes sometimes to The Cockerel and he managed to get me set on two months ago.'

'He knows nothing...?'

'Nay.' Josh shook his head emphatically. 'I told him we were doing badly at The Cockerel and I needed the coin. He believed me and I work with him which is useful, since he serves the Earl.'

'And you do, too?'

'On occasions, most days for this past week.'

'He is in good health?'

'Aye, he seems so, but with the pallor of the constant prisoner and the lack of spirit which goes with long confinement.'

Richard leaned closer, having looked round hastily to see if they were being observed or if another was close enough to their table to overhear what was said.

'I understand the prisoner, Perkin Warbeck, is now confined in the Tower.'

'Aye, and moved only two days ago to the apartment below that of the Earl.'

Richard gave a little angry intake of breath. 'Are they in communication?'

'I don't think so, not yet, but...' Aldred pursed his lips

doubtfully. 'I think it likely—soon. Naturally the Earl is very curious about his new near neighbour and would like to meet him.'

'That could spell certain danger for the Earl.'

'I know. That is why I got news of it to you the moment I knew Warbeck was being brought to the Tower.'

'As far as you know they have not yet met.'

'I swear by all the Saints they have not—yet. The Earl talks eagerly to his attendant about his new neighbour, wants to know all he can of the man. He has had little or no contact outside the Tower for years. He hopes to find a friend.'

'Is he aware of the man's possible identity or of his treason?'

Josh Aldred hesitated. 'It is difficult to know that. The Earl is childlike. Don't misunderstand, I don't mean childish. Whatever you may have heard, he does not appear to me to be dim-witted, but his thought processes are slow.' He stirred angrily in his seat. 'As yours or mine would be if we'd spent practically all our lives in captivity.'

'Just so, but that very trusting nature could heighten his danger—and that of the other.'

'Aye.'

'Could you get me in to see the Earl?'

'Not today. The King is at the Tower at a meeting of Council. The place is exceptionally well guarded and all men watched.' He grinned mirthlessly. 'You know Henry is very conscious of the danger to his skin. I think he never forgot how close he came to dying at Redmoor when the late King cut down his standard bearer. No, it's certain no stranger would be allowed entry to the Tower today. Perhaps later in this week or next I could get you in dressed as a jailor, on some excuse or other, but...' he frowned

'...you'll need to take care what you say to him. He'd not want to betray any soul but he's guileless.'

'I understand that.' Richard pushed back his stool and stood up. 'I'll try and get word to you when I can come to the city again. One of Jarvis's men-at-arms can be trusted with messages. At present I'm at the beck and call of my lady.'

'Is she as pretty as her sire is handsome?'

'As lovely as her mother and with her sire's imperious nature.' Richard's lips parted in a tender smile. 'And with the spirit to match. Sir Guy has promised me her hand, so, after this business is concluded, I intend to marry and retire to the manor with my lady.'

At the other's sceptical glance, he laughed. 'You don't believe I'm ready to give up the excitement of intrigue? Just wait, Josh, until you have seen my Anne.'

'You are in love with the maid?'

For the space of a heartbeat Richard stood still considering, then he said, softly, 'Aye, by the sweet name of the Virgin, old friend, I believe that I am, but she'll have none of me and is intent on snaring one of the King's gentlemen.'

'She's ambitious for a wealthy match, then?'

Richard gave the faintest of smiles. 'No, I honestly believe that is not the case. She thinks...' he hesitated '...she wants a quiet life on her own manor with a man loyal to the King to see her and her children secure.'

'Ah.' Josh smiled ruefully and nodded as Richard flung him a hasty farewell and made for the tavern door.

Richard was astonished and not a whit angered to discover, on his return to The Golden Cockerel that Anne and his party had already left.

Jake informed him of the circumstances. 'I doubt that

she wanted to go, Master Richard, but the young coxcomb insisted.'

'Coxcomb? Was this man tall, fair, dressed in an over-exaggerated fashion?'

'Aye, that he was.' Jake Garnet chuckled hugely, bringing on himself an attack of wheezing. 'He wore a feather in his cap nigh tall enough to topple a church steeple.'

'Hilyard,' Richard muttered under his breath. His brows drew together in a scowl.

'You know him?'

'He's one of King Henry's squires of the body.'

The innkeeper nodded. 'He had an escort of men-at-arms dressed in the royal livery.'

Richard said softly, 'Josh informs me the King was attending a Council meeting at the Tower. Unfortunate that Hilyard should choose this inn to quench his thirst.'

'You think he suspects some malfeasance on your part?'

'No, no, I doubt that. As I told you, I am considered just a servant in attendance on Mistress Anne at Westminster. That is not what disturbs me.'

As Jake stared back at him owlishly Richard gave a little harsh bark of laughter. 'The man has an eye for Mistress Anne.' He hesitated for a moment then added, 'You should know, old friend, she is promised to me.'

'Oh? She has agreed to the match?'

'By no means, and is constantly determined to wriggle out of the arrangement. We are not yet formally contracted, but her father has given his word.'

'And you want her, Master Richard?'

'Aye,' Richard said through gritted teeth. 'I want her, Jake, and be sure of this, I'll have her, whatever she has to say on the subject.'

He took his leave, promising to return in a few days if circumstances allowed. Though Jake asked no questions as to Richard's reason for meeting with his son-in-law, it was clear he had some intimation and approved.

Anne was concerned for Richard's welfare and that concern was not assuaged until he presented himself to her next day. They were alone in the chamber for a few moments as Mary had been summoned to the antechamber of the Queen's presence chamber to repair a tear in Lady Philippa's skirt.

'What happened?' Anne demanded as he bowed to her in the doorway then she hurried him inside and confronted him as he closed the door and leaned against it.

'Happened? When? I might pose the same question to you.'

'When you returned to Westminster, of course. John Hilyard gave me to believe he would make trouble for you.' She drew a quick breath as he continued to lean against the door casually. 'You know well enough I had no choice but to leave with Master Hilyard. He believed you are merely—'

'A servant?'

'Exactly, and it would have done neither of us any good to deny that fact. *Did* he make trouble for you?'

'Indeed he tried. The head groom summoned me and tried to accuse me of neglecting my duty and going off to carouse in some low tavern.' He smiled grimly. 'However, it was perfectly clear I was stone cold sober and he could not make the charge stick. He blustered about seeing that I received a sound thrashing, but I managed to get the fellow alone and assured him I would not suffer alone if he in any way brought that about. He saw my point.'

'Thank the Saints. I have been worrying—'

'How did you explain giving me leave of absence to Hilyard?' he posed the question abruptly.

'I told him you went on business for my father.' She frowned suddenly as she realised that might be dangerous. 'Did I do wrong?'

He shrugged. 'I doubt it. I imagine Hilyard was so intent on proving his interest in dancing attendance upon you that all other thoughts were excluded from his mind.'

She nodded, relieved. 'Did you…' she hesitated '…did you achieve your purpose?'

'Not exactly. I must delay for a few days then go into the city again.'

She turned from him, exasperated. 'I wish you would not involve yourself in these dubious matters. It could be highly dangerous…'

'So, you *are* concerned about me?'

'I was about to add, before I was interrupted, to all of us, including my father and mother,' she snapped.

He took advantage of Lady Philippa's absence to seat himself and Anne sniffed her disapproval which merely brought forth a cheery smile.

'Where is the lovely Lady Philippa?'

'Waiting upon Her Majesty and Mary is with her.' Again there was a sudden edge to her tone. Certainly he was not immune to the sight of Philippa's beauty, despite her extreme youth. As she had expected, Richard Allard was not the only man at Westminster to be so affected. Lady Philippa turned heads wherever she went, but her nature was so sunny and innocent of deliberate coquetry that Anne could not find it in her heart to pass censure.

She dismissed him loftily but could not help watching his departure wistfully. Was it only his need to remain within reach of his companions in this constant intrigue which kept him near her at Westminster or did he have some genuine regard for her and wished to remain by her side? She knew that should he need to be on the road again it would be a simple enough matter for him to make some excuse to leave her service, knowing she would be adequately protected by the loyal Simpkin and Wat.

Over the next few days Anne fell into the regimen of service at Court more easily than she could have believed. The Queen was, indeed, a kindly and generous mistress, and refrained from placing too-onerous duties upon the shoulders of her newest attendants. As she had said in her first audience, she wanted the two younger girls to attend on her when she was at leisure, to chat, to read to her, to play the virginals and lute.

Philippa proved to be accomplished musically and sang enchantingly which she put down, deprecatingly, to some of the Welsh blood in her veins. Mary had done a good job in altering and decorating her outmoded gowns and her great beauty caused her to shine in whatever she wore. The gentlemen of the King's Court were delighted to wait upon both her and Anne, to make room for them at high table in the great hall and to invite them to dance when the King's minstrels played in the gallery.

On each occasion John Hilyard danced with Anne and, several times, escorted her out on to the river terrace when the weather allowed under the watchful gaze of Mary Scroggins. Anne was aware that on those occasions she was also under the baleful scrutiny of Richard, although from a respectful distance.

Anne was delighted to see the Queen happy with her children for, sometimes, she would catch Elizabeth with a wistful, almost lonely expression which she hastily veiled, especially in the presence of the King, who came but seldom to her apartments and then only to discuss the financial affairs of the household.

Philippa laughingly remarked in private that the King

more resembled some wealthy merchant bargaining in the market at Bruges or Utrecht than the sovereign of a great people. For all that, Anne was sure he was a shrewd, informed and skilful ruler and sometimes her heart would miss a beat when she found his penetrating light eyes fixed upon her as if he would read through to her very soul.

The Queen missed her eldest child, Prince Arthur, whom she seldom saw, for he now, at thirteen, had a household of his own, but the Princess Margaret, a solemn child of ten years, liked to sit at her mother's feet, learning her embroidery skills. She was not outstandingly pretty but handsome, fair like her mother, but with her father's more pointed features.

When the nurse brought the Princess Mary Rose to her mother's chamber, Anne saw in the merry, lovely child the resemblance to her mother and thought how she must have looked when her father, King Edward, reigned and her uncle, then Richard of Gloucester, came to court to visit him.

Prince Henry, at eight, was a vividly handsome and precocious child who often came to chat with his mother and boast of his prowess at chess, riding and the martial arts at which he was proving accomplished. He had a round, vibrant face, with wide-spaced blue eyes which Anne thought missed little, and a mass of curling red-gold hair. She privately thought that, young as he was, he had an eye for the ladies of the Court who petted him continually and she thought perhaps he would resemble his glorious grandfather, King Edward IV, as he grew older.

Anne was emerging from the Queen's private chamber one morning in late October when she was hailed by a stranger, a tall, brown-haired man of about forty. He stopped in his stride down the corridor to beam at her and she stared at him, puzzled. Certainly she did not know him yet he appeared to know her. He had pleasant, open features and kindly brown eyes under somewhat bushy brows and his voice carried the lilting Welsh tone which Philippa used often.

Anne curtsied. 'I am sorry, sir, but I do not think I know you?'

'And why, indeed, should you, since I have not set eyes on you since you were a little lass at your mother's knee, but you are so like her I could not be mistaken. You are Mistress Anne Jarvis, I take it?' He came towards her, hand outstretched in greeting.

She nodded, still a little bemused, and he chuckled. 'I am Sir Owen Lewis and I was your father's squire.'

'Oh.' Anne's expression cleared. 'Of course, both he and my mother have spoken of you, sir, often. You—'

'Fought for the King Henry at East Stoke for which I doubt your father will ever forgive me,' he said ruefully. 'But, my lass, I am Welsh and my loyalties were torn on that occasion. I was able, later, to see to it that your father did not suffer too harshly for his own part in what may now be considered unsuitable loyalties. And now...' he spread his two hands widely '...though I am still in King Henry's service I am seldom at Court these days but spend most of my time with my wife and four little ones on my own manor near Conway.' He smiled at her warmly. 'Is your father present at Court?'

'No, indeed, Sir Owen,' she said regretfully. 'I doubt my father would ever be welcome here nor would he wish to attend, but the Queen has done me the honour of inviting me to wait on her with Lady Philippa Telford, and so I arrived here just a few weeks ago.'

'And heartily glad I am to see you here. You have a brother, young Ned, I understand. Is all well at Rushton?'

She smiled shyly in answer. 'Yes, I thank you, sir. My

parents are both well and will be pleased to hear I have met you.'

He nodded. 'And you are happy, well treated?'

'A little homesick, which is natural, but the Queen is very kind and I have Philippa's friendship. We are already very close.'

He bowed to her. 'Good. I hope I shall see you again during the few weeks I shall spend in London. Commend me to your father, mistress.' He strode off about his business and Anne stood for a moment, thinking of home and the talk she had heard about those long-ago days when Owen Lewis had served her father and of one occasion in particular when he had been injured as her mother had tried to escape her father's custody. Lady Jarvis had ever had a soft spot for her husband's former squire and regretted the circumstances which had kept them apart since Redmoor.

She was about to move on when John Hilyard emerged from another chamber and immediately came to her side, bowing low.

'Mistress Anne, I trust you keep well. You certainly appear to be so, for you are as radiant as ever.'

She curtsied formally in reply, lowering her head to hide her blushes at his exaggerated flattery. 'Very well, sir.'

'Are you excused service for the moment?'

'For the next two hours, yes.'

'Can I beg you to walk with me on the river terrace? It is a fine, warm day for late October. We are experiencing an Indian summer.'

Anne hesitated. She had seen little of Richard over the last few days and had intended sending Mary to summon him to her.

'Well, sir…'

'With your maid in attendance, of course,' he added, smiling. 'Could I attend you to your chamber while you fetch your warm cloak? The river breeze can be a little chill despite the unseasonable warmth.'

She was always chary of disobliging him. His manner was a mixture of authority and deferential attention and she nodded her agreement as they walked together towards her chamber door. If Mary was not present she could conventionally decline the invitation since Philippa was still in attendance and could not accompany her.

Unfortunately Mary was there and, even more unfortunately, so was Richard.

Anne stopped on the threshold and glared at him. She was conscious that he had avoided her presence lately and now that she could not give him her full attention he was here at her service.

John Hilyard hovered in the doorway behind her and she addressed Mary Scroggins first.

'I intend to walk on the river terrace with Master Hilyard. Will you find me a warm cloak, Mary, and your own, for I wish you to attend me.'

While Mary went to do her bidding she eyed Richard coolly. He had risen at her entrance for he appeared to have been lounging at his ease on a stool and, after casting one careful glance at her escort, he lowered his eyes, ostensibly obsequious.

His manner, so obvious a pretence, annoyed her further. 'Is there anything you wish to report, Master Allsop?' she demanded.

'No, mistress. I presented myself in case you had need of me.'

'You can squire Mary,' she said curtly, hoping, for some obscure reason she could not explain even to herself, that he would be put out by her order. She knew that John Hilyard's obvious attentions to her irritated him as much as she was churlishly angered by Richard's open admiration of Philippa Telford.

He bowed and came towards her with her cloak when Mary presented it. John Hilyard stepped forward neatly and himself draped it round her shoulders. She thanked him, her voice a little high. Why did she not feel the same tingle of pleasurable unease when he touched her as she did when Richard did so? Richard, for his part, did the same service for Mary and John Hilyard gallantly offered his arm to Anne to lead her from the chamber.

It was pleasant in the late autumn sunshine. Anne would have taken greater pleasure in it had she not been conscious of her two attendants trailing some polite distance behind. At least Richard would be unable to hear what passed between her and John, she thought, defiantly, though she was sure he would be straining his ears to do so.

John was chattering animatedly about the King's professed intention to take advantage of the unexpected warm weather to move the Court to the former hunting lodge of Sheen, now renamed Richmond, in honour of the King's former earldom.

'There will be some hawking parties and, if the weather holds, it should be very enjoyable,' John said.

Anne nodded. She was not listening very carefully, her mind occupied with Richard strolling behind her, and his neglect of her during the last few days. Had he been again to The Golden Cockerel and was his business there placing him in danger of arrest?

'The Queen has agreed to accompany the King this time and young Prince Henry can talk of nothing else. He loves hawking and hunting,' John was saying. 'I am sure the Queen will wish for you and Lady Philippa to accompany her.'

Anne smiled. The possibility of outings into the country was promising. Already she was becoming tired of being cooped up in the suffocating atmosphere of the palace of Westminster and the dank cold air from the river sometimes depressed her spirits.

'I shall enjoy that, if I am chosen to go,' she agreed.

'I imagine you miss Rushton,' he said suddenly, pausing near a tall hedge which gave some protection from the river breeze.

'Oh, yes,' she said eagerly, 'I do. I miss the openness. Ned, my brother, and I often went down to the river and—'

'I expect your father was often away from home so that you had considerable freedom?' he said casually.

Anne hesitated for a moment. That was an unusual gambit of conversation and she had the uneasy feeling that he was pumping her for information he was anxious to learn, rather than keeping her lightly engaged in chit chat. Years of careful attention to what was revealed concerning her father's movements, constantly drilled into her by her mother, made her deliberately cautious.

She said quietly, 'My father goes to Leicester and Northampton, too, sometimes on business connected with the manor, but he seldom travels further afield these days.'

'He does not come to London? He must miss Court life. I understand he was often in personal attendance upon the late King.'

'He has never said as much,' she said evenly. 'Naturally he regrets the passing of the old regime. He was a loyal servant to King Richard, as,' she added deliberately, 'he is to the present one and he would come to Westminster, I am sure, if he were summoned.'

'Of course,' he said soothingly. 'He must miss you. Is he an indulgent father?'

'Yes,' she replied, 'though I have never been spoiled. My mother sees to that.'

He chuckled. 'I understand they are still greatly in love. She would worry about him greatly were he to travel abroad.'

'I am sure she would,' Anne responded sweetly, 'but I have not known him to do so for several years.'

He was twisting a stem of laurel between his fingers, not looking at her directly. 'That fellow of yours was remiss in conduct to leave you unguarded in the Chepe. You said, in his defence, that he was well acquainted with the innkeeper and his father.'

Anxious to back up Richard, she said a little too quickly, 'He has been there often and trusts them. My father did go there once or twice on his rare visits to London.'

He turned a bland, smiling face towards her and she could have bitten her tongue in concern for her indiscreet remark. She said a little sharply, 'The sun is pleasant but it is getting cold. I think we should return to the palace, Master Hilyard.'

'Still so formal after we have been acquainted some weeks now. Will you not call me John, Mistress Anne?'

She made a little polite curtsy. 'You are kind. As you wish it, John.' She did not, however, add to that her permission for him to call her by her baptismal name.

The two girls were invited by the Queen to accompany her with some other chosen ladies to join the King's party to visit his hunting lodge at Sheen. Philippa, in particular, was delighted, as, only the day before, a trunk of clothing had arrived for her from her grandparents' home near Ludlow on the Welsh border.

Sir Daniel and Lady Gretton had written, expressing their pleasure in welcoming their granddaughter home to

England, for they had not seen her since babyhood when her mother had ventured into Wales on a fleeting visit to her parents, bringing with her her newly born daughter.

Sir Daniel announced that they would shortly arrive in London to see Philippa and sent a considerable amount in gold with the chest of fine clothing for Philippa's needs whilst at the English Court. Amongst the items was a well-cut riding gown in blue velvet which became Philippa mightily and she was duly anxious to show it off.

'They all fit excellently,' she said excitedly as she twirled for Anne's admiring attention in one after another of her new fashionable gowns. 'How do you think they managed that, since they have not seen me for so long?'

'I imagine your mother has kept them informed,' Anne said smilingly, pleased by her friend's delight in her new treasures.

'Now I shall be fittingly turned out for the hawking parties, though neither of us have birds,' Philippa said wistfully. 'To tell truth, Anne, though I shall enjoy the outings I never could be pleased to see the hawks stoop to their prey.'

Secretly Anne agreed with her. There was something extremely unsettling in the imagery, as if her family's enemies were poised to fall upon their expected prey at any moment.

She reported the invitation to Richard. 'I do not know if I can include you in my party without special invitation,' she added.

He smiled grimly. 'Certainly you will not go without me. Leave it to me to obtain permission.'

She was relieved. After the conversation with John Hilyard she was more and more determined to keep Richard near her, well away from any possible temptation to seek out his fellow conspirators in the city, too close for her comfort to the presence of the royal prisoners within The Tower.

She had not informed Richard of the probing questions John Hilyard had put to her on that supposedly leisurely walk on the river terrace, deciding, for the moment, that that worrying conversation was best kept to herself.

The hunting lodge at Richmond was small and, as a consequence, terribly overcrowded when the royal party descended upon in, yet Anne found its old-fashioned, rambling structure, set as it was near the river—a much cleaner, less crowded river than near Westminster—and surrounded by stretches of open and wooded country, utterly charming.

Though she and Philippa were forced to share dormitory accommodation with other ladies of the court they settled in joyfully, knowing it could be but a short time they would spend here before the weather worsened once more and they were forced to return to Westminster Palace. Anne was relieved to find Richard and the other two men from Rushton included in the hunting party.

The court was merry and constantly busied with one entertainment after the other, of which hawking proved the most popular, since the ladies could be included in this sport. Anne and Philippa were loaned small goshawks from the royal mews and joined the expeditions several times. Anne's bird made only one kill and Philippa's not at all, so they were not too distressed by the sight of the bloodied victims in the talons of their raptors.

The queen accompanied the King on only two occasions. The little Princess Mary Rose suffered a chill soon after their arrival at Richmond and the Queen made frequent visits to her youngest daughter's bedside to comfort and soothe her.

On the third proposed expedition the Queen insisted that

the two girls accompany the party though she herself declined and Lady Hartley remained at the Lodge with her. The girls felt happily free to be away from that lady's stern eye and rode joyfully amongst the company which consisted mainly, today, of many of the younger members of the Court.

The King had been over-busied at Westminster with affairs of State and seemed, on this day, to have put care aside and to be truly enjoying himself, indulgently watching the excited manouevres of his second son, Henry, who rode like a centaur despite his youth and was handling his goshawk with supreme skill.

Anne was conscious of the presence of her three watchful escorts riding in the rear of the party. When the company stopped for refreshment soon after noon, it was Richard who spread frieze blankets for them to seat themselves, taken from his saddle bags, and a fine, damask cloth on which the cold repast was laid out for Anne and Philippa upon the mossy ground within the small copse where they had recently been trying out the skill of their birds.

Fortunately the day was clear and the ground not too damp and Richard and his two cohorts waited upon them efficiently. John Hilyard had earlier offered Anne some attention but was now engaged in waiting upon his master and, eyeing him from a distance, she could only feel relief. Following the direction of her gaze and noting her absorbed air, Richard raised one eyebrow interrogatively.

'Is it that you miss the presence of your gallant admirer?' he whispered when, for a moment, Philippa's attention was engaged elsewhere.

Anne gave a little shiver. 'No. I am glad to see his attentions diverted,' she said shortly.

'He has been making a nuisance of himself?' Richard's questioning tone was sharp.

'No,' she whispered, 'it is just that sometimes...' she hesitated, her blue eyes clouded with doubt '...sometimes he is—rather too inquisitive about my father's affairs.'

Richard's brows drew together in a doubtful frown and his gaze once more returned to the subject of their talk. His mouth hardened in an attitude of intense distrust.

The air was keen and Anne should have found her appetite sharpened but, for the first time since they had come to Richmond, she merely toyed with her food. The sight of John Hilyard waiting so obsequiously upon the King sickened her. She could not have imagined King Richard demanding such a fawning display of loyalty and she recalled, with another inward shiver, that she had noted this attitude of wary alertness in the expressions of all those who served King Henry, even, she thought with a slight grimace, in the eyes of the Queen herself.

Young Prince Henry was anxious to resume the sport and the courtiers looked toward their king to see if he were agreeable to the breaking up of this pleasant hour of ease. Smilingly he rose to his feet from a saddle where he had been seated and gave his permission for the company to mount up once more.

Anne was somewhat reluctant to leave Richard with the work of clearing up the remains of the meal and packing up the cloths. She wanted him near her as the party proceeded and deliberately delayed until she and Philippa were in the rear of the party and she could see out of the corner of her eye that Richard and the two Rushton men had completed their work and were ready to mount up and ride after the royal party.

Prince Henry and the King rode in front. Beaters had been sent ahead to flush out prey and Anne looked away as the raptors soared high into the air to the delighted shouts of the sporting participants. She called imperiously to one of the huntsmen accompanying the party and handed over her hawk, who was struggling wildly in his jesses, anxious to fly free. His constant fluttering was spoiling her enjoyment of the afternoon.

Philippa thankfully handed over her own bird and the two girls allowed their mounts to amble while they themselves gratefully drew in the sharp wine-like air and looked about appreciatively at what was left of the golden brown leaves which were now few upon the bare tree branches.

Anne was so absorbed in her delight at the rural scene that when she first heard the excited and alarmed yells of the party ahead she did not, at first, take in the reason. She and Philippa had fallen some way back from the main party, though Richard and the Rushton men were close behind. The main group of courtiers were just in sight, approaching an area of deep covert while the King and young Henry had drawn ahead, their attentions on the soaring and hovering of their birds.

Excitedly the prince spurred his mount towards the undergrowth as his goshawk came fluttering down, her talons deep within the body of a lark, her latest prey. He rode nearer, calling her back to his wrist as she alighted on the grass and stood, wings quivering, cruel eyes scanning the dying throes of her victim.

Delighted by the triumph of his favourite, Prince Henry had, apparently, neither seen nor heard the crashing of the undergrowth directly ahead of him or glimpsed the black, snarling creature which emerged and made straight for the legs of his mount, red, feral eyes blazing, tusks lifted to strike in a frenzy of blood lust.

Now Anne understood the frantic warning yells of the men behind and the frightened keening screams of the ladies of the party. The King saw the danger too late and his horse reared up in sudden terror so that, for moments, he was incapable of riding to the assistance of the boy prince.

Suddenly a horse jarred hard against his gaily caparisoned black gelding and he was pushed aside so roughly that it was all he could do to remain in the saddle. His attacker reared aside and spurred forward desperately towards the boy's horse, which had reared and was whinnying, terrified at the sight of the wild black boar hurtling towards him. The prince clutched frantically at his reins, but was unable to remain in the saddle and toppled helplessly to the ground, one foot caught in the trailing harness so that he was being dragged ignominiously along the ground.

The boar turned, listening and staring defiantly at the horrified courtiers who seemed too stupefied to approach him, then rushed towards the hapless boy who screamed shrilly in an agony of fear.

The rider who had almost unseated the King rode straight at the maddened beast. He had snatched a sword from the saddle bow of one of the courtiers and was steering his own mount with a single hand towards the fallen prince and the boar. He jumped from the saddle as his horse reared off wildly, snorting in terror, and the newcomer stood astride the prostrate boy. He leaned down and sawed through the leather strap that bound the prince to his own plunging and rearing animal which, also, plunged off into the undergrowth.

Anne, with mounting horror, saw Richard tackle the snarling, frenzied animal which immediately leaped upon him, tearing at his unprotected legs. Richard stabbed down with his sword inexpertly, for he had no boar spear. This was not a hunting party as such and few of the huntsmen were prepared. Man and boy were beset and the approaching party drew their mounts back in a horrified semi-circle, their eyes searching for some practical but safe way of helping the pair.

Anne felt her breath catch in her throat as, between the gaps in the spectators, she saw Richard brought down in what was a snarling, struggling mass of arms and legs and tearing tusks. Over it all came the shrill screams of the terrified boy.

One of the huntsmen, it seemed, had come armed, however unexpectedly, and he charged into the fray, brandishing the barbed boar spear.

Anne could only stare helplessly while the fray seemed to continue for what seemed hours yet could only have been moments for suddenly it was all over. The beast lay dead, stabbed by Richard while the huntsman's boar spear held the creature down. Man and boy were able to draw clear of the still-heaving carcass.

Richard stood up, clutching with one hand at a wound in his sword arm; with that still-wounded arm, he drew the prince's quivering form to his feet. They were surrounded instantly by jabbering, expostulating courtiers, while the huntsman saw to it that the boar was unmistakably defunct. While all around her were dismounting, anxious now to determine the injuries to the prince, Anne alone could not muster either the will or the strength to do so.

She remained in the saddle, her eyes mutely searching the crowd for sight of Richard whose form was now lost to her in the general mêlée. She gave a terrible gasp of terror until she saw him at last withdraw from the mob of congratulatory men who sought to delay him. His eyes were seeking her and he gave a sigh of relief at sight of her. Now she was able to spring down unaided and run to his side.

'Richard,' she gasped. 'Dickon, are you—are you badly hurt?'

She could see blood pouring down his sword arm and he smiled at her wearily as his tired fingers let slip the borrowed weapon and he staggered in his stride toward her. His hose was torn and she thought he must have been badly gored in the leg, but he was able to remain on his feet so the wounds could not have been life threatening. She could hardly speak for the stupefying terror she felt for him.

The King had given commands, for one of the courtiers ran up with a flask of wine and some torn white cloth. Anne could not guess how he had obtained it. Presumably it had been torn from someone's shirt for it looked to be of the finest cambric.

'Come, man,' the nobleman insisted. 'Sit down here on this fallen log and let me cleanse and staunch the blood from your arm wound.'

Anne waited impatiently as the man tore off Richard's leather jerkin and exposed the ripped shirt and the long, crooked wound running from elbow to wrist. She would have preferred to tend Richard herself, but was forced to allow the young courtier to do her work for her. Richard's legs were gored but the wounds were not deep and it seemed that, barring infection, Richard would do well enough. In the distance Anne could hear the men about the prince and from their relieved tones judged that he had not sustained any real harm.

One or two of the more curious of the falconry party now came over to see what injuries the prince's rescuer had suffered. The little crowd was parted abruptly as the King stalked into the half-circle and stood, gnawing his under lip and staring down at Richard, who immediately attempted to struggle to his feet as his attendant did in the King's presence.

King Henry waved a hand testily. 'Stay where you are, man. You must be faint with pain and shock.' He paused for a moment, still regarding Richard intently. 'You have our profound gratitude. Without your prompt action I doubt that our huntsman with his boar spear could have reached my son in time. What is your name? I do not think I have seen you about the palace.'

There was a little stir of movement from the watchers as Richard sank obediently back upon the fallen log. Anne saw that he was very pale and he was still breathing erratically. He looked up at last fully into the eyes of his sovereign and gave a little shaky laugh, then knuckled his forehead in the timeless gesture of deference.

'I beg Your Majesty's pardon that I was forced to push you aside, but…'

The King's voice was stern but showed no trace of anger or irritation. 'Man, had you not have done so, you might have been too late to save young Henry. Your name, man, that I might know to whom I owe everlasting gratitude?'

'I am Dickon Allsop, sire. I—have come but recently to Westminster to serve Mistress Jarvis. I am in her father's service.'

'Ah.' The King's eyes narrowed somewhat and he turned to Anne, who was standing uncertainly with a nervous Philippa beside her at Richard's side.

'You are to be congratulated, Mistress Jarvis, at having so brave and resourceful a servant,' he said curtly. 'I trust you will allow me to reward him personally.'

At her nervous nod, for words had deserted her in her sense of fear and shock—she was still shaking—the King drew off a heavy signet ring from his embroidered leather gauntlet and, bending, offered the costly token to Richard.

For one dreadful moment Anne was afraid that he would not take it from King Henry's hand, but he knuckled his forehead obsequiously again and took the ring into a bloodstained hand.

The King nodded and gave a wave of dismissal to the gathered courtiers. 'Let us leave this fellow to rest for a while. We had best return to the hunting lodge.'

Richard said huskily, 'The prince, Your Majesty, he is well?'

'Thoroughly frightened but relatively unharmed. There are scratches and bruises and he will undoubtedly be stiff in the morning but you protected him well.'

His thin lips curved into a smile Anne thought was unusual in so stern and cautious a man. 'Henry must learn to be more careful of his own skin. He rode too far forward and too near the undergrowth for comfort. He is brave but rash. That will change—in time.'

He moved off, followed by his bowing attendants and Anne let out her breath in a relieved gasp as the nobleman attending Richard bowed to her and began to back away.

'He should do well enough now, Mistress. I suggest he stays where he is for a while and catches up the rest of the party later. One of the huntsmen can show him the way.'

Anne nodded her gratitude. 'Thank you for what you did for my servant, sir. I will remain with him. Will you escort my friend, Lady Philippa? One of my men from Rushton can stay with us and tend Dickon, should he need further assistance.'

Philippa demurred. 'No, no, Anne *chérie*, I will stay with you both. We shall be safe with our attendants even if it should grow dark.'

Anne was desperate to be alone with Richard. She swallowed back a sharp retort and forced a smile. 'Very well, Pippa. Will you see to it that Wat rounds up our horses and readies himself to escort us when Master Allsop feels recovered enough to mount?'

'Mistress,' Richard croaked, struggling to rise, 'I shall be perfectly well once in the saddle—'

'You will obey His Majesty and stay where you are for a bit,' she snapped crossly. 'I do not want you fainting in the saddle. That would do none of us good.'

He gave her a crooked grin as she stepped closer to feel that the improvised bandage on his arm was tight enough to remain in place throughout their ride. 'Very well, mistress.' He looked across to the young huntsman who had ridden to his help with his trusty boar spear.

'It's all right, man, you can follow the party. I know my way well enough and will see both my charges safely home before dark.' His lips twisted wryly. 'And thank you kindly. I don't know where either the prince or I would be now, in purgatory, like enough, had you not had the foresight to come ready for the possibility of a charging boar.'

The young man grinned in answer. 'I alus says you never know what you're going to find in forest land, best to take precautions.' He glanced back to where the gaily dressed hawking party was mounting up, ready to depart the clearing. 'They don't always see the dangers, if you take me meaning, like.'

He saluted Richard as he would an equal and strode off to his own horse which was waiting patiently, its reins looped to the low branch of a nearby alder.

Philippa was talking with Wat and Simpkin, and Anne turned to Richard. For moments they were alone.

'Sweet Virgin,' she muttered through gritted teeth. 'Do not ever alarm me so again. I thought—I thought…' Her voice trailed off as tears sparked in her eyes.

'I know what you thought,' he said softly. 'The same thought crossed my mind and—' his grin was truly mischievous now '—while risking my life to save the Tudor brat, of all people.' He looked ruefully down at the royal signet ring gleaming upon his finger. 'Well, he is Plantagenet, one-half of him, at least.'

Anne was about to answer tartly when Simpkin came over with a flask of wine. 'I think you should take a pull of this, Master Richard,' he said gravely.

Richard drank gratefully and Anne moved shakily to lean against the bole of an elm while she waited for Richard's colour to return so that they could mount up and turn for home.

Chapter Seven

Anne watched anxiously while Wat brought up Richard's horse and stood ready to help him into the saddle but, once he had had time to recover, Richard appeared to need no more assistance and vaulted into the saddle with no visible difficulty. When Wat helped her to mount she felt he must be aware of the fast pounding of her heart, for she needed far more time to accept the terrible nearness of Richard's brush with death. She managed a smile when Philippa rode alongside and they began to move off slowly.

Anne found it difficult to meet her friend's eye and she spurred ahead somewhat impatiently. If Philippa found her desire for haste ungracious, considering the condition of their injured servant, she made no comment. Eventually Richard overtook and rode beside Anne in the lead, since he apparently was the one who had noted carefully the way they had come. She stole a glance at him but he appeared serene and was riding without sign of obvious pain. She could not believe she had been so terribly affected. Even now she was shivering as if with an ague. Richard's peril had totally unnerved her.

She was so absorbed in her thoughts that she was not watching out for pitfalls on the track and when her horse stumbled she was almost unseated. Richard turned and she waved him on impatiently, but her momentary lapse of concentration caused her to be unaware of a hare which started at that moment across her path and her mare, already unsettled, gave a whinny of alarm and without warning plunged off at right angles from the track into the undergrowth.

Anne had not been properly settled in the saddle and now found herself slipping as her palfrey swerved sickeningly from side to side to avoid overhanging branches and increased its speed suddenly. Anne wrenched on the reins but to no avail and let out a cry of distress. She had always been an accomplished horsewoman and was able to stay in the saddle, though with an effort.

She gave up pulling at the reins, knowing that could only inflame her palfrey's fears and was grimly determined to hold on until the animal slowed and was capable of being controlled once more. Meanwhile she was being carried further off track and she set her teeth, praying that the headlong ride would not end by her meeting a tree trunk or other obstruction head on as a result of being flung over her mount's neck.

Anne heard a shout behind her and knew that either Wat or Richard was attempting to follow and check her frantic palfrey and she gave a little sob of relief. At least help was at hand but there was little prospect of riding alongside her on this narrow track. She bit her lip in concentration, hoping that the pace would slow soon and she would have the breath to soothe her frightened palfrey and bring her to a stop.

Suddenly a horse reared up ahead of her and the palfrey gave a neigh of fear and came to a shivering, bone-jarring halt.

Anne managed to retain her seat and her rescuer dismounted, calling to his own hack to stand still while he rushed towards her and placed strong arms around her waist, drawing her safely to the ground. She gave a glad cry when she felt herself pressed against Richard's jerkin and heard his voice, harsh with alarm, counselling her to rest still and catch her breath. She stood against him, her face hard against his chest, feeling the heavy pounding of his heart which was as frantic as the fast beat of her own.

'Sweet Virgin,' he murmured, 'you are not hurt?'

She shook her head mutely, too breathless to reply and very close to tears of shock, panic and utter relief. It was only when he gave a sharp cry of pain that she realised she was pressing against his injury and she drew away for a moment, glimpsing his features distorted with fear for her safety. Then, reaching up her arms around his neck, she drew his dear face hungrily down close to her own.

'Oh, my dear,' she whispered brokenly, 'I have hurt you. I—I am so sorry.'

His lips were nuzzling her hair which had burst free of its pins in that frightening ride. She had also lost that ridiculous, fashionable little velvet hat she had worn for the expedition. Her arms tightened around his neck and their lips met, his demandingly, and hers desperately in answer. It seemed that both of them needed reassurance that the loved one was still living, warm and alert, and neither cared for any consequences but gave way to the complete and overwhelming need to be one with the other.

He released her mouth for a second and she choked, 'My darling, I thought—thought back there that you would be killed. Never, *never* submit me to such agony of fear again...'

Any further expostulation was drowned as he claimed her mouth again and they clung to each other, speechless and yet conveying without any shadow of doubt the depth of their great love.

Moments later Anne felt Richard stir and his body stiffen and she broke free, staring up into his face as he looked beyond her to someone or something that had drawn close and was now in his line of vision. She turned abruptly to find that Philippa had ridden towards them on the parallel path and was staring, wide-eyed, at the sight of them in so intimate an embrace. Silently Anne leaned her back against Richard's taut body and faced her friend, her chin jutting defiantly. Warningly Richard put his two hands upon her shoulders. Neither spoke.

For seconds Philippa sat rigid upon her own palfrey, her blue-green eyes widening in astonishment, then she made an almost inarticulate little sound and turned her horse, a difficult feat on so narrow a path, and began to move back as if determined to head off Wat whose blundering progress nearby showed he must be following her closely.

Richard gave a great gasp and turned Anne gently but firmly to meet his gaze.

'That,' he said very quietly, 'could prove very difficult to explain.'

'We—we must tell her the truth,' Anne said quaveringly. 'She has the right to know…'

'To know what?' he coaxed even more softly. 'That you know at last that you love me, Anne Jarvis?'

'Yes, damn you,' she said forcibly. 'I love you, Richard Allard. I know that now, but…'

'But?'

She pulled away from him sharply, for his fingers were digging into the soft flesh of her upper arms so that she knew there would be bruises later.

'It changes nothing.'

'It changes everything.'

'No, this peril you deliberately placed yourself in tells me that, love you or no, I could not live with you. I could not stand the agony of suspense each time that…' She drew a quivering breath.

'My darling, when my business here in London is over I will devote myself to you alone and…'

'There you go again,' she stormed furiously. '"When my business is over." What I said just now is true. You deliberately flout danger. You had no need to run in just now, and face that boar alone and especially not to rescue the son of the man you declare you hate. There were others present equally capable of killing that boar and…'

'There was no time to hesitate, my heart. He was a child, a foolish child, I grant you, but just a boy, like your brother Ned. Would you have had me leave him to his fate? A moment later and the boar would have gored him. I had to intervene. I had no time to consider whom I was saving and if it was politic. I had to do it, and you know it.'

She drew a hard breath. 'But this other danger—no, do not try to convince me that I imagine things. You are courting danger now, every moment here in Richmond and in the city. Have you no time to consider what you do and—and put me first?'

It was an ultimatum and he swallowed and, momentarily, turned his head from her.

He said quietly, 'My honour compels me…'

'To put others first—the Yorkist prince in the Tower, I presume?'

He sighed. 'He too, though he is a man grown as I am, but he is a child in knowledge of the world at large. He needs others to help him as the boy did back there in the clearing. I cannot desert his cause while he lives.'

She said sadly, 'Then there is nothing more to say. Let

us get on our way or there will be questions asked if we are too long before returning to the hunting lodge.'

He helped her mount, as her palfrey seemed now to have got over her fright and was standing docilely.

Anne said softly, 'Has your injury been made worse by riding so fast after me just now?'

He shook his head. 'No, I told you it was just a long scratch. I'll see that it is dressed with care against infection.' More soberly, he said, 'About Lady Philippa? Can she be relied upon to be discreet?'

'Yes, I believe so. She is still very young, but her life has been spent at the Duchess Margaret's Court well steeped in intrigue. She knows when to hold her tongue.'

They returned to the main path and found Philippa with Wat in attendance, waiting anxiously. Philippa looked worriedly into her friend's face, but Anne merely shook her head gently in answer to the mutely posed question.

Richard said briskly, 'No harm done. The palfrey was frightened but Mistress Anne was not thrown.'

He took the lead and they returned to the hunting lodge as twilight was beginning to fall.

They were late to supper in the hall and Anne had little chance to speak with Philippa. She waited until they were in bed together that night and Mary had left the chamber upon an errand.

Philippa was silent, clearly embarrassed to frame the question she was longing to ask her friend; then, at last, she burst out, 'Will you not get Master Allsop in dreadful trouble with your father if it comes to his ears that…?'

Anne sat up against the pillows and looked directly at her troubled friend.

'You need to know the truth, Philippa, but I beg you will not speak of what I have to tell you again—not to anyone, not even to me in private. We can never tell who may overhear us. Master Allsop is not in my father's service. He is not a servant at all. He is the son of Sir Dominick Allard.'

Philippa's mouth rounded in a little 'oh' as she digested that intelligence. 'Sir Dominick is a friend of my father's and...'

'Just so. My own father was Sir Dominick's squire and our two families have always been closely associated. Richard, Dickon, that is, happened to be present at our manor when the summons came from the Queen calling me to Court. He offered to escort me south. I...' She hesitated, for the whole business seemed so foolish now and dangerous. 'I—told John Hilyard that he was my servant. We had just arrived and John Hilyard was assisting us to enter the palace at Westminster. There was some problem. The entrance was blocked and he helped to clear the way for us. I spoke on the spur of the moment, told him Richard was my father's steward and made up that name for him.'

'But why?' Philippa was clearly bewildered.

'I don't know.' Anne spoke hesitantly. 'I did not want him to abandon me at Westminster, needed to have him near me.'

She met Philippa's clear green blue gaze and swallowed hard. 'Obviously it would have been unwise for him to attend court under his true name. Like your father and mine, Richard's is disgraced after his father's unfailing support of the late King.'

Philippa inclined her lovely head as if she perfectly understood that.

'And you...' she paused deliberately, eyeing Anne coolly '...love him?'

Again Anne swallowed. 'Yes,' she said at last, so softly

that Philippa had some difficulty in hearing her. 'Yes, I think I do.'

'Your father would be angered if he knew?'

'On the contrary, he wishes me to be betrothed to Richard.'

'Then, once you are both back at Rushton, all will be well.'

'No,' Anne said stubbornly, 'it will not. Richard refuses to keep clear of intrigue and I will not ally myself with a conspirator. Philippa, you know the situation as well as I, for you have lived like that all your life, never knowing if your father will come back to you after one of his secret journeys in the Duchess Margaret's bid to oust King Henry from the throne she insists he usurped. I have met some of the widows of Redmoor. I do not wish to be left like that, striving to keep my manor free from sequestration. It is not a life for a woman.'

'Yet you confess that you love Richard.'

Anne's voice was harsh with unshed tears. 'With every fibre of my being.'

'Then how will it help to continue to love him, whether he is near to you or not, for you will not be able to help yourself.' Despite her lack of years Philippa was astonishingly practical. 'You will long for him, constantly fear for him every time his name is mentioned. There will be no happiness for you with another man.'

She added shrewdly, 'Even if your life together is short and you live constantly on the edge of the fear of losing him, you will have those moments and—if the worst happens—the memories to look back upon. At least, that is what my mother has always said about her abiding love for my father. She willingly gave up everything to be with him.'

She looked away for a moment, then she said, 'I know

you have the same amount of courage, *ma chère* Anne, and—I long to experience such a love. It is not granted often. I pray to know it as my parents do.'

Anne was very close to tears now. She reached out and took her young friend's small hand. 'You are so wise, Pippa,' she said in a little choked voice. 'Far wiser than I am.'

'You will think about what I have said?'

'Of course, my dear. The dilemma is with me all the time since—since I have known for sure that I love Richard.' She sighed. 'If only I could convince him to leave the capital and go home to Yorkshire, to extricate himself from this constant plotting...'

There was a knock upon the door signalling Mary's return to their chamber and Anne called in answer. Then two girls hugged each other in companionable silence.

As Anne had promised Richard, Philippa never indicated by look or word to him that her attitude to him had altered in any way. She continued to treat him as a servant in her usual courteous manner that she had towards all her inferiors. Neither did she mention seeing Anne in his arms again to her friend.

Three days later the royal party returned to Westminster and the girls were once more settled in their old chamber.

The days had shortened and grown colder and the palace rooms and corridors grew more and more chill, so that it was necessary for Anne and Philippa to wear their warmest gowns and hooded fur-lined cloaks when walking on the river terrace or in the bare brown gardens.

John Hilyard continued to pay noticeable attention to Anne, which embarrassed her. She could not rid herself of the notion that he had been set to spy upon her, learn tidbits of knowledge from her about her father's activities. She had thought it best to keep away from Richard as much as possible after the two shattering events in Richmond park, and so she had little opportunity to inform him of her suspicions concerning the young squire.

Just once Philippa posed the question which disturbed her, the only oblique reference she made to Anne's declaration of her intentions.

'Master Hilyard seems greatly taken with you, *chère* Anne. Do you reciprocate his feelings, I wonder?'

Anne could not repress a shiver of revulsion and her reply was sharp.

'Certainly not. I—I have no particular interest in Master Hilyard though, I confess, I find his attentions to me flattering. He is so much in the King's favour that I could not believe he would consider an alliance with my house possible, even if he had such desires. He is,' she added through gritted teeth, 'very interested in the activities of my family, their comings and goings and our manor at Rushton.'

Philippa's lovely eyes opened wide in sudden understanding and she passed instantly to talk of something else. Anne was sure that she had said sufficient to warn her friend to be equally cautious in her dealings with Master Hilyard.

Despite her sudden desire to avoid his company she was forced to be civil with him when he paid his usual courteous attentions to her on the second night after their arrival back at Westminster.

John Hilyard presented himself to her in the hall at the close of the meal and begged her permission to talk with her apart on one of the oriel window seats. Not wishing to offend him, she withdrew from Philippa's side and accompanied him, but kept a wary eye to ensure that Mary Scroggins had risen from her seat at the foot of the table and had moved closer to her mistress to be within call.

Anne had looked round earlier but Richard did not appear to be in his place with the other servants so, apparently, was absent from supper in the great hall.

John Hilyard gallantly saw to it that she was seated comfortably in the cushioned embrasure and requested permission to sit beside her. She granted it graciously, though she wished she had not the need to be so close in contact with the man.

He said enthusiastically, 'The King has spoken much of the unfortunate affair in Richmond park and mentioned several times how grateful he is to your servant, Master Allsop. He has commanded me to enquire after his health. I believe he was injured by the boar quite severely. Have you visited him to see if the wound is healing well? The King wishes to know if his own physician is needed to tend your man?'

'I have sent to enquire after him, of course,' Anne said diffidently. She was sure it was essential that she reveal no particular anxiety for her servant, yet it was necessary for her to show the normal concern a mistress would feel for an injured member of her household.

'He is very well recovered. I am sure there is no need for further tending, for he rode back to Westminster without assistance. He is not doing anything too energetic as yet and he will soon be back to normal. Thank His Majesty for his very gracious concern.'

'The man was very brave—and very quick thinking. The reaction could almost be described as that of a military man, would you not say, Mistress Anne?'

Anne caught back a sudden ejaculation of surprise and turned guileless blue eyes upon her companion.

'A soldier? Master Allsop? Oh, no, to the best of my knowledge he has never seen service on any campaign. He is certainly not old enough to have fought at Redmoor, at least I do not think he is, and I would not have thought he could have been present at East Stoke either.'

Too late she realised that her own knowledge of that encounter with rebels against the King could only have been related to her by her own father and she wished fervently that she had not mentioned the latter battle. It also occurred to her that Hilyard was hinting at a possibility that Richard could have been involved in the Warbeck rising in the West country and she was by no means certain that he had not.

'No, no, I was just wondering if he had seen military service abroad? He carries himself well and handles himself well, too. It merely occurred to me…' He smiled at her blandly. 'But it appears that I must be mistaken. The King, naturally, made it clear that he would like to be apprised of anything known about Master Allsop so that he might reward him further.'

'Dickon would not wish for any further reward, I am sure.' Nor any further interest in his doings on his sovereign's part, she added inwardly, then said aloud, 'He considers he was merely doing his duty as any loyal subject would do or indeed any man would who saw a child in danger. I am glad to see that Prince Henry appears to have taken no serious harm from the encounter with that ferocious animal, nor does he seem too shaken.'

John Hilyard shrugged lightly. 'The young see little danger and are resilient. The prince is a veritable young lion but his mentors must see to it that he takes greater care for his person over the next years.'

He passed to talking of other matters, commenting on the dress and behaviour of some of their mutual acquaintances at court, several of his courtier friends and Anne's younger companions among the Queen's ladies.

Anne was relieved to leave the subject of Richard and

his background and chatted pleasantly enough over the next half-hour. They both expressed relief that the Queen's youngest child, the Princess Mary Rose, was much improved and her mother considerably less anxious about her. All the time her mind was abstracted. She could not rid herself of the notion that John Hilyard's probing questions about Richard heralded danger for him.

Though she had kept from Richard's side for some days, receiving bulletins on his progress from either Wat or Simpkin, she determined to speak with him personally as soon as that might be managed in private. Richard must be warned that, unfortunately, his heroic behaviour in saving the King's son had aroused that monarch's interest to a dangerous degree.

She was grateful next morning when her somewhat drawn features, which she attributed to a severe headache, drew the notice of the Queen, who sympathetically declared that she must go to her chamber and lie down for the rest of the morning. Anne was relieved of duty for the rest of the day.

She hastily dressed warmly and, with Mary in attendance to watch for her, she sped through the palace corridors and out through the door opening out on to the courtyard which led to the stables. By this time the guards were well used to her comings and goings and made no objections to her leaving and entering the palace.

She saw Richard emerging from the stables in close talk with Wat Glazier and hastened over to the pair, after first ensuring that there was no one around at this moment to observe her.

Without ceremony Anne interrupted Richard's instructions to Wat.

'I must see your urgently. Is there anyone in the stable?'

'Not at the moment, but...'

She did not wait for his objection but turned at once to Wat.

'Please stay outside with Mary and warn us if anyone is heading this way.'

Imperiously she hastened Richard inside and pulled the door closed behind them.

The familiar, warm horse smell assailed her nostrils and, for one moment, it seemed that she was at home at Rushton preparing to ride out with Ned. Richard's frowning face loomed up before her in the shadowed dimness and she pulled him hurriedly towards the far wall, murmuring soft words of reassurance as the horses in their boxes whickered and moved restlessly, nervous at being disturbed by someone they did not know well. Anne's palfrey whickered with delight and she was forced to go to her favourite and stroke her nose affectionately.

'There, Cleo, it is all right, it's only me, Anne. We will ride out for exercise later. Quiet, girl, quiet, you'll attract the notice of one of the grooms.'

'Just why are you here?' Richard demanded sternly. 'We have decided it is unwise for us to meet so often. If you needed me you had only to summon me to your chamber. You know I would have come immediately.'

'What I have to say should not be spoken within the palace walls,' she said urgently. 'There is always a possibility that someone will overhear and innocently repeat what they heard to some other person who could be dangerous.'

'So,' he said drily. 'I see you have quickly come to understand and beware of atmospheres within palaces.'

She nodded impatiently and her hood slipped back so that he had a tantalising glimpse of her strained young face shadowed by the gable-shaped headdress. Tendrils of her glossy dark hair had escaped from the confining velvet hood and he longed to finger them, then bend to kiss the white column of her slender throat as she leaned towards him.

'I think all that. Why do you think I have sought you out here?'

He shrugged uncomprehendingly and she said huskily, 'You should leave Westminster at once, Richard. John Hilyard is beginning to ask awkward questions about you and I am growing more and more convinced that the man is dangerous. Sweet Virgin,' she murmured agitatedly, 'why was I so foolish as to keep you here with this stupid ruse? I could well have endangered your life.'

He reached out and took her hand. 'Hilyard?' he said, his brows drawing together in a sudden scowl. 'What has he to do with me? In his eyes I am hardly worthy enough for special notice. I think you need to explain yourself.'

'I did not tell you before as I did not wish to alarm you, nor,' she added hurriedly, 'to make you jealous of the man, but—but several times lately, when he has been outwardly paying court to me, he has been asking probing questions about my father.'

'Ah.'

'I think he has had his orders to do so from—from the King or from one of the King's spymasters.'

'Highly likely, but I doubt if he has discovered anything treasonable concerning your father. He has been most circumspect since the failure of Lovell's rising at East Stoke, in '87, far too long ago to raise suspicions in the mind of one of Hilyard's kidney.'

'The King has a long memory,' Anne said sorrowfully, 'and though he appears to pardon men, he never releases them from surveillance, I have discovered. Perhaps you are right,' she added thoughtfully. 'He has his own reason for allowing the Queen to summon Philippa from exile just now.'

He glanced at the door and, seeing it still firmly closed, drew her down beside him upon an upstanding bundle of sweet smelling hay.

Quickly she told him of her talk with John Hilyard the previous evening.

'So, you see, your impulsive act in saving young Henry has aroused the King's interest. He wants to know more about the fictitious Master Allsop and when he realises there is little to tell and that Master Allsop does not in reality exist, he is going to become extremely curious about your real reason for coming to London—and in disguise. Dear God,' she said piteously. 'I could not believe my innocent prank could put you in this peril.'

'You cannot blame yourself,' he reminded her mildly. 'It was I who brought myself to His Majesty's notice.' He gave a grim chuckle. 'Perhaps it is more than significant, or will be believed so by the King, that I saved the Tudor cub from a boar, of all creatures. He has never convinced himself that the whole new dynasty is not in danger from the former followers of the Plantagenet White Boar.'

'You could be questioned,' she said throatily, 'and it will come out that you are Sir Dominick Allard's son, here on a secret mission for the Duchess Margaret of Burgundy perhaps, or why else should you lie about your name?'

'I think you make too much of this aimless curiosity of John Hilyard,' he said, cupping her determined little chin in his hands. 'I am of no importance to the man. Why should he pry further?'

'There was that incident at The Golden Cockerel. He was angry about that. Suppose he began to make enquiries there and...'

She saw his start of concern then and the black frown again creased his brows.

'They are involved then, in this mysterious business of yours?' she questioned almost angrily.

'They are not actively engaged in treason, but I would not wish them to be drawn into any involvement with me—or the purpose of my visit to London.'

She sprang up then and faced him, more and more terrifyingly aware of his peril.

'Richard, leave Westminster at once, this afternoon.' She turned her head away from him for a moment, unwilling for him to see the frightened tears pouring down her cheeks. 'If—if you will do what I ask, you can carry a message to my father that—that—I will agree to our betrothal.'

He jumped up immediately and turned to her, enfolding her in his arms. 'Then you do truly love me?'

'I have told you I do, but—' she gulped '—you must agree to give up this insane business, go back to Wensleydale and—and when the Queen releases me from service I will marry you and go home with you.'

His lips took possession of hers triumphantly and she gloried in the wild passion she felt surging up in him. Against her hair he muttered, 'I wish I could take you with me soon…'

'I do not like to leave Philippa without a friend in this court,' she said anxiously. 'Oh, Richard, I wanted so much to come, to be in attendance, in the thick of it all. Now all I want is to be safe at home or with you, only you. Do not risk yourself again, for my sake, Richard. Promise me, promise me.'

They were so intent on each other that, once again, as they had been in the wood when Philippa had come upon them unawares, they were unaware of anything around them, not the challenging angry voice of someone outside nor the muttered embarrassed answer of Wat Simpkin. They only realised their privacy had been invaded when the stable door crashed open. Then and only then did they guiltily spring apart and turn to face the intruder.

Sir Owen Lewis stormed into the stable, cloaked and booted and spurred for a journey.

'What the Devil is going on in here? Fellow, if you wish to fondle your serving wench do it somewhere else, not where you are in the way of your betters.'

His angry tone died away and he stared, frowning in utter shock and bewilderment, at the pair who faced him, only too clearly just freed from each other's arms.

'Mistress Jarvis, you shame yourself. I cannot believe your father…' His voice trailed off again as he peered more closely at her male companion.

'By all the Saints, Dominick Allard! No, that cannot be. By the Virgin, man, you so closely resemble your father I thought for a moment you must be he.' He stepped nearer, bending his head to look more intently into Richard's angry grey eyes. 'Tell me I'm right, you are Allard's cub?'

Richard placed a protective arm round Anne's shoulders. 'Yes, sir, I am Richard Allard, and Mistress Jarvis and I are soon to be formally betrothed with the consent and the good will of her father. She has done nothing of which she need be ashamed, I assure you.'

Sir Owen Lewis faced them still frowning, both hands now upon his hips.

Anne introduced him to Richard hurriedly. 'This is Sir Owen Lewis, Richard. You must know he was my father's squire.'

'Who, I heard, left him, disloyally, before Redmoor, and returned to his father in Wales.' Richard's tone was contemptuous.

Sir Owen Lewis's colour darkened visibly and he gave a hiss of anger.

'I was recalled by my father, sir,' he snapped, 'who also had loyalties. I do not consider my conduct in the least dishonourable. I explained to Sir Guy, who agreed to release me from service. I have never lost my respect for your father, Mistress Anne, and was ever grateful for the training and care I received at his hands.'

Richard gave a heavy sigh. 'Forgive me, Sir Owen. I had no right to impugn your honour. We all hold our particular loyalties dear.'

'Indeed, young man, and that is why I ask myself what you are doing, plainly incognito, at the Court of King Henry? Why should I not summon the King's guard and have you taken into custody and questioned?'

'No, please, Sir Owen.' Anne went impulsively up to him and took his hand. Her voice was very low and pleading. 'Richard meant no treason. The reason he is here in the guise of my servant is due to my foolishness. It was,' she murmured pitifully, 'meant merely as a joke. I would not for the world have placed him in danger.'

'I see.' In the dimness of the stable Sir Owen's expression was hard to read. At last he sighed and said, 'I can see for myself that he is very dear to you, Mistress Anne. I would not wittingly cause you harm nor bring harm, by association, to your father, but you must understand that my primary duty is to His Majesty, in whose service I am. I must demand of Master Allard exactly what his intentions are here in the capital. He knows full well former Yorkist supporters are not welcome at King Henry's Court. Come, sir, you came here with a purpose to aid the Yorkist cause. Do you deny it?'

'No, sir, but I do not consider that purpose treasonable.'

'Suppose you tell me what it is, so that I might decide that for myself.'

Richard was silent for a moment and Anne watched him anxiously. At last he said quietly, 'I am charged by Her Grace the Duchess Margaret of Burgundy, his aunt, to see and speak to the Earl of Warwick and to report to her on his health and welfare.'

Sir Owen said expressionlessly, 'And how do you intend to accomplish that, Master Allard, since the Earl is the King's prisoner in the Tower?'

Richard shook his head. 'I cannot in honour speak of that, sir. Others would be hurt by my admissions. I only ask you to believe me when I say no harm is meant to the King's cause by me or any others who aid me.'

Anne could hear Sir Owen breathing somewhat heavily. 'Can I take your oath on that? You intend no harm to his Grace the King nor any member of the royal family and, further, that you do not intend by any action of yours to foment rebellion?'

'Yes, sir, I swear that by everything I hold holy and by the love and devotion I bear Mistress Anne Jarvis.'

Sir Owen released his pent breath. 'I can understand your concern for the Earl. His fate has been hard these fourteen years. During my time of service to Sir Guy Jarvis I did meet the young man, though he was then still a child. Like you I wished him well then and I do now—but I do understand that for the King to release him would prove dangerous to his own hopes of a peaceful realm. He would be at the mercy of any fool with ambition to use the Earl, who is known to be somewhat innocent in matters politic, for his own purposes.'

'The Duchess Margaret realises that only too well, sir. She is anxious at this time, while he is penned so close to the other pretender, Perkin Warbeck, to ensure that the Earl is not tempted to make any move to plot rebellion or attempt to escape which would undoubtedly doom him.'

Sir Owen listened carefully and, in the end, inclined his head gravely. Anne stared at first one man then the other and stirred restlessly, clearly disturbed by what she had heard. She could not understand the necessity of speaking with a prisoner in the Tower without an avowed intent to try to aid his escape.

On the contrary, Richard was saying categorically that he intended to advise the Earl to refuse any offers to help him do just that. To her it made no sense and she could not contemplate why Richard would put himself in danger for so slight a reason.

Sir Owen cleared his throat. 'Will you solemnly swear that this is your sole purpose in seeking to enter the Tower?'

'I do, Sir Owen.'

'Then I will help you to do that, simply to enter the Tower, so that you are not challenged to prove your identity. How you obtain access to the Earl after that is your own affair and I will not question you further about your associates. Tomorrow I intended to send one of my servants to the Tower armoury with a message to check certain equipment held there. The King has ordered me to do just that. I will entrust you with the message. That will give you entry into the Tower itself. You will return to me with the answer I request from the master of ordnance.' He paused deliberately. 'You understand what you do afterwards is entirely at your own risk?'

Anne said hotly, 'This could pose a personal risk to you, too, Sir Owen. You should not aid Richard in this. Indeed, he should not go himself.'

Sir Owen Lewis gave a tired smile. 'I do not see any significant risk. Naturally, should there be repercussions to this visit, I shall deny any involvement, simply say I entrusted a safe conduct to a servant I trusted, without knowing the man had any other intention than to fulfill my errand.'

He shrugged. 'What risk there is I am prepared to take—for the sake of old loyalties, but,' he added, leaning towards Richard earnestly, 'should there be difficulties and you, my young friend, be taken and questioned, you understand that I shall take no steps to extricate you from your perilous situation?'

A smile curled Richard's lips and he gave a little formal bow. 'I understand perfectly, Sir Owen, nor would I ask or expect more of you than you grant me. Indeed, I am more than grateful for the opportunity you provide.'

Sir Owen gave a little satisfied grunt. 'Very well. Present yourself to me in my apartment at eleven of the clock tomorrow morning.' He gave a little wintry smile. 'I take it as read that your mistress will give you leave to visit the city.'

Anne was tempted to storm that she certainly would not. She could not believe her ears, that Sir Owen Lewis, who had placed himself in the King's service against his natural leanings towards his former master's cause, should do this for an avowed Yorkist. This was sheer criminal folly.

She watched helplessly as Richard and Sir Owen grasped hands as on a bargain then the older man turned and nodded to them both, bowed to Anne, who curtsied in answer, then withdrew to the rear of the stable and gave his attention to his horse as his intention had been to ride out.

Richard drew Anne to the entrance and bent to speak softly in her ear. 'I shall be gone merely a few hours. There is no risk...'

'There is *every* risk,' she replied furiously. 'Only just now I was begging you to leave Westminster. Did you not heed what I said? Already both the King himself and John Hilyard are becoming interested in you. To go to the Tower now is rank folly. If you love me you will leave this task undone and return to Yorkshire as I asked.'

He took both her wrists in his strong grasp and, in the clearer light from the stable door which was slightly ajar, she saw that his expression was showing real anger. His grasp tightened and she gave a little gasp of discomfort bordering on pain.

'If you love me,' he said bitterly, bending his face almost to touch hers, 'you would make no conditions. Have I not said this is a matter of honour for me? Sir Owen understands that.'

She shrank back from him, tears pouring unchecked down her cheeks. 'I understand only too well that honour is more important to men than love. My mother understands it too, so does yours. If you go, you go without my leave or my blessing.'

With that she tore her hands free and, forcing open the stable door with some difficulty for it had stuck, she ran from him. She was still crying when she emerged into the courtyard and Mary viewed her with some disquiet. Before she could frame a question Anne snapped at her. 'I must return to my chamber—now.'

She was so wrought up in her own distress that she did not notice John Hilyard cross the court and open his lips to greet her, but she passed him as if he were not present. He pursed his lips thoughtfully, looking towards the stable from which she had emerged. At that moment Sir Owen Lewis led out his own horse and a groom hastened to attend him.

Hilyard nodded a greeting then, as Sir Owen mounted and began to walk his horse towards the courtyard arch, he saw Dickon Allsop come to the stable door and signal to his man. Wat Glazier hurried up to the door and they moved off together towards the servants' quarters.

Hilyard's brows drew together in a curious frown. Mistress Anne had appeared disturbed, so much so that she had not noticed his presence. What had occurred to distress her? Was her favourite palfrey unwell? If so, surely there would have been more urgency by her steward to investigate the cause of the ailment? Women took these matters hard, he knew, grew unaccustomedly attached to their pets and their horses.

He had seen her in talk with Sir Owen Lewis before and ascertained that the man had formerly served her father. Hilyard chewed his nether lip. It appeared that the three had been in the stable together. There was something about that man, Allsop, which irritated him. The man was too familiar with his mistress yet—surely—that was often so in the behaviour of servants of long standing.

He stood looking after the man and determined to have a watch kept on the fellow. The King was impatient to know more about the saviour of his son. It would pay him, Hilyard, to see that he discovered more of the man's history and why he continued to stay in Westminster after his task of escorting his mistress safely to court had been concluded.

Chapter Eight

Anne woke after a hopelessly sleepless night with a splitting headache. She had tried to lie still and quiet, unwilling to ruin Philippa's opportunity for rest, but the younger girl saw at once that Anne was deeply unhappy and, after Mary had gone out of the chamber as usual to fetch water and towels for their morning toilet, she questioned her friend, her brow crinkling in sympathy.

'What is it, Anne, *chérie*? Are you unwell again, or is something very wrong? Has something happened between you and Dickon?'

Anne was about to reveal the source of her unhappiness but thought better of involving Philippa in the treasonable business she had heard discussed in the stable. It was not that she did not trust her friend—she would have done so with her life—but it were infinitely better for Philippa if she knew nothing of what Richard planned. Her own background was suspect, as Richard had said on more than one occasion, and Anne was beginning to believe that both she and Philippa were being watched very carefully by the King's agents within the palace. Also, there was the safety of Sir Owen Lewis to be considered now.

She said hurriedly, 'I am not recovered. My head is splitting—' which was perfectly true '—and you are right, Richard and I have had a disagreement.'

As she saw Philippa's brows rise enquiringly, she said, 'I want him to leave Westminster, Pippa. Master Hilyard was questioning me about him the other evening and I think it safer for Richard if he returns to Yorkshire. Either Wat or Sim, or both of them, could be left with me. We shall be safe enough under the Queen's protection.'

'And he refuses to go?'

Anne nodded. 'He is unwilling to leave me here.'

'Do you not wish to leave with him?' Philippa's tone was wistful. 'I am sure if you asked permission to leave the Court the Queen would grant it, especially if she knew you wished to marry.'

'I could not do that. I came here so recently at Her Grace's request and—' impulsively Anne hugged her friend '—I would not leave you here at Westminster, at least not until you have forged other friendships.'

Philippa's lovely eyes sparkled with tears of gratitude. 'Indeed, I know I should feel rather lost without you, *chérie*, but I would not wish to spoil your hope of happiness.'

Anne shook her head decisively. 'I was asked to come on the understanding that I would befriend you and I will not forsake that intention now. At any rate it would make no odds. Richard is determined to stay in London—for his own reasons,' she added, looking away from her friend's shrewd glance.

'Since you are still unwell, shall I ask the Queen to excuse you from attendance this morning again?'

Anne nodded eagerly. 'I would be grateful.'

She had mulled over her last quarrel with Richard so many times during that hateful night and had, at last, come to a determination. If he could not be persuaded from this dangerous course of action she would go with him into the city. She would not stay behind here at Westminster worrying all day. That could not be borne. She bit her lips uncertainly as Mary came back with their toilet requisites and cast her mistress a doubtful glance. Mary must not come with them, Anne decided. She, too, must be protected from any consequences of this proposed folly. Anne would be adequately chaperoned with her intended betrothed. The problem was, how to convince Richard of her desperate need to accompany him.

Accordingly she sent Mary off to prepare a tisane for her headache after Philippa had gone to report to Lady Hartley in the Queen's apartments and, donning cloak and sensible shoes, ran off to the stables to enquire after Master Allsop. To her relief she found him actually preparing to mount up in the stable.

'You are leaving early,' she said nervously as he dismounted at sight of her and stood warily, keeping his distance. 'I thought perhaps you were still with Sir Owen.'

'I presented myself early and, fortunately, found him alone. I have his letter for the master of ordnance and the safe conduct.' She saw his brows draw together in a frown and knew he was still angered by their last encounter. 'If you have come to attempt to dissuade me—'

She cut in instantly. 'I have not. I know that would be useless. I have come to accompany you.'

His frown grew still blacker. 'This is pure nonsense and you know it.'

She drew close to him, her eyes appealing. 'Richard, please listen to me. I know your sense of honour compels you to this and I cannot but applaud your motives.' Tears spiked her luxuriant dark lashes. 'I have been thinking of this all night and I understand, or I think I do, what it means to you to try to save the Earl of Warwick, but to me you are all important now. You cannot ask me to wait here in hopeless dread while you risk yourself.

'Oh, I know I cannot go with you to the Tower but you can leave me with Master Garnet at The Golden Cockerel. At least I shall be near you and will know immediately whether your mission has been successful. Also, I can lend verisimilitude to your journey into the city. It is natural that you should escort your mistress on her command. There will be fewer questions asked amongst the menials here concerning your absence from the palace.'

He remained frowning, one hand impatiently slapping his riding glove against his thigh, then he shrugged in reluctant submission to her wishes.

'Very well. What you say is true. It is wiser that there be no talk about my reasons for leaving Westminster.' He called to a tow-haired groom standing idly just outside the doorway chewing a wisp of hay. 'Boy, unsaddle my horse again. I have changed my mind. My mistress is anxious to go to Chepe side. We will travel by river. It will be more convenient and comfortable for her.'

He hustled Anne somewhat ungraciously to the King's steps and summoned a ferryman. After he had assisted her into the boat she sat silent while the oarsman pushed off and Richard sat apart from her in the stern obviously wrapt in his own thoughts. From time to time she stole a glance at him but looked away again swiftly, unwilling for him to catch her gazing at him so anxiously. He had made no comment about Mary Scroggins's absence from her side and she considered he had come to the same conclusion as she had, that the fewer people involved in this the better.

When they alighted at London Bridge she gazed back with a premonitory shiver to where the grey bulk of the Tower dominated the sky line. She prayed fervently that the head of the man she loved would not be added to the tally of heads on its ramparts.

As they approached St Paul's churchyard and came somewhat surprisingly into a small oasis of separation from the thronging crowds in the narrow streets—for the church, she knew, was frequently as busy—she halted and faced him, chin tilting decisively.

'Richard, while we are not momentarily surrounded by people, tell me honestly why you are anxious about the Earl's safety. He has been the King's prisoner so long, surely he can be in no danger where he is.'

He sighed heavily. 'Have you not heard the rumours rife in Westminster that the King is planning a strategic alliance with the Spanish King and Queen for a marriage between their daughter and his son, Arthur?'

She nodded. 'Yes, the Queen is naturally excited by the prospect of welcoming a daughter-in-law to the Court.'

'And you think Ferdinand and Isabella will be ready to allow their daughter, the Infanta Caterina, to come to England where the King still sits somewhat precariously upon the throne?'

'But King Henry does not,' she faltered. 'The early rebellions have failed and the last threat to him, made by that man, Perkin Warbeck, concluded with his defeat in the West country and he is safely ensconced in the Tower also.' Her expression clouded. 'The man confessed he was not a Plantagenet. And how can this effect the Earl of Warwick who was not involved in that rising?'

'He *did* confess, though that really proves nothing. Were I prisoner to Henry, I might be persuaded to confess to anything the King wished.'

'Then you truly believe Warbeck *is* the Queen's brother?' Her lips parted incredulously.

'What I believe matters nothing. The truth of the matter

is that young Warwick *is* a true Plantagenet and the King cannot deny it.'

'You think...' she hesitated '...that the King wishes to execute the Earl?' Her blue eyes were now revealing a sense of horror. 'But they say he is very slow witted and... Oh, Richard, that would be so very cruel.'

'Exactly, that is how it would be generally regarded by the common people. In order to accomplish it the King would have to have a genuine excuse.'

'What you were saying to Sir Owen, that you think he might be urged to escape—would that be considered grounds for charging the Earl with treason?'

'Yes. Warbeck has been moved near to his quarters in the Martin tower. The Earl is my age but not, as you say, worldly wise. He will, perhaps, not see for himself the obvious dangers, wishing, as any man would, for his freedom and companionship. He must be warned and from the lips of his aunt, the dowager Duchess of Burgundy. I am her trusted messenger.'

'Would you—' she breathed the question awkwardly '—if the time was better, would you—encourage an escape and a rising in the Earl's favour?'

'I think not,' he said steadily. 'Though my heart would urge me to such a cause, my head would warn me of the unsuitability of the Earl to reign. You have so often preached to me the advisibility of securing peace in the realm for the good of us all that I am reluctantly prepared to agree with you, but—such an endeavour would not be for me to decide. For the present it is deemed most necessary to safeguard the life of the Earl.'

'But will he listen?'

'I pray God he will,' Richard said through gritted teeth. He looked round as his ears caught the sound of approaching footsteps. 'Come, we must go quickly to The Golden

Cockerel now. I have an appointment at the Tower, but I must first discharge my errand for Sir Owen before keeping it.'

When they arrived at the inn they were made instantly welcome by Bess, who conveyed them immediately through to the private solar at the rear, where the landlord, Jake Garnet, was seated near a roaring fire. He stood up, bowed and held out both hands in greeting to Anne.

'Mistress, how good it is to see you again at The Golden Cockerel. You must be cut to the bone in this fierce wind especially if you happened to travel down river. Bess, will you see to it that food and the best wine is brought for our guests?'

Bess smiled and bustled out. Jake conveyed Anne to the chair by the fire and turned enquiringly to Richard.

'Jake, I ask you to care for Mistress Jarvis once again whilst I am gone on an errand.'

'Of course.' Jake made no enquiry as to where. He said simply, 'You will find Josh waiting at the agreed time and place.'

'Good. I have safe conduct into the Tower itself.'

'Oh?' The bushy eyebrows were raised in surprise.

'I have been entrusted with a message to the master of ordnance.'

'Ah.'

'I shall not tarry overlong. Jake, I wish you to keep Mistress Jarvis here in the solar. I do not wish a repeat of the embarrassing meeting we had last time. I do not want anyone at Westminster to know she has been here.'

'I understand, Master Richard. You can be assured everything will be done as you ask.'

'You are going now, before you take refreshment?' Anne rose agitatedly to her feet, her eyes appealing. Jake moved towards the door, aware suddenly of the need of his guests to be alone for a short time.

'I'll—er—see to it that my wenches are bustling in the kitchen.' He was gone and Richard came hastily to Anne and enfolded her in his arms.

He said huskily, 'You must not be alarmed. Jake will keep you safe.'

'You know it is not *my* safety which concerns me,' she murmured, her cheek pressed against the leather of his jerkin. 'Oh, my love, be very, very careful. Though your message to the Earl is innocent enough, it is in direct contravention of the King's intent, if what you suspect is true. If you are found with the Earl you could be arrested. Suppose he talks of your visit—afterwards?'

'I shall be well away by then for, my heart, once this is done and I have delivered you safe back to Westminster, I shall ride for Yorkshire. He will not know my true name for I shall introduce myself as Dickon Allsop. I cannot think of anyone else at Westminster, save you and Sir Owen Lewis, who will know of my visit to the Tower and I can trust Josh Aldred with my life.'

He bent and kissed her full upon the mouth. 'Keep this for me as pledge of my love, my brave heart.'

She gave a tremulous smile in answer for she was feeling anything but brave—indeed, a wild panic was rising within her—but she answered his kiss with fervour and drew away that he might not feel himself held back by a show of her true fears for him.

When he moved to the door he saw only that she was smiling as she turned towards the chair. He did not realise, she hoped, that she had turned quickly so that he would not see the welling tears or the trembling of her frightened body.

* * *

Richard met Josh Aldred in the tavern outside the main gate of the Tower as he had done several times before. While they sat together over leather jacks of ale Richard told Josh of the safe conduct he had obtained.

'There will be no need to smuggle me in, Josh, as we thought you would have to do. This makes it easier but there are still risks to you. Time is of the essence now and I must see the Earl today. Immediately after you have managed to let me into his apartment you are to leave the Tower and return to The Golden Cockerel. You cannot be found on the premises if anything should go wrong and I am arrested. Make some excuse for going off duty. Say you are taken ill. There may be suspicions afterwards but nothing can be proved against you.'

Josh Aldred shrugged. 'As it happens it will be near time for me to go off duty so there'll be no need to dissemble, but I would rather stay on and see that all goes well with you.'

'I repeat, I would rather you were far from the scene, just in case. Josh,' he said impatiently, 'your safety is important both to Bess and Jake, but even more so for your continued usefulness to the rest of us loyal to the Yorkist cause.'

Josh grunted reluctant agreement.

'I have left Mistress Jarvis at The Golden Cockerel.' As his companion's eyes widened in alarm he said hastily, 'She insisted on accompanying me and there could have been problems had I demurred. I know she will be safe enough with your father but, Josh, she is my heart's love, my whole world. If anything should go wrong and I not return to The Golden Cockerel in good time you must get her back to Westminster safely. Swear to me that whatever happens you will do that.'

'Of course I will. You can trust me.'

'I know that.' Richard gave a wintry, forced grin. 'It is just that I know Mistress Anne. She will not go willingly if she is in the least alarmed about my fate. You must see to it, despite all opposition, that she does so.'

Josh Aldred nodded. His expression was dour. He knew, only too well, that his wife, Bess, could give trouble on occasions such as these.

'Did you manage to get what I asked?'

'Yes, safely hidden in one of the store cellars within the Constable's lodging.'

'Good, then I will meet you behind the house after I have finished my business with the master of ordnance.'

Again Josh inclined his head then finished his ale and, pushing back his stool with a grating sound across the floor, he stood up.

'One last thing, Master Richard. What if your name is mentioned after this visit? As I've told you, the Earl is not entirely discreet. Even if you manage to impress upon him the need for silence as to the identity of his visitor, he is liable to speak of you afterwards. He gets so few that a new face is a novelty and he is like to boast about it later.'

'Yes, we've thought about that. Since I am known as Master Allsop at Westminster I shall use that name when speaking with the Earl. Later it will be impossible to link that name with the Allards who live so far from London. Mistress Anne, naturally, will keep silent. I intend to leave Westminster shortly and she will simply say I have discharged my duties satisfactorily and she has dismissed me for other service. I cannot think she could be implicated in any way.'

'She is to remain at Court?'

'Aye.' Richard gazed moodily ahead of him. 'I wish it could be otherwise but she cannot leave until she is released from her period of duty and there is the young daughter of the Earl of Wroxeter to be considered. They are close friends and Anne is determined to remain by her side while there is need. I hope, soon, they will be able to leave Court and Anne and I can marry.' He thrust out his nether lip moodily. 'I do not believe that it was entirely wise or safe for either of them to be summoned to Court, but Guy Jarvis could hardly defy the Queen's direct request.'

Josh nodded, then turned and left the tavern while Richard sat on for a while tracing patterns in the spilt ale upon the table before him.

He waited until he knew Josh had had ample time to reach the Tower before him for, on no account, did he wish them to be seen together within the confines of those grim walls if it could be avoided, then he paid his own reckoning and left the tavern.

He was greeted by the master of ordance within the Tower armoury without any sign of surprise. The guards on duty at the gate had passed him through after simply glancing at the seal upon his safe conduct so he had had no problem getting into the courts of the massive walled area that housed both a royal palace and several prisons confining commoners and noble prisoners.

His errand completed, for the master promised faithfully to send a reply quickly to Sir Owen Lewis at Westminster, Richard withdrew from the armoury and made his way to the rear of the Constable's lodging where he knew there was a small garden and orchard. Richard had been several times to the Tower during his short period of service as page to the late King. Though there had been some changes, they were slight enough to give him no difficulty in finding his way to the trysting place agreed with Josh Aldred.

It was now dinner time and, as they had hoped, the small

garden enclosure was deserted. After a moment's wait he was relieved to see Josh coming towards him.

'It's a good job it's so cold this morning,' Josh observed as he fell into step beside Richard. 'All the guards off duty are more inclined to find some welcome brazier inside the guard house than linger outside. Occasionally this garden can be a meeting place for flirtations with serving wenches at such times, but not today, praise the Virgin. The lasses are as anxious to remain within doors in the warmth as their swains.'

He led the way into the lodging through a back way and down steep stairs to the cellars. The two pushed their way along cobwebbed walls and barrelled ceilings, brushing by casks of wine and salted fish and meat into a low ceilinged recess at the far end.

Here Josh produced a bundle of clothing and, in the dim chilly silent place Richard pulled off his cloak, leather jack, holland shirt and donned more serviceable garments of rough homespun such as Josh himself was wearing. Josh hurriedly bundled up Richard's own possessions.

'Do you intend to leave as one of the jailors dressed as you are now or use your safe conduct to get out?'

'I think it best if I do not return here or meet you again. I'll leave as I am. Have you keys to the Earl's apartment in the Martin Tower?'

'My own.' Josh handed over his leather belt with keys attached. 'I'll convey your own clothes back to The Golden Cockerel and you can change there. I'll provide you with a tray laden with the Earl's dinner. I managed to get assigned to that duty myself.' He drew his brows together. 'It would have been safer had I spoken a warning to his lordship, Master Richard. It is still not too late for me to do this if you give me the message entrusted to you.'

'He is unlikely to listen and heed you,' Richard said

crisply. 'He sees you too often. He is unlikely to accept you come from his aunt, Her Grace of Burgundy.' He sighed heavily. 'Truth to tell, I have not too great a hope he will heed me either. I can but make the attempt.'

He halted suddenly as they made to leave the cellars. 'Wait, I must rid myself of these first. They are hardly appropriate for my jailor's disguise.' He removed his own heavy gold family signet and handed it to Josh and then with a sardonic smile added the King's gift, his reward for the rescue of the young prince that he'd so reluctantly accepted on that memorable occasion.

Josh gazed at it curiously, noting its worth and then, without comment, placed both rings within the purse suspended from his belt.

Armed with a filled food tray supplied from the kitchens by Josh, Richard was finally shown the jailors' entrance into the Martin Tower. Josh checked, looking beneath the linen napkin which covered the tray that Richard had all that he needed for the Earl's dinner. He gave him a hasty glance to assure himself that his companion would pass muster, then stood back and nodded towards the door.

'Do not forget what I said earlier,' Richard murmured softly as he saw what appeared to be two jailors coming towards them across the courtyard. 'Go off duty now. You should not be present here this afternoon, just in case.'

Again Josh nodded, but his expression was still troubled. 'You recall what I said about the Earl's apartment? You can find your way? You do not want to appear strange to your duties.'

'I shall manage. Now go, my friend, and reassure Mistress Jarvis that all has gone very well so far.'

The two men passed them, giving Josh nods of greeting to which he responded with a friendly wave. He turned only once more to grin at Richard who was fumbling unfamiliarly with the laden tray and the key to the main door of the tower.

As he stepped forward to offer help, Richard hissed, 'I tell you I can manage. I must. Now go away.'

The key turned at last as Richard balanced the tray upon his hip. He smiled to himself a little bleakly as he recalled that, over the years, he had lost his paging skills. In those days he had been adept at balancing bowls of rose water and, so laden, kneeling before noble guests that they might refresh their greasy hands, without spilling one drop, while serving at Court banquets. These skills would come back to him, he told himself sternly, and made his way into the building.

Immediately the grim walls appeared to close around him and he halted for a moment in the entrance to stem the trembling of his hands which held the tray and would have resulted in embarrassing breakages, a spoilt dinner and the need for awkward explanations. A guard sauntered up to the guardhouse door, scratching himself idly. He gave Richard a cursory look and Richard thought it necessary to explain his presence.

'I'm the new man, taken over from Josh Aldred. He's gone off duty. I was told to report to him and he's sent me with the Earl of Warwick's dinner.'

The guard showed no surprise and continued to scratch his thigh without looking fully at the newcomer.

'Along the corridor, first door to your right. Hurry along now before it gets cold.'

Richard did not wait to see him return to his guard post and made for the door indicated.

He knocked and a light, slightly high-pitched voice bade him enter. To this inner door there appeared to be no key in the lock so Richard had no problem entering with his load. He paused in the doorway to look round the apartment before coming forward hesitantly and placing the tray down upon a table in the centre of the chamber. He deliberately avoided looking directly at the prisoner as he wished it to appear at first that he was a newcomer, strange to his duties, and nervous in the presence of so exalted a political prisoner as the young Earl of Warwick, cousin to the Queen herself.

He saw at once that it in no way resembled a cell, though the one high-placed window in the thickness of the wall was barred from the outside. It was sparsely though pleasantly furnished with an oaken table, two stools and a carved armchair. There was a curtained section behind which Richard presumed was the Earl's sleeping quarters and probably an entrance to a private garde robe. A meagre fire burned in the grate, for the place seemed unaccountably chill, with a carpet in front of it in place of rushes; seated in the cushioned armchair before the fire was the man he had come to see at great risk to his own safety.

The Earl turned at once at his entry and smiled at him in genuine welcome. Richard knew him to be about twenty-seven years old, very close to his own age, but his movements, as he swung round eagerly in the chair, and the pale smoothness of complexion—due undoubtedly to his confinement, for so long excluded from the sunlight and hard exercise so normal for most young men of his age, which would have tanned and roughened his skin—and the totally guileless smile from wide-set pale blue eyes made him seem much younger.

He was dressed in doublet and hose of fine wool in murrey, slightly outdated, and a little rubbed, Richard noted, at cuffs and collar, and the gold braid which adorned the doublet was tarnished, though had been of fine quality. He had a mass of golden curls falling full on to his shoulders and Richard recalled instantly the child he had first seen on his visit to Sheriff Hutton and how his father had told him the boy resembled his father, the late George of Clarence.

Richard turned and made fast the door, then went immediately to the Earl's chair and fell upon one knee before it. 'My lord, I am here to serve you,' he said quietly.

The blue eyes opened very wide as the Earl looked down at him. It was clear that he was utterly bewildered by Richard's behaviour. The stare continued for so long that Richard did not think he would obtain permission to rise and wondered if the Earl had become so used to having his nobility ignored that he had forgotten how to deal with servants and courtiers, but, at last, Edward said slowly, 'Please rise. I am sorry. It is long since anyone addressed me like that.'

Richard leaned forward and took one slim white hand in his and kissed it, then he rose to his feet and returned to the table.

'I have your dinner, my lord. You should eat before it grows cold and while you do I will explain why I have come.'

Again the Earl cast him a strange, enquiring long glance then he nodded and waited while Richard lifted the small table and brought it to him, then poured out wine.

The Earl took a sip and regarded him over the rim of his wine cup. 'I do not think I know you. You are not one of my regular servitors.'

'I am not, my lord. I am—' Richard hesitated '…I am a friend of Master Aldred. My name is Dickon Allsop, but—but I am not a jailor.'

The Earl had been carving meat from the joint with a small knife he took from his hanging purse. Richard noted that it did not appear sharp and the Earl had some difficulty carving with it. His guardians were taking no chances, he thought quizzically, yet the young man seemed docile enough—indeed, he had had no training to make him otherwise. Warwick was looking at him again, enquiringly, but there appeared no sign of alarm nor undue curiosity in his mild gaze.

'You say you are not a jailor? Did—did my cousin the King send you to me?'

'No, no, my lord. I am here secretly. I beg you not to speak of my visit to—anyone, nor to mention what I say to you.'

The Earl swallowed and looked at Richard, then down at his plate. It seemed it took him some considerable time to consider any answer to what was said to him. Richard watched him carefully. Was the Earl as dull-witted as people had intimated? Her Grace the dowager Duchess of Burgundy had enjoined him to find out the truth of the matter. Richard pursed his lips as his thoughts raced, then the Earl said, consideringly, 'I would never divulge what someone asked me to keep secret, Master—Allsop?'

Richard smiled a trifle grimly. He was now convinced Edward of Warwick was no half-wit. He took time to think and answer because his ability to confer with others had always been limited. After the death of his parents he had been handed over from one guardian to the other, nobody taking pains to see he was educated and finding his presence in the household something of any embarrassment until King Richard had come to power and insisted that his nephew be removed to the Yorkist stronghold of Sheriff Hutton with other royal princes and princesses and be prepared for martial training.

Alas, that brief interlude had been too short, hardly more than a year before the boy, then about thirteen years old, had found himself a prisoner again, a focus for Yorkist intrigue and kept securely within the grim confines of the Tower to safeguard King Henry's interests. Richard suspected that he was rarely visited at all and never by any noble who wished him well. No wonder he was slow of thought and somewhat naïve.

Richard advanced closer to the table and said quietly, 'No matter how I obtained entry here, my lord. It is sufficient for you to know that I come from your aunt, the dowager Duchess of Burgundy who wishes you well, as she dearly loved her brother, your father, and never ceases to pray for your well-being.'

'My Aunt Margaret?' The Earl nodded and a smile curved his lips, one which Richard recognised as being a smile he remembered occasionally upon the lips of his paternal uncle, King Richard.

'Yes, my lord, your Aunt Margaret.'

The Earl's expression was wistful now. 'I would like to see her.'

'Yes.' Richard's grey eyes grew troubled. 'I am sure you would, my lord, but—' he drew a fast breath '—I beg you to be very cautious of speaking of that longing to anyone.' He paused as the pale blue eyes looked at him wonderingly. 'That very wish could be interpreted as a desire to escape.'

The Earl's lips parted eagerly. 'Escape?'

'Do not speak the word, my lord. Do not even think of it.'

Edward of Warwick's eyes grew even more wistful. 'Is it wrong, Master Allsop, to want to leave these quarters and see the world, to breathe the clean air of the Yorkshire moors again, smell the sea? We used to travel to Scarborough Castle sometimes,' he recalled with a sigh, 'and walk on the beach and throw flat pebbles into the sea, the pages and squires and…' He paused and looked anxiously at Richard as if he dared not speak the names of others he had known in those days and Richard remembered that the present Queen had been one of the number of the royal household kept there.

'My lord, I know how desperately you desire your freedom, but at present it could be dangerous for you to consider taking any steps to accomplish a proposed escape.' He paused for a moment then leaned forward, speaking earnestly. 'My lord, can I ask if you have been approached by any who has put such an idea into your head, even formulated a plan?'

'We have talked of freedom.' The reply was somewhat irritable, as if Richard was foolish in the extreme to ask such a question.

'You speak of "we", my lord. Whom do you mean beside yourself?'

'Why, Pierre Warbeck and I. Naturally we have talked of it. He has told me of the places he has been and the sights he has seen…' The Earl broke off suddenly as the door latch was rattled from outside and a pleasant, light voice with but the trace of a French accent, called softly, 'It is I, Ned, Pierre. Why is your door fastened? Cannot I come in?'

The Earl looked from the latched door to Richard and his soft boy's mouth fell slightly open. 'It is my friend and fellow prisoner, Pierre. If we do not admit him at once guards will come and they may separate us. Open the door, Master—' The shrill voice sounded petulant and he had forgotten Richard's name in his agitation.

Cursing softly under his breath at so inopportune an interruption, Richard hastened over and unbarred the door, admitting the Earl's visitor.

The young man who entered and glanced hurriedly at Richard was tall and slim and fair. Seeing him for the first time close to Edward of Warwick, Richard was forcibly struck by the thought that they so closely resembled each other. He had seen this man before though never at really close quarters, but he recognised him immediately as the man now known as Perkin Warbeck.

He had previously claimed to be Richard of York, the younger of the sons of Edward IV, who had been last seen in the Tower of London during the summer of 1483 when their uncle, Richard III, had been acclaimed as King of England. The grounds were the illegitimacy of the two boys due to the bigamous marriage of their father to Elizabeth Grey, previously Woodville, their mother.

After a disastrous campaign the rebellion had failed and Warbeck had surrendered himself to King Henry's mercy and had confessed that his claims had been bogus. He had been declared an imposter and was now imprisoned within the Tower in apartments close to his alleged cousin of Warwick.

Catching the Earl's eye and seeing the look of embarrassment and guilt plainly emblazoned there, Warbeck firmly closed the door again and latched it. His gaze again returned to Richard who was standing by the Earl's chair.

'I do not think I have seen you here before, fellow,' he said haughtily, in the voice that bore still the faintest of foreign intonations. 'You are new in service here?'

Richard glanced at the Earl, who clutched at his sleeve anxiously, and replied quietly, 'I have just been explaining to my lord here that I am not a jailor. I have borrowed my clothing from another man in service and came to speak with his lordship on a matter of grave importance.'

The imperious frown on the newcomer's face deepened and he moved in closer to the Earl and seated himself on the nearby stool.

'Ned, you should be very careful,' Warbeck warned. 'I hope you have said nothing to this man which could be interpreted as treasonable.'

The Earl let out his breath in a little gasp and looked entreatingly towards Richard.

'The Earl has said nothing of such a dubious nature, sir, and I came expressly to warn him against any so doing, in particular to avoid embroiling himself in any attempt to escape.'

'Indeed?' Warbeck's expressive eyebrows rose in interrogation and, again, Richard was struck by his resemblance to the Queen. He was Neville fair, like the Earl, with curls which reached to his shoulders, clear-cut features and a slightly over-large nose, the Plantagenet nose, Richard thought ruefully. Like the Earl he was well clad in dark blue velvet doublet and hose which was rubbed and bore marks of long use and had been skilfully darned upon the sleeve at some point. Despite their shabbiness his garments were elegantly cut and worn with an air.

Richard bowed to him. 'My lord, I served you, fought with you at Exeter and managed to make my escape after the failure of that battle. I assure you that my presence here is in the service of the dowager Duchess of Burgundy and for the benefit of both of you. Since you are here I will be glad if you will listen carefully to what I have been endeavouring to convey to the Earl here.'

Warbeck started and his piercing blue eyes surveyed Richard closely and then the imperious glare softened and he inclined his head in a little nod of acceptance.

'So, you are for the cause. Praise be. You have seen the Duchess recently?' The words were spoken eagerly and Richard thought with a pang of pity that there seemed a genuine longing to know about the woman who some believed to be the imposter's mother, born to her and her adviser, the Bishop of Cambrai.

'Indeed I have, sir, only some months ago and I can assure you the Duchess is in good health and spirits, only...' he hesitated '...she is naturally anxious about the welfare and safety of—both of you.'

He knew he was treading dangerous ground here. If this man was an imposter which he had confessed himself to be, then Warbeck himself could pose considerable danger to his easily led fellow prisoner. If, despite his enforced confession, he was whom he had claimed to be—and seeing him now, Richard could almost be convinced as to the truth of that—then he was owed all Richard's devotion and loyalty. He sighed slightly.

Turning to the Earl, he repeated his former warning. 'If either or both of you should be approached as to a plan formulated to allow your escape, I beg of you both to have nothing to do with it. The Duchess has enjoined me to plead with you to avoid any such offer—and, in fact, to declare yourself loyal to King Henry's interests. Such a plot could doom you both, prove a ploy, a clever stratagem to allow the King to move openly against you.'

Warbeck frowned. 'I do not understand. The King has been merciful to me and though his lordship has remained a prisoner throughout his rein, the King has not endeavoured to rid himself of him. Even during the Lovell rising of 1487, when Lambert Simnel declared himself to be Edward, he merely showed him to the people but in no way acted against him. Why should he wish to execute him now, for that is what you imply, Master—?'

'Allsop,' Richard supplied.

'Just so, and I say again, why now?'

'You have received no news of the King's intention to ally himself with Spain by a marriage between his son, Arthur, and the Spanish Infanta?'

Warbeck shook his head. 'We hear little here of court politics.'

'But if Prince Arthur is to wed the Spanish princess, that

can pose no danger to me and to Pierre here, surely?' The Earl's voice was shrilly petulant.

Richard saw that Warbeck realised the insinuation instantly and his blue eyes blazed in sudden alarm.

'Because, Ned,' he explained softly, 'King Henry will be more than ever anxious to rid himself of all remaining Plantagenet heirs so as to convince King Ferdinand of Spain that in due time his daughter's position as the future Queen of England will be unassailable.'

For moments the Earl remained staring at him as if he could not comprehend the meaning of what was said, then he made a little, inarticulate sound in his throat and turned from Warbeck to Richard and those pale blue eyes now revealed understanding and a sense of unbelievable horror.

'They will execute us?' he appealed hoarsely.

'No, my lord, if they have no grounds. The King will be anxious still to retain the good will of his people and show mercy to all his subjects, even those who have rebelled against him—at least,' Richard said dully, 'those he knows very well are no real danger to him. That is why he kept the pretender, Lambert Simnel, within the palace kitchens, humiliated but not physically harmed. You must see to it that you two talk of nothing that could be construed as treasonable.' He turned enquiringly towards Perkin Warbeck. 'How long since you have been granted admission to my lord's apartments?'

Warbeck considered. 'A few days now. It seemed that we acquired a sympathetic jailor who turned a blind eye to unlocked doors.' He gave a faint Gallic shrug. 'It was very tempting. I had not seen my…' he hesitated and then added '…my fellow prisoner and we met and became friends.' He looked pointedly towards the Earl.

'Ned has need of friends. He has not been able to develop his potentiality. He reads but not well. I was able to help him with that and he has found my descriptions of places outside these walls fascinating. He has seen so little of the world. We have not,' he stated vehemently, 'spoken of a wish to be free, at least only as a vague possibility natural to all prisoners. We have never, and I mean that, criticised His Grace the King nor have I mentioned the names of any of my former followers with the exception of Mayor John Atwater who is imprisoned here with us in the Tower.'

Richard remembered the man as being Perkin Warbeck's most faithful Irish adherent. He had heard that the former mayor of Cork had been injured and was in a bad way. Though his son had managed to escape from captivity, Atwater had been forced to remain behind.

'Has Mayor Atwater been in communication with my lord Earl?'

Both men shook their heads emphatically and Richard gave a sigh of relief.

The Earl said almost tearfully, 'Does this mean that we can no longer see one another? Pierre has become my first real friend since—since I was a boy.'

Richard looked meaningfully at Perkin Warbeck and the former pretender said comfortingly, 'It would not be wise for us suddenly to cut off our meetings, Ned. We will still meet occasionally, but we must be very careful what we say to each other and reject firmly any offer of help from anyone, however much that person may seem to be our friend and trustworthy.'

The Earl nodded and Richard could see the slight trembling of his lips. He had been badly frightened. In many ways he was childlike but Richard was reassured that this immaturity did not signify that the Earl had failed to grasp the possibility of his own danger. No, he filed away the thought to report back to the Duchess at Malines. Edward of Warwick was not simple minded. Once brought out of confinement and carefully tutored, he would prove to have as good a mind as any other man.

Perkin Warbeck had moved to the high-barred window and was listening carefully for any sounds he could discern outside.

'There are jailors moving about. I can hear their talk and I thought I heard sounds of arrival from the water gate. You should go, Master Allsop. We thank you from the bottom of our hearts for your fair warning and promise we will heed your words. Do not endanger yourself further by delaying here. The tray should be returned to the kitchens. There is always such confusion there you will not be noticed, but any other man coming in search of it could recognise the fact that you are a stranger to the company and that could spell trouble.'

Richard went to the Earl and made obeisance again, then he turned back to Perkin Warbeck who was holding out his hand towards him in farewell. Impulsively he bent and kissed the long fingers in homage and when he raised his head again he found that Warbeck's blue eyes were awash with tears.

'Thank you, Master Allsop,' he said softly, his voice a trifle hoarse with emotion. 'Convey to my…' there was the faintest of hesitations again '…my patroness, the Duchess, my fondest love and tell her I pray continually for her well-being and happiness. She knows, I am sure, that circumstances have made it impossible for me to fulfill my mission here and that all is not as it seems to common folk.'

'I will do, my lord.'

Grey eyes met blue then, hurriedly, Richard turned to retrieve the tray with its used dishes.

He was bending to pick up the tray when he froze as he heard booted footsteps outside. There came a heavy hammering upon the door and a voice he thought he recognised demanded, 'Open this door immediately.'

Richard stood upright instantly and looked first to one and then the other prisoner. Both men showed expressions of alarm.

The Earl began, 'What shall we...?'

Perkin Warbeck gestured him to silence and Richard nodded for him to obey the demand. There was little point in refusal to obey since the door could be broken down with the help of an easily summoned battering ram.

Warbeck approached the door. 'Very well. Just one moment, the Earl and I were at prayer—'

His explanation of the latching of the door was interrupted peremptorily.

'Open the door at once, I say, in the King's name.'

Warbeck fumbled with the latch. Outwardly he appeared calm but Richard could see his fingers were sweaty with fear and he could hear his own heart hammering within his chest. He turned just once to see the earl had stumbled to his feet and the wide-set pale eyes were wide in horror.

As the latch gave the heavy door was unceremoniously pushed wide by the heavily built soldier who accompanied John Hilyard, for Richard had known at once who the new arrival would be. The man stood arrogantly, feet astride, hands on hips, coldly surveying the three men in the chamber. Richard could not help noticing that even in this role, Hilyard was extravagantly dressed as usual in an overlong furred over-robe over a fashionably short doublet revealing an elaborately embroidered cod piece.

Hilyard did not move to enter the room but pointed an accusing finger at Richard.

'Arrest that man. He has no right of entry here. He is dressed as a jailor, which I know he is not. Clearly he is engaged in treasonable communication with the King's prisoners. Take him to the dungeons below the Wakefield Tower where I will question him at my leisure.'

His chilling gaze dwelt on the trembling form of the Earl as he said shortly, 'My lord, I have to tell you that you, too, will be questioned as to your converse with this man. You, sir,' this last in contemptuous tone was addressed to Perkin Warbeck, 'you know only too well what to expect by consorting with the King's enemies. You had best return to your own apartment and remain there until the King's officials decide what is best to be done with you.'

Two men-at-arms who had accompanied Hilyard had already moved in and roughly bound Richard's arms behind his back. He did not struggle. There was nothing to be gained by antagonising these men and giving them further excuse to manhandle him. He shot a hasty glance at Warbeck, exhorting him to silence and the man inclined his head briefly. Richard was hustled out into the corridor. Behind him he could hear the light, high-pitched voice of the Earl protesting at such rude treatment afforded his servitors.

Richard was pushed along and forced out of the door. He had a glimpse of the scandalised guard who had greeted him earlier and given him directions to the Earl's apartments. No wonder the man appeared transfixed. He, too, would be afforded blame for his negligence in this business and would be lucky to come out of the affair with a whole skin.

After the dim light in the Martin Tower corridor, the wintry sunlight outside on the green momentarily blinded him. He staggered, finding it hard to retain his balance after a final hard shove from one of his captors. As he attempted to straighten, he found himself staring into the apparently incurious eyes of Josh Aldred who, in the company of other jailors, looked to be on his way to the gatehouse to go off duty.

Richard gave him one meaningful glance which Josh patently ignored, then he was impelled brutally forward across the green. The little group of jailors did not move, then he could hear them continue with their conversation as if nothing unusual had occurred. Grimly he realised that such sights were common to them. He had only moments as he was breathlessly hustled along to wonder if Josh could have betrayed him, a thought he instantly dispelled.

No, he would not believe that, yet the next fear that beset him was the thought of how Hilyard had known he was there in the Martin Tower and, if he had followed him to the Tower, was he aware that Anne was awaiting his return at The Golden Cockerel? He could only pray, as he almost fell down the steep stair which confronted him on the entry to the Wakefield Tower, that Josh would be able to keep her well hidden from any arresting agents who came to the inn and, eventually, escort her safely back to Westminster palace.

Chapter Nine

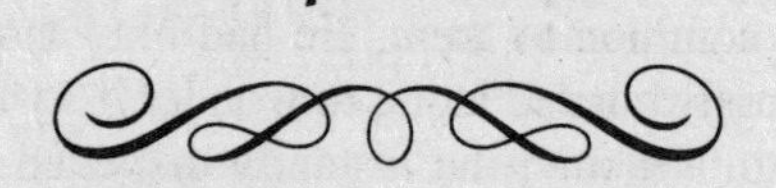

Anne had been made very welcome at The Golden Cockerel and, for a while, she had allowed chatter about the customers who frequented the inn and stories about the times her father had visited to occupy her mind and distract her from the gnawing worry about what was happening to Richard on his mission to the Tower. She ate politely of the excellent food provided and served by the smiling Bess Aldred but, in truth, she could not taste it. Eventually she sat moodily silent and Jake Garnet signalled silently for Bess to leave them.

He rose and went gently over to Anne. 'You are very concerned for him?'

She nodded, lifting her face to search his directly. 'You must be very worried all the time about your own son-in-law. Haven't you tried to persuade him to give up his allegiance to what has to be accepted as a lost cause?'

He shook his head solemnly. 'Josh goes his own way, as does your father, and Sir Dominick and, of course, Master Richard. They know the score. It is not for me to rebuke them for their earnest attempts to right what they see as a grave wrong.'

'But it is hopeless,' she murmured brokenly, 'and dangerous. Master Garnet, if I were to lose Richard now...'

Her lips trembled and she turned away from him.

'You love him deeply.'

'With every fibre of my being. I want him to go home, now, before he loses his life in this mad venture. He owes the dowager Duchess of Burgundy nothing. He has served her long enough. I shall miss him terribly when he is gone from Westminster for I have come to look for sight of him every hour of the day, but if he is well out of London I shall wait patiently, knowing he is safe in Yorkshire until I can join him as his bride.'

His expression continued grave and he gave a heavy sigh. 'You know, Mistress Anne, that were he to do that, without making every effort to complete his mission, he would never rest content. He would be with you in body, but his soul would be in torment. He would be constantly castigating himself for cowardice and, in the end, it would come between you.'

She turned back to him and her blue eyes were bright with tears. He thought how very lovely she was and so very like her mother.

'I know.' It was the merest of whispers, scarce more than a breath.

He moved away, ostensibly to collect dishes on to a tray, but really to give her time to collect the remnants of her courage.

At last she said, 'If—if Richard is successful, will Master Aldred continue to work at the Tower?'

'He has intimated that he will continue to do so for a while in order to watch out for the Earl's interest—while he can.'

'And—should anything go wrong and he is suspected of aiding and abetting the Earl to escape, or worse, of plotting with Yorkist sympathisers outside, what—what will you and Bess do?'

He lifted his shoulders and blew out his lips. 'That, Mistress Anne, is something which continues to haunt me. Naturally my first concern will be for Bess. It may be necessary to get her safely out of London, but, like you love Master Richard, she loves Josh. I fear she would not heed my advice. She will want to stay near him—to the end, if necessary.'

Anne bit down upon her bottom lip until she tasted blood. They were seated behind the taproom in the parlour and no sounds from the busy Chepe reached them here nor could she look out on to the famous thoroughfare as the glazed window here looked out on to the small flower and herb garden, bare and brown in the chilly November air.

She tried to summon a smile for Jake Garnet's sake and continued to remain looking into the hearth fire's bright scarlet heart. Jake went to the window and stared out unseeing, his own thoughts busy with the doubts Anne had placed in the forefront of his mind. Josh's activities at the Tower had been innocent enough until now and had been set up for just this purpose, the facilitating of admittance for any trusted Yorkist supporter who needed to see the Earl in person. Today that need had to be met and afterwards—who could tell the outcome?

They were both silent, lost in their own thoughts when suddenly the door to the taproom was opened abruptly and Bess and a newcomer burst into the room. Anne turned to them both with a little frightened cry.

'Richard?'

Jake gestured for Bess to close and latch the door, for he could see by both their expressions that something had gone gravely wrong, then came hastily forward to grasp the hand of his son-in-law.

'Master Richard is not with you?' He turned, as Anne started out of the chair, to explain. 'This is Bess's husband, Josh.'

The man was breathless as if he had been running fast but he waved away Bess's offer of mulled wine testily.

'Not now, lass.' He looked anxiously at Jake, then at the frightened woman near the hearth. His father-in-law nodded imperceptibly.

'Mistress Anne, Master Richard's betrothed?' he asked.

'Where is he?' she begged, hands outstretched beseechingly.

He made no attempt to soften the blow. Of what use could that be?

'He is taken,' he said grimly. 'I saw him bundled out of the Martin Tower by two men-at-arms. They were commanded by some popinjay I have seen only once before when the King himself came to a Council meeting at the Tower some days ago.'

'John Hilyard,' Anne cried. 'John Hilyard! Oh, sweet Virgin, how could he have known and followed us from Westminster?'

'You know this fellow?' Jake asked.

'He is a squire of the body to the King. The way you describe him, so simply, it could be no one else. He—has been paying me some attention recently. Lately I have become suspicious, believed that he was sounding me out about my father's activities and I have tried to avoid him—but—but I could not think...' She covered her face with her hands and sank back into the chair, weeping.

Jake said gently, 'It is not your fault, Mistress Anne. You cannot blame yourself for this. Master Richard's arrest could be accidental, simply a result of the man's unexpected arrival at the Martin Tower. The discovery of an unknown jailor there might have urged him to have the fellow questioned as a precaution.'

'No, no, he knows Richard.'

Josh Aldred came quickly to her side and bent down over her. 'He knows him, you say, as Richard Allard?'

She lowered her hands and looked at him distractedly. 'Why, no, he thinks he is my servant, Dickon Allsop, but that cannot help the situation, can it?'

'Does he know that you are here at The Golden Cockerel?'

She shook her head. 'I don't know. If he followed us or sent other men to watch me—I don't know.'

The two men exchanged hasty glances.

Josh said grimly, 'I think I should convey Mistress Anne back to Westminster by river immediately. The man is too busied at present to follow her here. We have a little time unless, as she says, there are men outside, but I saw no one strange either out there or in the taproom. Master Richard's orders are implicit. I was to get her out of the city whatever happened.'

'But you should think of yourself first,' Anne said. 'You could be in grave danger if it is known that you have helped Richard.'

'He will not talk,' Josh said in a clipped, harsh tone. 'At least, not yet. I know Master Richard.'

Anne was too numbed and in shock to properly take in what Josh Aldred was saying but she did understand, though dimly, that she should do as Master Aldred said and leave The Golden Cockerel. If John Hilyard connected Richard with Josh Aldred he, Jake Garnet and Bess, all of them here, could be in danger. For their sakes, she must go—immediately. Yet she could not contemplate leaving Richard in the hands of his enemies at the Tower...

She turned a frightened face to Josh Aldred. 'I will not hinder you. I will come with you at once.'

Jake Garnet came to her and took her chilled hands within his huge ones. 'Try not to be too alarmed, Mistress Anne. Master Richard has had close calls like this many times before now and managed to get himself out of danger. Things look black, I grant you, but they have nothing definite against him. It may well be they will let him go...'

His voice trailed off miserably as she turned and faced him directly, despair clearly written on her pale, lovely face.

He bent and, taking the liberty of a trusted friend, kissed her fingers. 'Do not despair, my dear, we will pray for you—and him.'

She inclined her head. She was not fully aware of the tears spilling on to his huge paws, but she tried to smile bravely. 'Be very careful, Master Garnet, if—if they should come here and ask questions. I know Richard would want to keep you from harm.'

'Aye, mistress, I know.'

She allowed Bess to put her warm cloak around her and, impulsively, she hugged the woman. 'Thank you for all you have done for him—in the past.'

Josh was impelling her gently towards a back door from the parlour which led out into the garden. She went with him blindly and found herself finally in the busy street again and, at length, near the wharf at London Bridge. Josh had not hurried her once within the Chepe and though she knew he was taking note of all passers-by, ostensibly he appeared calm enough, a man escorting a gentlewoman to the ferry.

She waited, not moving from the spot where he left her for minutes, until he hailed a ferryman and assisted her into the boat, jumping down immediately afterwards and taking his seat beside her in the stern. She did not speak until the ferryman had pushed out into mid-river and was heading towards Westminster, then she said in a whisper, 'What will you do now, Master Aldred?'

His expression was grave and his eyes compassionate. 'We must wait, Mistress Anne, as we have done many times, to see what will transpire.'

She stared out over the pewter grey waves of the river. 'Will they—will they torture him?'

It was so soft and tentative a question he only just caught it. For a while he did not answer then, unable to evade it finally, he sighed and said, 'I am afraid they will.'

He saw a terrible shudder pass through her as she implored, 'I know there must be many of you, fellow conspirators. Is there no way of helping him to escape?'

'From the Tower? I fear not, Mistress Anne.' He was silent again for moments. 'From what I understand, the King is anxious to act against the Earl of Warwick. That is the reason why Master Richard was so anxious to speak with the Earl, to warn him. Now the King has a prisoner, it is likely he will take all steps necessary to force Richard to name accomplices and to embroil the Earl in the suspected plot to escape.'

'But there *was* no plot, Richard said.'

'No, Mistress Anne, but it would be to the King's advantage to prove there was one.'

She gave a despairing little moan.

In order to distract her from her worst imaginings, he told her briefly what had occurred at the Tower, how he had procured jailor's garb for Richard so that he might gain access to the Martin Tower.

He shook his head irritably. 'I had no time to retrieve the clothes, which are hidden in the cellars beneath the Constable's lodging, but he *did* entrust to me this ring. It appears to be very valuable.' He held it out to her and she took it, her eyes widening.

'It is the ring the King gave to him.'

He stared at her in amazement. 'You say it was a gift from the King himself?'

'Yes, the day of the hunt at Richmond. Richard saved young Prince Henry's life from a wild boar which threatened him and the King rewarded him with the ring.' She gave a tight little smile. 'He did not want to take it from the King's hand.'

'I can imagine,' Josh said grimly. 'Does the King know his true identity?'

'No, no. Richard was riding with the hunt as my servant.'

'Thank God,' Josh returned fervently. 'The trail cannot yet lead back to his father—or yours.' He considered, gazing bleakly across the dull expanse of the river. They were speaking very quietly and the ferryman's full attention was on his rowing and the avoidance of other craft nearby. 'It might—just might—be worth appealing to the King for mercy if the worst happens.'

'You mean if Richard is sentenced to a—traitor's death?' The horror of her tone was fully apparent even in so low a whisper.

'Aye, Mistress Anne.'

'If things are so bad, you must all leave London, Master Aldred.'

'I intend to get Bess and her father away the moment I get back to the inn. Jake owns a country house in Blackheath. We could go there for a while until we think it safe to return to the city. First I had to keep my word to Master Richard and see you safe.'

'There is no hope—is there?' she said dully.

He turned back. His face was in shadow now since dusk

was beginning to descend upon the Thames as they were approaching the King's steps at Westminster.

'I have to be honest with you, Mistress, but I fear not,' he said, then slowly he added, 'There might be just one way. Go to the Queen.'

Anne was startled. 'The Queen? But surely she could not nor would she wish to countermand the King's wishes...'

'The Queen has always had her own loyalties,' Josh said doggedly. 'I cannot explain to you now, but I know for a fact she has secret correspondence with—those you would not expect her to. If you throw yourself on her mercy, show her this ring. Your Richard saved her son's life. I do not know what she could accomplish, but I think it is your one hope.'

The ferryman was heading for Westminster quay now and Anne turned despairingly towards the grey hulk of the palace ahead of her. Her lips were trembling but she managed to summon a grateful smile as Josh lifted her from the boat then jumped back in himself after giving the ferryman instructions to row him back to London Bridge.

Anne stood for a moment, watching the small boat pull out into mid-stream and eventually disappear from her sight into the grey gloom of twilight. She uttered a swift prayer to the Virgin for all who had been imperilled at The Golden Cockerel then turned and faced the palace buildings.

There were few people about; what servants and officials there were were intent upon reaching the warmth of the palace or its environs. For a moment she thought she would not be able to force her stiffened limbs to move, but at last she found the strength to go forward slowly. Already she could see the brands had been lit on the outside of the palace and appeared particularly bright along the river terrace and the main entrance.

She needed to reach the sanctuary of the chamber she

shared with Philippa. There she could try to think what was best to be done—if anything. As yet she could not make up her mind whether she could confide in her friend. Suppose she brought Philippa into danger too! Tears sprang to her eyes again and angrily she dashed them aside with the back of her hand. She could not play the coward now, fail Richard, and sit about weeping like some foolish green girl. She had to decide what could be done to aid him. Josh Aldred had made a definite suggestion. Dare she take his advice?

Richard shifted uncomfortably on the dirty straw of the dungeon beneath the Wakefield Tower where Hilyard's henchmen had finally flung him. One wrist was manacled to the dank stone wall above him but he had enough leeway to sit. His free hand explored his bruised face. His head ached abominably where he had been flung backwards off the stool on which he had been seated during preliminary questioning.

Hilyard had struck him several times while his two burly men-at-arms had held him hard down on the stool and he discovered now that his mouth was cut on the left side and was seeping blood. There was another bad bruise on his forehead and the back of his head was also seeping blood, he found.

He grimaced and leaned back against the rough wall. So far he was relatively unharmed. They had contented themselves by repeatedly questioning him, Hilyard had sneered at him and spat in his face when he had remained stolidly silent and then the men had brutally ill used him with their fists.

They had not as yet so much as shown him the instruments of torture, but he knew what must come soon and if he remained obdurate the pain would begin in earnest. But, so far, he had been left to ponder his fate. Hilyard must consult one of the King's officials of the Star Chamber and that worthy must be present before Richard could be more closely questioned and his replies carefully noted and reported to the King.

He groaned inwardly as he realised his capture had furthered the very intent he had hoped to thwart. They would make every effort to get him to involve the Earl and Warbeck in the supposed escape plot. Had he doomed them both by his very presence in the Tower? After consideration he decided that he was blaming himself unnecessarily.

That decision had been made long ago by the King and his most trusted advisers when the very proposition of a marriage alliance with Spain had been bruited. There must be others at the Tower, paid by Crown officials, to see to it that the Earl and Warbeck were allowed to meet and discuss their longings to be free. Natural enough, but such desires in royal prisoners could be made to appear treasonable. Were these men to be exonerated, promised their freedom after their supposed negligence had had the correct effect? He gave a harsh, dry laugh. Now they had a real culprit on which they could unleash all blame. He had played into their hands.

Again his wearied brain attempted to figure out how Hilyard had found him in the Earl's prison apartments. Had he been betrayed and, if so, by whom? He dismissed the thought of Sir Owen Lewis. He, certainly, would not have wished to associate himself with Yorkist royalists, even to accomplish such a betrayal, thus connecting himself with the slightest taint of treason.

No, Hilyard must have had Richard watched. But why? Surely Hilyard had not suspected him from the beginning. If so, the man possibly knew his true identity and, if that were so, he could be connected with his own family and

Anne's, placing both their fathers in direct jeopardy. Yet, he thought about that seriously, Hilyard had not challenged him with the knowledge of his true name. Surely he would have done so if he were in possession of such information.

Grimly Richard determined to remain silent on that matter, whatever it cost, but a cold shiver went through him when he considered that braver men than he had not been able to keep that resolve.

Once more his tortured thoughts returned to Anne. Josh Aldred had realised his plight and would go at once to The Golden Cockerel. He would see to it that Anne was safely conveyed to Westminster but—and here was the terror which gnawed at his peace—it was essential that Anne keep silent about her journey to the city and her involvement with him.

She must deny all knowledge of his whereabouts and seem amazed to discover that Master Allsop had been arrested, disguised as a Tower jailor and closeted with the King's royal prisoner, the Earl of Warwick. He gritted his teeth savagely. He had been a fool to agree to escort her to Westminster in the first place and, even more heinously stupid to go along with her ploy of keeping him near her. He loved her desperately and the temptation to have her within his sight each day had been more than he could bear.

How long had he loved her? Certainly very soon after their first meeting on the Rushton desmesne. He had known always that his father had wanted the match and, though he had only seen Anne previously as a child, had reluctantly acknowledged the fact that he would eventually wed Sir Guy Jarvis's daughter. After their several fiery encounters he had known without doubt that the lovely dark-haired girl had captured his heart.

Now, soberly, he faced the fact that he would die without knowing the sweetness of possessing her. He prayed to the

Virgin and all the saints that he had not endangered her. She had pleaded with him to give up this mission and he had put his honour, his debt to the dead King who had treated him with kindness and consideration, before his longing for security and peace at home in Yorkshire with his beloved Anne.

She had lived in dread of this very happening, had confessed that it was her secret fear that she would be torn from the arms of some Yorkist lover, as so many widows had been after Redmoor. For this very reason she had sworn never to give her heart to such a man but, Richard smiled in the darkness of that stinking dungeon, she *had* done so. Anne loved him, as he did her, and, by God's help, he would see to it that no word torn from his tortured lips would doom her or injure one hair of her father's head.

Anne sat bleakly alone in the sanctuary of her Westminster chamber and considered her next move. She had been thankful to find that Philippa was, apparently, attending Her Grace the Queen, and Mary Scroggins was off about her own pursuits for the present. It was beginning to grow dark but she made no move to light the candles.

At first, after the numbness of realisation had worn off, she had given way to her terror and grief and sobbed passionately into her pillow. She had had just enough self-awareness to do that so that no sound of her weeping would be heard from outside in the corridor. Now that wild outpouring was slaked and she sat on her bed and faced the situation starkly and clearly and without the confusion renewed panic would bring.

She would not give way to hysterics again. Richard was in dire peril of dying horribly at Tyburn, a traitor's death of disembowelment, and somehow, she must save him.

Josh Aldred had pointed her in one direction only. He

had advised her to go to the Queen and plead for her help, yet Anne was still very doubtful of following that course. If she failed, she would not have then the advantage of her secret knowledge of Richard's activities and the vague possibilities of alerting fellow conspirators to his plight with the hope of enlisting their help in a rescue.

Should she send one of her men to Rushton, to her father? Surely he would know of comrades-in-arms who could be appealed to but, no, she dismissed that notion. It would take too long for Wat or Simpkin to even reach her father, let alone for him to summon assistance for Richard.

She shuddered throughout her being. Richard could, even now, be being put to the question. Josh Aldred had not spared her his own fears because he had considered her brave and resourceful. Her thoughts raced desperately. There was so little time. Hesitate now and she could lose Richard. If he were made to confess his association with Yorkist sympathisers, even his reports to the dowager Duchess of Burgundy, he would be condemned and dispatched without mercy.

No, she decided, Josh had been right. She must take the terrible risk of approaching Her Grace, Queen Elizabeth. If she knew of Anne's great love for Richard she would understand. She had known love herself, experienced the agony of losing loved ones in her own family. She was the only person Anne could appeal to who could possibly plead for Richard's life and Josh had reminded her that Richard had saved the life of Prince Henry. Surely that one act of brave folly must stand to his favour!

Her resolution once made, she went at once to the Queen's apartment and found her closeted with two of her older favourite ladies, Philippa at a footstool at her feet singing and accompanying herself on the lute.

Anne curtsied deeply and immediately begged a private audience.

The Queen glanced at her sharply and then waved away her three attendants without questioning Anne further. She saw at once that the girl was in a distraught state.

Philippa looked anxiously at her friend as she rose and carried her beribboned lute to the door. Lady Hartley looked as if she would expostulate, but at one imperious glance from the Queen she shooed out the others, curtsied and retreated backwards through the door.

The Queen signalled for Anne to approach her chair.

'Come, sit on this stool, child. You look still unwell. Aren't you recovered?'

Anne came forward and stood uncertainly, twisting her hands in nervous strain.

'Your Grace,' she plunged in before her nerve failed her, 'I am in grave trouble and only you can help me.'

A frown gathered on the Queen's brow and she held out her hand once more, indicating that Anne should come close and seat herself.

'Child, you know I will do so if it lies in my power. What is it?' She leaned down to peer into the youthful face lifted in pleading to her own and was further alarmed to see the tears begin to gather on the lustrous dark lashes. 'Anne, you are not—with child?' The final words were uttered very softly. 'If it is so, you must rely on me to approach your father and…'

'No, no, Your Grace, I have done nothing to harm your good opinion of me.'

'But you are greatly troubled. If I know anything of life and the experiences of my lady attendants, I can recognise the fact that some man has caused you this distress. I know John Hilyard has been giving you special attention. Is it that you wish those attentions to cease?'

'Yes, Your Grace, I mean no—' Anne stumbled uncertainly into speech again. 'John Hilyard is not the cause of my anguish, at least not in the way you mean.'

The Queen sat back again in her chair and nodded. 'I am relieved that you are not disgraced. Tell me what is it that so alarms you. Is your father ill? If so, you must go North at once. I will find you an escort…'

'No, no, Your Grace, it is not that. I cannot—must not leave Westminster.' She choked a little, then pressed on doggedly. 'Someone I love is—is in grave danger of losing his head, worse, of dying a terrible, traitor's death at Tyburn. He has been arrested and held in the Tower. I fear he will be put to the question very soon and…' The tears were falling unhindered now, splashing on to the silk of her gown. 'I cannot bear to think—of—his suffering…'

'A man you love, a prisoner in the Tower? I do not understand. I have not seen you in close talk with any of His Grace's courtiers, or, at least, not so close that I would believe your heart to be engaged, other than young Hilyard…'

'He is Dickon Allsop, Your Grace, my father's steward. We are betrothed.'

The Queen's expression was revealing utter bewilderment now and Anne hastened to explain. It was necessary though it might further doom Richard for the Queen to know his true identity.

'That is not his real name, Your Grace. He is Richard Allard and my father is in favour of the match.'

'Richard Allard? Dominick Allard's son?'

'Yes, Your Grace. He offered his services to escort me when I was summoned south and I—I told John Hilyard he was my servant—and—and I could not take it back later…'

'He agreed to this deception?'

'Yes, Your Grace, but only to please me. He had no intention of spying at Court. You must believe me.'

The Queen's expression was inscrutable as she said quietly, 'I think you had better tell me everything and slowly. I need to know how it is that Dominick Allard's son is held under guard at the Tower and how he can be accused of plotting against the King.'

Miserably, haltingly, Anne told the tale, how she had foolishly tried to keep Richard by her, how she had feared he was embroiled in some Yorkist plot and how, finally, he had told her he wished only to warn the Earl of Warwick that there were those plotting to harm him and bring him to the scaffold.

The Queen betrayed neither anger nor surprise at this revelation. She listened without interruption until Anne came to a pathetic stop.

'So, you see, Your Grace, he was disguised as a jailor and John Hilyard burst in upon him closeted with the Earl and Master Perkin Warbeck, and he is now lying in a dungeon somewhere within the Tower accused of treason.' Passionately she added, 'He meant no harm to the King's cause, Your Grace, I swear it. He wanted only to safeguard the Earl whom he—whom he…'

'Regards as his true sovereign,' the Queen finished drily. 'Yes, I understand Master Allard's dilemma. And how, do you think, did Master Hilyard discover him in so damning a position?'

'I think, Your Grace, John Hilyard followed me. I should not have been foolish enough to insist on accompanying Richard to the city.' She gave a slight sobbed hiccough. 'I think, perhaps, Master Hilyard is jealous of…'

'I do not doubt it,' the Queen said grimly. 'Well, this is a coil, indeed. Your Richard is in very deep trouble and, as you say, like to lose his head. The question is, how are we to extricate him?'

Anne sprang up from the footstool. 'Oh, Your Grace, you will consider helping me? I thought—feared—'

'You feared that I would regard him as a traitor and rejoice at his arrest and punishment?'

'I did not know what to believe, Your Grace, but—' Anne's eyes filled with tears again '—I know you are my only hope.'

'I hope that it is not misplaced,' the Queen replied grimly. 'Now, sit down, Anne, and let us think what may be done.'

Anne subsided once more on to the stool and lifted her face to the Queen's.

'First, if it is possible to extricate Master Allard from the Tower, is there somewhere where he could be taken where he would be safe from the King's officers? For, I tell you frankly, even then he might be re-arrested.'

Anne stared at her bewildered. 'I thought an escape would not be possible.'

'I doubt that it would, but—there may be other means at my disposal. However, even should your Richard be freed from the Tower as I have said, he might yet remain in danger until it is possible for him to leave England. Where could he be hidden, Anne?'

Anne tried to marshall her chaotic thoughts. 'He has—friends in the city. I understand they have a house near Blackheath...'

'That would be excellent, well out of London and on the way to one of the ports.'

The Queen lifted a small silver bell on the table by her side and rang it once. Almost immediately the chamber door was opened and Lady Hartley stood framed against the lintel.

The Queen summoned her forward and when her attendant obeyed and came to her chair and curtsied, she said very softly, 'Jane, has our previous visitor left?'

'He was on his way to seek a ferryman, Your Grace. Have you further need of him?'

'Yes, summon him back to me if that is possible. If not, never mind, we must shift without him.'

Lady Hartley glanced briefly and curiously at Anne, whose eyes were so obviously red-rimmed with weeping, and withdrew at once.

The Queen was pacing the room now, her lips compressed. 'Your Richard told you of this…' she hesitated '…ruse—to rid the King of the Earl of Warwick? He is quite sure of his facts?'

'I believe so, Your Grace. Of course he did not reveal to me the source of his information.'

Anne was uncomfortable. She understood that the Queen's position in this political posturing was extremely difficult. On the one hand she had to think of the welfare of her children, Henry Tudor's children, and the security of the realm. On the other, the Earl of Warwick was her cousin, close kin and—Anne shuddered at the terrible dilemma which faced Her Grace—Perkin Warbeck might very well be, in truth, her own younger brother, despite the confession forced from him.

Anne wondered, fleetingly, if the Queen had ever set eyes on the pretender or if the King had forbidden her to request a sight of the man. For the first time it was borne in on Anne that the Queen was, herself, a royal prisoner, whether willingly or not. For the sake of the union of her Yorkist house with that of the Tudor, she had been forced to sacrifice her own loyalties.

The Queen gave a heavy sigh. 'It would seem that I have no other course but to seek audience with the King and beg mercy for your Richard. Have I your sworn word that no other plot was envisaged but this desire to warn?'

'Yes, Your Grace, I swear it on all I hold dear, but...'

'But? Is this not what you want?'

'Oh, yes, Your Grace, but I would not bring down the King's anger on your head.'

The Queen gave a faint wintry smile. 'It would not be the first time, Anne, and it is in a good cause. I would allow you to petition him, but I fear you would not receive a favourable reply to your appeal. Nor,' she added ruefully, 'can I be sure of such a one. Send one of the pages outside to the King's apartments and request an immediate audience for me.'

Anne rose with alacrity and moved to the door. 'Shall I summon Your Grace's attendants to accompany you or—' she swallowed hard '—I could perhaps go with...?'

'I do not think that would be at all wise, child. No, I would rather go alone. It is better so. The page will accompany me to the King's door. There are guards in the corridors. I shall be quite safe and adequately chaperoned.'

A page was dispatched at a run as Anne impressed upon him the urgency of the Queen's request. She came back into the chamber to find Queen Elizabeth staring dreamily from the window at the brown earth of the winter garden below.

Hesitantly Anne said softly, 'I do not know if this would have any weight with the King, Your Grace, but he himself gave this ring to Richard in gratitude for his rescue of Prince Henry from an attacking boar.' She held out the ring Josh Aldred had handed to her. The Queen took the costly thing and regarded it, her eyes widening.

'Henry gave this to Master Allard, personally?'

'Yes, Your Grace, I was present.'

The Queen gave a little gasp which ended almost in a

choked laugh. 'The King must, indeed, have valued Master Richard's services highly, for he is not normally so wont to—well, no matter. Certainly that should be a great help in my bid to persuade him but, Anne, I must warn you, that it is possible, no, probable, that I shall fail. The King brooks no treason and however well meant, this act of your Richard's was treason against the King's sovereign will, if what you were told was true.'

'I know.' Anne's reply was a mere whisper and choked with tears of distress.

'Take heart, child, if the worst comes to the worst, I shall petition His Grace to remit the sentence to one of hanging which would give your Richard a quicker and more dignified death.'

Anne bowed her head and gave way to a bout of weeping again. The Queen moved to her and touched her head beneath its velvet hood fleetingly. 'Let us hope and pray that I succeed and you can convey your Richard to safety in Blackheath. You realise…' She hesitated, then said a trifle hoarsely, 'He may not be in the best of conditions? You may need to organise a wagon and some trustworthy man to aid you.'

'I have two stalwart men, Your Grace.'

'Good, and I have—' She broke off as the page tapped and entered, bowing low.

'His Majesty is within his own private chamber and will be glad to receive you, Your Majesty.'

The Queen nodded and moved to precede the boy through the door. Anne stooped and kissed the velvet hem of the Queen's skirt as it rustled by her. She waited until the door closed and then sank down on her knees to pray at the Queen's carved prieu dieu in an anguish of fear, tinged with but a glimmer of hope.

She sprang to her feet a few moments later as the chamber door was opened abruptly and Lady Hartley re-entered, accompanied by a tall figure of a man, swathed in a rust-coloured cloak and hood of homespun wool.

She glanced round quickly. 'Her Grace is occupied elsewhere. Wait here, Sir Adam,' she said crisply.

Anne said hesitantly, 'The Queen has gone to an audience with the King, Lady Hartley.'

Lady Hartley showed no emotion. She nodded, tight-lipped. 'This is Mistress Anne Jarvis, Sir Adam,' she said. 'No doubt you were acquainted with her father, Sir Guy.' Without more ado she left the chamber, drawing the door to softly, behind her.

The newcomer advanced nearer to the fire and threw back his russet cloak. Anne saw that he was about her father's age, his dark hair beginning to thin a little and turn grey. However she thought his lean muscular body appeared as fit and agile as that of a much younger man and his long features were weatherbeaten, as if he had spent considerable time out of doors or possibly at sea. His dark eyes danced as he studied her closely.

'So you are Margaret and Guy's daughter, and a beauty, as I might have imagined.'

'And you, sir?' Anne murmured anxiously.

'Sir Adam Westlake, Mistress Anne, and very much at your service should you ever need me,' he returned crisply and she curtsied low.

'My father has spoken of you often, sir, but—but I thought you were at Malines in the service of the dowager Duchess of Burgundy.'

White teeth gleamed in the dark-complexioned face. 'So I am, Mistress Anne, but—occasionally, I return to England, let us say, as a courier.'

'To the Queen?' Anne's blue eyes rounded in wonder.

He inclined his head.

Her thoughts were racing again. So he had come to England to see the Queen urgently, to give her the disturbing news concerning the Earl of Warwick? Yet the Queen had been so anxious to have these tidings confirmed. It must be extremely dangerous for Sir Adam Westlake to enter the country and to risk himself at Westminster! Anne gave a little gasp of admiration. He had been on his way home and the Queen had sent for him to return, had dispatched Lady Hartley to find him. Was this in connection with Richard?

He was still eyeing her curiously and she moved awkwardly. Without waiting for invitation he seated himself in the window seat at ease, crossing his long legs as if he had all the time in the world to ruffle it here amongst his enemies. Anne knew him to be a firm supporter of the late King, as her father had been and actively engaged, as Richard was, in work for the Duchess in plans to thwart and harry King Henry. Clearly he trusted the Queen and she him. Anne was becoming more and more amazed as this terrible day progressed at what she had learned of those at Court.

He said gently, 'Are you in trouble, Mistress Anne? You seem distressed. Do you need my help?'

She drew a hard breath and decided to trust him. Briefly she told of Richard's peril and his dark brows drew together in a frown of alarm.

'Josh Aldred is to take Jake and Bess to Blackheath, you say?'

'You know them all? Yes, that is what he told me.' She gnawed her lower lip. 'If—if the Queen is successful in her plea for Richard—I—I hope to take him there until we see if he is well enough to proceed.'

Sir Adam's face revealed both scorn for Richard's jailors

and concern for his welfare. 'Aye, Mistress Anne, you do well to expect he has been put to the question.'

'They could be killing him even now…' Her lips trembled and he shook his head.

'Never fear, there is time yet. They'll not want to kill him.'

She knew the corollary to that, unspoken, was 'not yet, until they have extorted information and have no further use for him'. She turned away, her tears blinding her.

It seemed hours to the watchers before the Queen returned. In actual fact it was less than one, and Anne was assured that Lady Hartley kept watch outside lest anyone dared to break in upon them. Obviously she was used to keeping these visitors to the Queen as safe as it was possible for her to do so and, apparently, most times, she had been successful.

Sir Adam seemed totally unconcerned about the length of time he was kept waiting in so compromising and dangerous a situation. He had spent the time thinking quietly, as if he were considering ways in which Richard might be helped. His very presence comforted Anne, as her own father's would have done.

He rose at once to bow as the Queen entered and she extended her hand to him as she moved towards him. He bent and kissed her fingers.

'I am right glad Jane managed to catch you, Sir Adam,' she said, then turned at once and faced Anne.

Without preamble she said steadily, 'I have managed to obtain a pardon for Master Allsop.' She stressed the name, indicating that she had not revealed Richard's true identity. 'I have a warrant for his release from the Tower and you should send one or both of your men to fetch him and convey him to where we spoke of recently. He is barred from Westminster and indeed from London on pain of re-arrest and he is enjoined to speak nothing of his arrest nor the reason for it to any he meet upon the road or later. You understand?'

Anne nodded. Richard was to keep silent about the King's intention regarding the Earl. She was prepared to make any promise so that she might save Richard and was impatient now to dispatch Wat and Simpkin to procure a wagon instantly. Richard must not languish more than a moment longer than she could help while he might be suffering pain or deprivation. She took the warrant from the Queen's hand and, like, Sir Adam, bent to kiss the cold white fingers.

The Queen turned a wintry smile upon Sir Adam who stood, one eyebrow raised enquiringly, as she seated herself in her padded armchair near the fire. She shuddered as if she had taken a sudden chill in the King's apartments.

'It seems His Grace is willing to grant immunity to several of the jailors involved in this...' she paused delicately as if she was too disgusted to frame the word, '...affair. They are to be freed, those who have confessed to aiding the Earl and the pretender to plan an escape, so it was not too difficult to obtain a release for Master Allard. You know of all this?'

'Mistress Anne has been telling me.'

'Good. It saves time.' The Queen looked at him steadily. 'Tell my lady aunt Margaret it is impossible to save them. You understand?'

'I do, Your Grace.'

There was a little rasp to the Queen's voice. 'And—and I want you to do something for me, Sir Adam. I wish you to convey Lady Philippa Telford home—immediately.' Her voice was a little hoarse as if she were holding back tears. 'I should never have sent for her. I—I wanted to see her.

Her mother and I were once—very close, when I desperately needed friends, but she should go—now. You will see that there will be repercussions to this affair and—and I do not wish Philippa's father's hands to be tied, as they would if she remained here at Henry's Court.'

He inclined his head, his dark eyes grave.

'I have dispatched Lady Hartley to see that she is packed and ready to depart within the hour. It will be a long journey and she will need somewhere to stay tonight.' She turned briefly to Anne who was anxiously hovering, awaiting permission to leave. 'Perhaps she could stay within the house of your friends at Blackheath?'

'I am sure that can be arranged.' Sir Adam's tone was firm and confidently businesslike. Obviously he was totally sure of the loyalties of Josh and Jake Garnet.

'I shall go with Richard, wherever he wishes, Your Grace, if you will excuse me from service,' Anne said nervously. 'I can see to it that Philippa is not unduly alarmed by this sudden removal from Court.'

'Then go with God, child. That will certainly be for the best.' The Queen sighed. 'I shall miss you both, but pray constantly for your happiness—all of you. Off you go now, Anne, and make your arrangements. Your maid will travel with you and can attend Lady Philippa, too. Have you coin enough for the journey?'

'Yes, Your Grace, my father provided for any sudden need.'

Sir Adam said, 'I think we should all leave the realm for a spell, though I think it might be wise to remain in hiding for a few days before we set off for the port. In all events Richard may be...' He did not continue on that line of thought and the Queen's lips compressed again.

'An excellent plan. Take my most fervent prayers with you, Sir Adam, and take no unnecessary risks upon the journey.' Her lips trembled slightly. 'You know it would be useless to try to...'

'Aye, Your Grace, I know that only too well. Be assured. I shall see to it that my rash young friends understand well your warning.'

He knelt at her feet and kissed her fingers once more. Anne, curtsying at the door, could not avoid seeing how white and haggard the Queen's features were now revealed in the uncertain early evening light from the oriel behind her.

Chapter Ten

Once clear of the Queen's chamber Sir Adam Westlake drew Anne into the deserted antechamber, cautioning her to quiet.

'Mistress Anne, I will await Lady Philippa at a ferryman's boat house about half a mile down river. The man is in my pay and can be trusted. Tell her she must bring nothing but necessities for we must proceed by ferry and I will obtain a covered wagon when we are in the city and then go on to Blackheath. You, too, should bring nothing but your essential needs if you are to travel with Richard. You will go to the stables to send your men to the Tower with the Queen's warrant to free Richard, I take it?'

She nodded. 'But I shall go with them.'

'I think it best if you come to Blackheath with us.'

'No, I must go to Richard.' She was whispering, as he was, in case her voice carried beyond into the corridor but it was quite emphatic.

He gave a faint sigh. 'Very well, but prepare yourself for difficulties and dress sensibly to meet the weather you'll find out there. Send your maid to the boat house with Lady Philippa. You should be well protected with your two men, who are, I'm sure, trusted by your father or he would not have sent them here with you. Your maid will remain with us until we meet up in Blackheath.'

'Yes, Sir Adam. Mary is thoroughly trustworthy, too.'

'There is a red-headed fellow, a groom who has been bribed to carry messages between me and Lady Hartley. He will conduct Lady Philippa and your maid to the boat house.'

Anne was a trifle breathless with her longing now to go to her chamber and pack what she required for herself and Richard, for she might need her herb chest and considerable amounts of clean linen for bandaging. She felt her whole body was nerved now to reach him and every second she was forced to delay was a torment.

'Wait for a moment while I leave first. I have no wish for you to be found in my company should anything go wrong.'

She nodded again and he slipped out through the door. She stood tapping her foot impatiently until she believed he was clear. Sweet Virgin, how dreadful to live a life such as he did, every moment thinking he might be taken and questioned. And he was in touch with the Queen whose reputation must be safeguarded at all costs.

Anne remembered with a pang of pity her mistress's final words to him: 'Tell my lady aunt Margaret it is impossible to save them.' That dreadful cry of torn allegiance. And now the stricken Queen must be parted from the two young attendants she favoured!

She slipped outside at last when she thought it safe to do so and made herself proceed to her chamber without the haste which could attract undue notice.

She found Mary helping Philippa to push changes of clothing and undergarments into a saddle bag. Philippa's face was white and set but there was no panic. Young as she was, she had known other such emergencies in her short life.

Lady Hartley had left after delivering the Queen's orders and Anne thought she was off about some other secret business for her mistress.

Philippa said brokenly, 'Do you know what has happened, Anne? The Queen is in no danger?'

'No, no, but Richard is. I will explain everything when we meet again in Blackheath. Richard is imprisoned in the Tower, but the Queen has managed to procure a warrant for his release. He may be—hurt.' She avoided Philippa's horrified expression mirrored in her eyes. 'The Queen is anxious that you should not be kept here, a veritable hostage, against your father's activities. She has provided an escort for you in Sir Adam Westlake. You know him?'

'Yes, I do. He is a special companion of my father's.'

Anne was urging Mary now to pack necessities for herself. 'We may need medicines, Mary, particularly poppy juice. See to it.'

She said to Philippa, 'I want you to wait within the stables where our horses are until a man comes to take you to Sir Adam. He will convey you by river to the city.'

'You are not coming with us, mistress?' Mary's voice was sharp with alarm.

'I shall go with Wat and Simpkin to the Tower.'

'Mistress…'

'Not one word, Mary, there is no time. Richard will need me. I shall join you soon enough. Your task is to attend Lady Philippa.'

Grudgingly Mary fastened a second saddle bag and handed it to Anne, who had already changed into a simple woollen gown and donned cloak and hood. She nodded approval as the other two women did likewise. It would be cold on the river and on their journey to Blackheath and, besides, hooded cloaks helped anonymity. She had no wish for them to be recognised by any palace officials as they left the environs of Westminster.

Together they successfully navigated the palace corridors and were not challenged at the main rear door. They were accepted now as the Queen's attendants and could well be visiting the stables to cosset their pet mounts, though as it was now growing late, Anne had feared they might be questioned as to their need to leave the palace proper at this hour. Fortunately none of the other attendants or courtiers were about as they hurried to the stables and a quick enquiry of one of the boys, engaged in brushing down a horse newly brought in, succeeded in finding Wat who came instantly at his mistress's command.

She drew him outside while she outlined hurriedly her need and Richard's plight. She felt, rather than saw, his gathering alarm in the gloaming of the stable yard.

'Find Simpkin. Bring what you both need for a protracted journey and procure a covered wagon for me. I'll wait in the stables.'

He did not argue, which proved how quickly he recognised her urgent need and she returned to find Mary in talk with a red-headed groom whom Anne thought appeared both slovenly in appearance and shifty in manner. Apparently Sir Adam trusted the man to hold his tongue, so she was forced to do so also. She watched his departure with her two companions with some relief that they were now clear of the palace, though Mary's backward glances betrayed both her fears and her disapproval.

It seemed an age before Simpkin came to her side. She had been bidding a somewhat emotional farewell to her palfrey and he said softly, 'Never fear, Mistress. I am sure the Queen will see to it that your horse is safely returned to Rushton.'

'Of course she will. Have you managed to get the wagon?'

'Aye, though at this hour I was forced to purchase it at too great a cost. The horse coper would have asked too many questions else,' he grumbled. 'We shall need all the gold we have left to see us to the nearest safe port.'

He took from her the saddle bag and led her quickly across the Abbey yard to where a travelling horse-drawn wagon stood waiting, Wat on the driving box. Simpkin lifted her into the wagon and saw to it she was comfortably seated on the wooden bench, placed the bags near her feet, then he took his place beside Wat and they moved off, taking the road north to London.

Anne shivered and drew her cloak closer around her. Tucked into the bosom of her gown was the precious release warrant. It was growing quite dark now and she saw that brands were being lighted along the streets of the city as they rattled across the cobbles. Even now she was afraid. Suppose the Constable of the Tower refused to accept the warrant or that even before she could reach him, other officials had been sent ahead of her to rescind the order.

Her body ached to see Richard, hold him close to her, assure herself that he was alive and not too badly affected by his brief sojourn within the grim walls of that terrible fortress. The wagon trundled along so slowly that she wanted to scream at horse and driver to hasten but knew only too well that Wat was driving as fast as he dared.

It was dark and he wished to prepare himself both for potholes and dangers of the darkened streets and the attention of any robbers whom he knew to haunt the streets and alleys of the city, despite the vigilance of the Watch as they made their rounds. The wagon stopped at last and Anne made to scramble down even before Simpkin came to her side. Instantly he restrained her, firmly but gently pushing her down upon the bench again.

'Are we there, at the Tower?'

'Yes, mistress. At the main gate. Give me the warrant.'

'I will come myself.'

'Mistress, it is not seemly. Master Richard himself would not wish it.'

She peered down at him pleadingly, her face white and stricken in the uncertain light from a flaming brand set on the gate house wall. 'You will brook no denial?'

'The warrant has the King's seal, hasn't it, mistress? Who will dare gainsay his will? Now wait quietly here and I will bring Master Allard safely back to you. I swear it,' he insisted gently and she released his hand. Then he took the precious parchment and moved forward to instruct Wat to look to her safety. She heard his footsteps receding from the wagon then the harsh word of challenge delivered to him from the yeoman of the guard on duty at the gate house.

She huddled miserably within the wagon, thankful for its protection from the piercing wind. Wat could be heard murmuring to the elderly nag and at length he walked it for a while along the deserted street and back again when he had found a suitable alley where he could back the animal and turn the vehicle round. He peered once inside and enquired if she was warm enough.

'Yes, Wat, do not fret. I am just anxious to have Master Allard back with us.'

'Me, too, mistress.' He moved awkwardly from one foot to another. 'You think the warrant will hold good and they'll let him go?'

'I pray they will, Wat.'

He was voicing her own dread fears. She gazed out from under the front canvas covering towards the black shape of the looming gatehouse. Dear God, how many prisoners had died within the walls of this terrible place? And the Earl, no older than Richard, had spent most of his life here?

She experienced the dull ache of pity for the young man whom the Queen had believed was shortly due to die here. She could distinguish nothing in the gloom but the rough stone wall and the two yeomen with their halberds guarding the gate.

Her thoughts went to Sir Adam Westlake with Philippa and Mary. Her maid, she knew, would be overcome with anxiety. She prayed Sir Adam would get them safely to Blackheath for the Queen had undoubtedly thought that Philippa's freedom was threatened by this latest intrigue at Court and was determined to return her to her parents in Burgundy. She would never have insisted on such stealth and haste had she not thought it necessary.

Anne was stiffening within the wagon and thought at least an hour must have passed since Simpkin had left them to enter the Tower. Wat had walked the horse again, fearing it would take cold and some ill from its enforced, lengthy wait in the chilly night air. They must depend on the beast for their journey out of the city and on to Blackheath.

Another fear struck Anne with some force. Surely the city gates would close soon now. Would they be allowed to proceed tonight? They must get clear. This was her one abiding desire. Richard must leave London ahead of any possible pursuit dispatched by a King who might come to rue his act of clemency given in a sudden moment of weakness to his Queen.

They were back near the gatehouse again and Anne's ears were strained to catch any sound of men coming to the gate.

There it was, the noise of booted feet approaching, slow, stumbling, and her heart misgave her as she crouched near the entrance of the wagon, unwilling to disobey Simpkin and show herself but longing to catch the first sight of him when he emerged. Had he Richard with him? Were those awkward, stumbling steps those of her love?

Wat murmured something indistinguishable and scrambled down from the driving seat, making for the gate. For a moment his bulk cut off her first sight of the two men who came into the eerie glow of the brand set on one side of the gate.

She could hear voices, good-humoured enough by the sound of them—answering questions or giving advice? She could not tell, then the steps seemed to advance more quickly and she saw Wat and Simpkin supporting Richard between them as they moved towards the wagon.

Simpkin's voice was calm, showing no sign of the concern he must be feeling. 'Up into the wagon, Master Richard. Can you manage it? Mistress Anne is waiting there for you. Once you're settled we'll be off at once.'

Through a blurring of tears Anne moved towards the rear of the wagon, stretching out her arms to receive him.

'Richard, oh, my dear, have they hurt you?'

She heard him give a muffled laugh as he hoisted himself up on to the bench beside her. 'Not so very badly, my heart. Thanks, Simpkin, I'm up now. All is well.'

She could not see his features well enough and his voice sounded strong. She could feel the rough homespun of his jailor's garments as her arms closed round his beloved form.

'They have tortured you? Sweet Virgin, forgive them.' Her tears splashed on to the wool of his jerkin and he lifted one hand to stay her.

'There, sweeting, it is not so bad. One of my legs is twisted.' Again she heard that half-mocking, rueful laugh in the darkness of the wagon's interior. 'The result of a short spell on the rack, but very short, I praise the saints. God's teeth, I had not believed it possible I've come out of that hole alive. Tell me how you managed to achieve that, my heart, but, for the moment, let me rest while Simpkin gets us away from here.'

She drew his head against her heart then recoiled hastily from him as he gave a sharp vocal expression of pain. He was further hurt, beside the leg he complained of. When could she get him to a safe haven where she could begin to tend him and afford him some relief? If only she could see him properly. He was alive, here in her arms, and she must thank God for that mercy with all her heart but now she was longing to give him comfort and relieve his pain with the poppy cordial.

Simpkin called back to her from the driving seat, 'Don't fret, mistress, I have obtained a pass which will allow us through the wicket at the city's east gate. We shall be on the road to Blackheath soon when we've crossed London Bridge.'

Anxious not to hurt Richard further she kept herself slightly from him but he moved closer, reaching out wondering fingers to touch her as if he could not believe she was there with him.

'I still cannot think I am really here with you, my heart,' he murmured brokenly.

'Richard, my love, I am afraid to touch you, hurt you further.'

'Don't be,' he said fervently. 'Your nearness comforts me. I can inhale the sweetness of you. God, can you imagine what it was like in that fetid place? Sweeting, does my stink offend you? I seem to have been in that dungeon days, weeks even, instead of the few short hours of actual time.'

'No, no, my darling.' Her voice was still hoarse with tears of relief and fervent gratitude for his safe delivery. 'I need to feel you, hear your voice, smell you, to be sure I have you safe. Even though I carried the Queen's warrant for your release I was afraid they would not let you go.'

They were lurching over the bridge now and Anne could imagine the nearness of the shops and houses which lined the giant structure. She was almost willing the elderly horse to move faster, further and further from this air of menace and very doom the nearness to the Tower engendered.

She had drawn his head down on to her knee as she sat uncomfortably sideways to support him against the jolting of the travelling wagon. He winced once or twice then settled quietly against her heart.

'How else are you hurt?' she demanded, her chin cuddling his dishevelled hair.

She felt the slight shrug of his shoulders. 'Oh, the guards hit and kicked me. My ribs are bruised, I'm sure, and I was flung down into the dungeon but all will mend. Don't be frightened when you see me in the light. I imagine I'm quite a sight. One of my eyes feels half closed and I've a lump on my forehead where I fell, as well as a cut lip where that son of Belial, Hilyard, hit me wearing a sharp-edged ring.'

She forced back the tears again and hugged him closer.

'You say the Queen arranged my release?'

'She went to the King and begged him. I—I told her everything.'

'Did you, by God?' He gave a strangled laugh. 'Even so, despite her courage I doubt she would have had quite that amount of influence on Henry.'

'You *did* save the life of his son.'

Again there came the rueful explosion of a laugh. 'There, I knew that would be of use to me one day.'

The wagon seemed to be making smoother progress now. They were challenged at the gates and there was a delay until the wicket gate was opened and the wagon was allowed to trundle through then, at last, they were on the road to Canterbury, heading for Blackheath.

It was quite dark now and Simpkin stopped once while Wat kindled two lanterns to fix upon each side of the driving seat. Anne, gazing out to the front between their two solid forms, could see only the few feet of road illumined before them as the horse ambled steadily on.

Eventually, lulled by the movement of the wagon and extreme exhaustion and pain, Richard slept.

Grey dawn light was beginning to brighten the blackness before Wat turned and informed her they were almost there. He had seen only one mile engraved upon a Roman milestone on the roadside.

Anne suddenly realised that she did not know which house to make for.

'I did not enquire of Sir Adam exactly where the house is,' she said worriedly.

'I know it, mistress,' Simpkin said quietly, 'so does Master Richard. It is on the south side of the heath and somewhat secluded. We shall be safe there.'

She leaned back, reassured, and, as the wagon negotiated a turn to the right of the main highway, Richard stirred as if he sensed they were at their secure haven.

Simpkin turned on to a rough path, then through a stone gatehouse and drew the wagon to a halt. Anne peered forward anxiously and could just discern the wattle daub walls of a house with overhanging thatch and, instantly, as if the inhabitants had been waiting for their arrival, a door opened and the sturdy form of a man emerged, lifting high a horn lantern.

Simpkin scrambled down and moved towards him. 'It is Simpkin Cooper, Master Garnet. Do you remember me?

I've been here with Sir Guy Jarvis, my master. I have Mistress Anne Jarvis and Master Richard Allard in the wagon.'

'Thank the living God,' Jake Garnet breathed fervently.

'He's not in good shape, Master Garnet, and he'll have stiffened further in the wagon. He'll need help to get him into the house.'

Richard was moving awkwardly, trying to force himself up on the bench and Anne gentled him. 'Lie quiet. We are here at the Garnet house at Blackheath. Wat and Simpkin will help you down.'

'God damn this weakness,' he cursed as he managed to hoist himself out of the wagon only to give a sharp cry of pain as his injured foot took his weight on the ground.

Anne found Sir Adam Westlake at the rear of the wagon peering in at her. He gave a half-stifled laugh at the sight of Richard.

'God's teeth, man, I've often seen you looking less than civilised, for you've never been a court fop, but the sight of you now makes even me shudder. Take my arm and let's get you inside.'

Anne was helped down by an attentive Wat and she, too, found it hard to walk for she had stiffened, sitting awkwardly as she had through the night hours nursing Richard's head against her heart. Simpkin and Sir Adam were helping Richard over the step into the hall and she followed, on Wat's arm.

Everywhere streamed with light, for Bess stood fully dressed at the foot of the steps and it seemed she had lighted every pricket and candle in the house to welcome them.

Seeing Richard, she tutted her concern and led the men into the rear solar where there was a cushioned settle.

'Here, put him down, carefully now. Mind his hurt leg.'

There was a light clatter of footsteps as Anne made for the comforting warmth of the solar as Philippa and Mary hastened down the stair. Both were wearing nightclothes and bedgowns.

'Thank God, mistress,' Mary cried at sight of Anne. 'You'll be fair exhausted. We must get you to bed at once.'

'Not until I've seen Richard settled,' Anne retorted firmly. Thankfully she allowed Mary to draw off her cloak and moved to a stool near the fire, for she could see that Richard was in good hands under Bess's determined tending. She and Mary quickly produced hot water, clean linen and medicaments for the bruising.

'I have hot broth in the cauldron waiting for you all,' Bess said briskly. 'We have been praying that you would arrive soon.'

Adam said, smiling, 'He's not so bad, Mistress Anne. We'll soon have him fed and bedded and he'll be more himself later in the morning, a trifle worst for wear, true, but I've seen Dickon like this before.'

'Tortured?' she demanded angrily.

'No, I cannot recall that, but he's been in dangerous scrapes before and come out wounded and just as soon recovered.'

Anne turned to watch as Bess and Mary between them peeled off Richard's stained homespun shirt and saw clotted blood matting his chest hair and terrible purple bruises darkening the paler skin of his shoulders and side.

'Dear God,' she said, rising and crossing to his side. 'How could they have so manhandled him?'

Richard grinned at her as he opened the badly disfigured eye. 'Very easily, my sweet. I was very fortunate it stopped so soon.'

'How was that, Dickon?' Sir Adam queried.

'I'm damned if I know, Adam.' Richard winced as Bess

sponged down his bruised chest. 'They'd scarce started. I had said no word, thank God, though it was in my mind that I might not be able to hold out, when a jailor burst in, much to Master Hilyard's fury, and said he was wanted by the Tower Constable outside.

'He stalked out, only to return a few moments later in an even greater rage and curtly ordered the tormentors to untie me and return me to my dungeon. There I found several very scared-looking men who'd been shoved in there during my short absence. My jailors threw me down and I could see by their looks and their avoidance of me that my newly arrived companions in misfortune were very scared indeed.

'When the jailors left us and barred the door, one of them began to babble that they all had promise of the King's pardon. He was unceremoniously hushed by a strategic kick to a very sensitive spot which left him gasping.

'Even in my state, where I could think of nothing but my own aches and pains, I was wondering who they were and what that was all about. None of them said anything more on the matter.'

Anne was bathing his bruised face and then began to smooth in healing salve. She tried to quieten him, fearing that to talk would further weaken him, but he pushed himself up on the settle to peer up into Sir Adam's and Jake's watchful countenances.

'It occurred to me that these had been put there as seeming miscreants to trick me into a confession. Naturally I was mindful of that and kept silent. I made no mention of any companions, certainly nothing of how Josh had helped me.'

Jake sighed his relief. 'He's seeing to your horse, Mistress Anne, and hiding the wagon with your two men,' he said.

At length Richard was helped up the stairs into a small but starkly clean bed chamber and Bess went to prepare a hot posset. Anne supposed she would add some drops of poppy cordial. Mary came up with a wooden mazer of broth but Richard managed to swallow only a little, waving away the rest with a grateful apology.

'Thank you, but I can take no more,' he murmured, then, stretching out his hand to grasp Anne's he said, a little more confidently, 'Do not fret, my sweet. I'll be well after I've slept. And you must rest, too. Insist she does, Adam.'

Protesting, Anne was led down to the solar where she was provided with broth and small white manchet loaves and ale. She enquired after her two men and was assured they were being fed and accommodated in the barn near the stable.

Josh came in later, his homely face worn with alarm and fatigue but visibly relieved at the sight of her with Richard.

'So, I hear you took my advice, Mistress,' he said, looking smilingly to Sir Adam, 'and went to the Queen.'

'It seems you knew more on that score than I did,' Anne said fervently. 'You are sure we shall be safe here? If you are known to the Queen…'

'Be easy, Mistress Anne, we are not. We are simply servers in a chain of loyal Yorkist helpers. She would not betray any one of us even if she knew our identities, but we keep ourselves to ourselves. It is necessary for survival. Each man knows whom he should contact for assistance and that is all there is to it.'

Sir Adam said, 'You must obey your betrothed and get some rest.'

'I want to stay by him,' she protested.

Sir Adam shook his head firmly. 'You must sleep with Lady Philippa and your maid. I shall stretch out alongside Dickon on the bed. I promise I shall summon assistance if it is needed. I doubt that, though. Our Bess has so dosed his posset he should sleep soundly for hours.'

Anne allowed herself to be persuaded. As if aware of her bone weariness and heartsickness, neither Philippa nor Mary questioned her as to the night's events, seemingly satisfied that they had turned out as they had, and, at last, she fell into a sound sleep beside Philippa in a bed on which the sheets were blessedly clean and scented with lavender and rosemary.

But Sir Adam's prediction that Richard would soon recover proved over-optimistic. The next day he seemed fevered and only the ministrations of Bess and Anne kept him comfortable, and doses of poppy cordial allowed him relief from pain and fitful sleep. Anne realised it would be days before he would be fit to resume their journey to the port of Bishop's Lynn.

'Should you not start off without us and take Philippa on?' she asked of Sir Adam.

He frowned, looking down at Richard anxiously. 'No. We should be secure enough here. The discovery of Lady Philippa's unprecedented withdrawal from Court should cause some anxiety and anger in high places but, as yet, no one knows where she is. It may be better for us to stay hidden for a while, then we can all proceed together.' He moved restlessly to the small horn window overlooking the heath to the south. 'In all events I would prefer to wait for a few days and see if we can discover what news, if any, from London.'

'You mean concerning the Earl?'

'Aye, Mistress Anne, and I am sure your Richard will be unwilling to leave England until he hears the tidings, for good or ill.'

* * *

The following day Anne found that Sir Adam had left the house and no questioning of her two men gave her a satisfactory answer as to why he had done so. She was alarmed. Had he gone into London to discover the tidings he sought and, if so, was he not in danger of arrest? She conveyed her anxiety to Simpkin who shook his head decisively.

'I don't know where he is, Mistress Anne, but this I do know. Sir Adam is a wily bird and knows well how to look after himself.'

She returned to the house where Bess was overseeing one of her two young maids in the preparation of breakfast for Richard.

'He seems much better, this morning, Mistress Anne,' she informed her. 'It appears that the fever has broken and he's more himself. I reckon as he's still in a mite of pain, though. At least he says he has an appetite for breakfast, so that's a good sign. I've told him to stay in bed until later this morning and see how he feels then.'

Anne hastened to his chamber and was relieved to see Richard propped high against pillows and, though still pale, looking much better.

She bent and kissed him and he returned the kiss heartily.

'I'm feeling fine, sweetheart. I shall be fit to ride tomorrow if Simpkin can get us some good nags.' He looked round thoughtfully. 'I haven't seen Adam this morning. Is he below stairs?'

She evaded the question. 'I think perhaps he's in the stables,' she said hastily. 'He may be instructing Wat and Simpkin about horses. Philippa is down and gathering winter savoury in the herb garden with Mary.'

He did not press the matter and she was thankful. She did not want Richard worrying himself about Adam, to add further distress and worsen his condition. She watched anxiously as he fed heartily and was gratified but, she noted, as Bess had done, that he moved restlessly in the bed as if his ribs and leg still pained him.

The bruises on his face had turned from black into violent mauves and yellows and Anne felt a vivid rush of anger against John Hilyard who had stood by and ordered this. And she had quite admired the man when first they'd met!

She left Richard to doze again, for he soon seemed to tire for all his brave words about journeying in the morning, and went down to the parlor to greet Philippa.

'Bess says Richard is better.' Philippa's lovely aquamarine eyes appealed for confirmation.

'Yes, he is, but he's dozed off again now and, for all he says he wants to get up soon, I still think he's suffering quite a lot of discomfort.'

Philippa sighed. 'I cannot accept the need for these cruel methods of obtaining information, yet my father and his companions talk as if they are quite normal and sometimes necessary.'

Anne said tartly, 'For all they say, men are hardly logical. Surely it must be plain to them that men in severe pain will say anything to have the torture stopped, whether they confess the truth or not. Answers must be extremely misleading. Fortunately, for all I hear, Richard was not tortured long enough for him to wish to say anything compromising to his many friends, but for all the short time he suffered, enough damage has been done.'

She had eaten sparingly herself, her mind still occupied with anxiety for Richard, and now for Adam Westlake and the problems of meeting the journey ahead of them.

That evening when Sir Adam returned and she saw the black fury plainly written upon his face mingled with some intense sorrow, she castigated herself inwardly for not having given sufficient thought to the fates of the royal prisoners in the Tower. Compassion for their plight had been thrust aside in her mind, overridden by more personal worries.

Richard had by now dressed, helped by Wat, descended the stairs and come into the parlour. Simpkin had managed to procure him clothes suitable for travelling so he had been able to discard the jailor's garments he'd been wearing when released from the Tower. Richard had a change of clothes also, since Josh had thought to bring his own garments, retrieved from their hiding place in the cellars of the Martin Tower when he'd left London with his family.

Before Anne could speak, Richard addressed Adam in a harsh, revealing tone which betrayed the source of his suspicions.

'Your face tells all. You have obtained tidings. They are condemned then, both of them?'

'Aye, I heard yesterday from a chapman travelling east. The prince was hanged today at Tyburn. The Earl is condemned to be beheaded and will die very soon. Atwater suffered with Warbeck.'

If anything Richard's countenance went even paler. 'You went—to see?'

'Yes, I thought I ought to be there. It was the last and only thing I could do for him.' Sir Adam looked steadily back at the younger man. 'Do no distress yourself, Richard. It is over now. There was nothing any one of us could have done. The Duchess will know that and expect nothing more of us. You risked your life for them and were not well enough to go with me. You were sleeping so soundly this morning, I decided not to consult you.'

Richard said stiffly, 'He—suffered the full penalty, disembowelling?'

'Yes.' The single word was baldly delivered as Philippa

gave a little distressed cry and Anne turned tortured eyes on Richard. Jake Garnet and Josh Aldred had entered the parlour and looked as shocked as the rest of them.

Adam added, slowly, 'He died well, as I knew he would. He made no speech on the gallows that could embarrass the Queen.'

In the quiet little chamber each of them crossed themselves reverently.

Richard made a faint inarticulate sound, turned and fled the parlour, pushing Josh unceremoniously out of his way as he headed for the chamber he had shared with Adam.

Anne had noted the single word which had betrayed the reason for all their concern, 'prince'. Was it true? she thought bleakly. Was the pretender, Perkin Warbeck, truly the Queen's brother, Richard of York? If so, and the King had known it despite the earlier confession, how could he have subjected the man to that terrible public humiliation and agonising death?

Almost immediately she realised the truth of it. He could not afford to do any other. He had declared Perkin Warbeck a common upstart pretender and, whatever his own thoughts and suspicions on the matter, the man had had to die as a common traitor died.

They had all stood silent as the sound of Richard's blundering, uncertain steps ceased on the landing and the door to his chamber slammed shut. Anne waited for no more but lifted her skirts high and ran after him. She was relieved to find the door unlocked from the inside and pushed it open and entered.

Richard was kneeling near the bed, his head turned from her and she was horrified to hear the sound of his sobbing. She hesitated only momentarily, thinking perhaps he would prefer to have his grief unwitnessed, but she choked back her own tears and, coming forward very quietly, knelt by his side and reached up to touch his shoulder.

'Oh, my love, you must not torture yourself so. You heard Sir Adam. You almost lost your own life trying to save them. It was hopeless from the start. In your heart you know as much.'

Blindly he turned his head towards her and she half sat upon the floor, cradling him to her, while he gave way to his innermost emotions and the worst storm of his grief passed at last. He sat up, half pushed her away, dashed a hand across his smarting eyes and said hoarsely, 'What can you think of this display? I am unmanned. For a while I became the child I once was at Court again. I could not serve my King at his last battle, nor could I prevent the public humiliation his body was subjected to and now I have failed in the last task I set myself in his name, to save his nephews.'

'My darling,' she said very softly, 'do you think Sir Adam is any less affected, or my father and yours, when the news is given? They have all suffered for their loyalty to the Yorkist cause and I, in my foolishness, castigated them in my heart for it because I believed they neglected their own women to do so.

'I was wrong, my heart. They were all honourable men who risked life and fortune, and those women who loved them suffered agonies of fear too. I am proud to be one of their number, Richard. I love you with every fibre of my being but I cannot regret that you risked everything, our love and future happiness for what you thought to be honourable, and I suffer with you now in your great grief.

'The late King must have known many griefs, too. He lost his wife and son, and even before his death knew men blamed him unfairly for the deaths of others. Prince Edward of Lancaster, the old King, Henry VI, and even for that of his brother, George. He suffered in private and recovered in public, led his men bravely and died on the field…'

He was about to interrupt her and she guessed at what he was trying to say and she plunged on determinedly.

'I know you feel now that you would have rather died in the attempt to save these last two princes of the House of York, but what would it accomplish? The Queen bravely faces her own fate and thinks now of the well-being of the realm. It is what her father and uncle would have wished her to do and she knows it.

'Your task now is to help Sir Adam bring Philippa safely back to her father. The Queen laid this upon Sir Adam Westlake. I was present and guessed at the extent of her own suffering, for these men who die are her kin and must be still dear to her. Philippa must be returned to Burgundy; if she falls into the hands of King Henry and becomes a hostage to the crown, Lord Wroxeter's own hands will be tied in any future effort he may make in the Yorkist cause. The Earl of Warwick has a sister. There are yet other Yorkist heirs.'

She shrugged. 'Who knows what the future holds? Her children have Yorkist blood.'

He was leaning back on his heels, breathing heavily, his grey eyes shadowed, and she waited in an agony of dread for his response. How could she find the words to comfort him?

Instinctively she knew that words would never be enough and she leaned forward again and drew his head and shoulders towards her. At first she felt him stiffen and try to withdraw, then he gave a great gasping sigh and scrambled towards her, reaching up wonderingly to touch her dark hair that was tumbling loose from its confining linen coif.

She remained very still as his fingers gently explored her forehead and nose, tracing her lineaments as if he was becoming acquainted with them for the first time. Her lips trembled at his touch and then she shuddered with emotional release and pleasure as his fingers lingered on the sensitive flesh near her ear lobes and throat, then continued on to explore the deep swell of her breasts revealed by the low cut of her gown.

Almost without knowing it they rose to their feet together and he pulled her close to him, desperately, savagely, kissing her lips which parted eagerly beneath his, then her throat and breast. She made no resistance as his passion mounted and he drew her impatiently towards the bed.

She could never say afterwards that she was unaware of what would happen. Deliberately she allowed him to unhook her gown so that it fell in stiff folds of brocade from her body to make a sussurration of sound upon the floor beside the bed. Her own body was longing to feel naked flesh against his as he was to fondle her, and she simply gave way to her own repressed longing and surrendered to his need.

Her own fingers found their way to the fastenings of his shirt and hose and she heard, through a dazed wash of overwhelming release, his little groans of pain, for his injuries still troubled him, and knew the moans were of ecstasy too, as her own little whimpers of need were. They lay naked together at last and she gloried in the wonder of his touch.

If she had been afraid that in his desperation he would not heed her virgin state and subject her to rough handling and undue pain, she need not have doubted. His great love for her, despite the intensity of his longing, bestowed restraint and his wooing of her was gentle until together they were one and could mount into a passion of rapture which she thought would never end.

He lay replete, breathing harshly again, and her fingers

stole to his loved face and the dear, shaggy mop of brown hair he could never comb into the neat curled bob fashion required at Court and she had some time past admired. Damp curls clustered upon his brow and his mouth curved into a tender smile.

'Oh, my love, forgive me. I should have waited. Though you are my betrothed and there is no sin, your father would have exhorted me to patience.'

'I have no regrets, Dickon, my heart,' she murmured, her fingers tangling in the strong curling hair upon his chest and avoiding the dark bruises which even now could give pain. 'You needed me and I only wished to give comfort. That you gave me pleasure beyond my wildest dreams is something I could not have hoped to know. I am your wife, lacking all but a priest's blessing, and shall have that soon enough. That is,' her lips curved into a teasing smile, 'unless you intend to reject me as wanton.'

He gave a great triumphant laugh and took her to his heart once more.

Much later she turned towards the door and said in a little horrified whisper, 'I did not lock it. What if Sir Adam had wished to...?'

He laughed merrily. 'Adam has far too much tact and so has your maid. As for Philippa...' his eyes twinkled wickedly '...I believe Philippa is much more worldly wise than her lack of years would lead one to expect. We are safe enough, my darling, from prying eyes but...' he stretched arms wide above his head, momentarily releasing his possessive hold on her '...I think we should dress and rejoin the others. We should be planning our journey now and Adam will wish to start tomorrow.'

For a split second the warm light faded from his grey eyes as he added softly, 'There would be little point in remaining until the Earl dies. They would not let us near him.'

She dressed hurriedly as he did and he played maid again and hooked up the back of her gown, smiling tenderly at her awkward efforts to put to right her dishevelled hair and set her headdress straight.

'I think it is useless to hide our guilt from the others, my heart.'

'Dickon, what have we done?'

Her dismay further amused him. 'I swear you have done no wrong. As I said, we are betrothed, though no official ceremony was performed. Your father will not censure you. From the first you were destined to be my bride.' He reached up and touched the loveliness of her dark hair, now half concealed beneath her hood. 'I had to wait until you were grown. Now I know that was right, too, pre-ordained.'

They held a council within the parlour after supper. Wat and Simpkin were summoned from the stables to attend and Sir Adam, as the elder of the two gentlefolk, presided.

He glanced briefly at Richard and, on the determined lift of the younger man's chin which acknowledged his firm intention to leave in the morning, began to list their needs for the journey.

'We have obtained suitable horses,' he said. 'Simpkin has done wonders and purchased them cheaply and without too many awkward questions asked from a neighbourhood horse coper. Bess will pack food and supplies for us. I disembarked at Bishop's Lynn, as I believe you did last, Dickon. There the boatmen are sympathetic to our cause, but it would be too difficult now to cross the Thames estuary again. I think we should head for Rye and depend on our abilities to bribe some worthy owner of a suitable and seaworthy cog.'

Richard inclined his head.

'We have spare horses for Wat and Simpkin to return home later and the wagon can be disposed of in Rye. I think you should drive the wagon, Richard, for the first part of the journey. No.' He held up one hand to prevent Richard's heated protest at this indignity. 'You are still unfit for long hours in the saddle and will only delay us if you insist on trying. That would be plain foolishness.'

He glanced at Josh, who with Bess and Jake were listening in silence. 'Will you accompany us, Josh, to Burgundy? There might be questions asked at the Tower and some repercussions.'

'I've considered that, Sir Adam. We've decided to ride North, make for Yorkshire where we have sympathetic friends.' He sighed. 'Jake has agreed the good old Cockerel will have to be sacrificed. I am thinking of making for Barnard Castle.'

To this Jake gave a rueful grunt and Sir Adam glanced at Josh sharply as if his intended destination held some significance for him. Josh continued. 'We'll keep this house as a refuge. Only our friends know of our possession of it, so, in time, we can return here if there is need.'

Sir Adam was visibly relieved. To add a count of further persons to his company on some small cog, for which he would have to pay a considerable price to keep the owner from talking too freely, would have proved more difficult. Their plans for the morrow once made, he dismissed them all to their sleeping places, since an early start was necessary tomorrow, as soon after sunrise as was expedient.

Within her chamber with Mary and Philippa, Anne felt her colour heightening. She had been too intent on their council in the parlour to be embarrassed by what had taken place earlier between her and Richard and which she was sure was known to the company but neither girl looked at her oddly. When they were in bed together later, Philippa's hand stole out and gripped Anne's as a mark of her silent approval. Anne gave a deep sigh of gratitude and allowed herself to drift into sleep, her mouth breaking into a smile of contentment.

Anne had expected Richard to object next day to taking his place upon the driving seat of the wagon but he did not. They took affectionate farewells of the Aldreds and Jake and, with Simpkin and Sir Adam, mounted and taking their places on each side of the wagon, Wat beside Richard upon the driving bench and the spare horse tethered behind, they trundled out upon the highway once more to ride south.

Anne, with Philippa and Mary, had been provided with cushions to ease the discomfort of the hard seats and with their packs and basket of food beside them, settled themselves for the long hours ahead of them.

Anne's thoughts were blissful, despite the constant jolting. Soon Richard would take her before a priest and make her his wife. Then she would be able to sleep openly with him in the chambers of any inns they frequented. The crossing might be stormy at this time of year but she feared nothing if he were by her side and she looked forward eagerly to the new sights and sounds she would encounter at the Duchess's court at Malines.

Though she was now merely dowager Duchess of Burgundy, Margaret of York still wielded great power and influence in the province. If Anne was aware of the fact that she might not be able to return to England and Rushton and parted for a while from her parents and Ned, it carried but a momentary pang. She and Richard would not starve. The Duchess was known to be generous to Yorkist sympathisers and would see to that and, besides, her Dickon was resourceful.

Early in the afternoon Sir Adam led them off the main highway onto a narrower road. Clearly he knew the byways in this district and was used to making his way across rough country, but the road here was bad and the jolting of the wagon increased so much that the three women found themselves tossed from side to side until they became breathless and feared they might even be thrown out.

Mary grunted ominously but she made no complaint. Obviously it was necessary to quit the common highway where the wagon might be seen and identified, though Anne hoped and believed that once clear of London and after some days since Richard's release from the Tower, they would not be pursued. She gritted her teeth, held out her hand to Philippa, who grasped it hard, as they tossed and bounced together, determined to endure whatever discomfort without whining until they could take to a less rutted road again.

The road widened at last and became less strewn with boulders and potholes so that they were able to rest once more, bruised but still uncomplaining. Anne wondered how Richard was faring since he had been restless with pain yesterday, and if he would have been less uncomfortable if he had ridden. He turned and grinned at them.

The early morning had been cold and they had been glad of the sheltering canvas but it had become warmer now and the women settled themselves to doze. There was little to interest them on this unfrequented way bar one or two farm carts and a labourer trudging to or from his fields.

Anne was woken from an uneasy doze by a shout from Simpkin who had fallen behind when the road had narrowed again and now rode up to the wagon. Peering out the front between Richard and Wat Anne could see he was agitated.

'Mounted men behind us,' he panted, 'quite a company by the sound of them, and the glint of weapons or armour I glimpsed above the hedges as they rounded that bend over there. Why should such a company leave the main highway, sir, if it wasn't to catch up with us?'

Richard had pulled up the wagon close to Sir Adam who had been riding ahead. The knight turned in the saddle and shaded his eyes to look back to where Simpkin Cooper was pointing.

'He's right,' he said grimly. 'There are at least six of them, I'd say, judging by the sound of their horses' hooves, though I can't be sure yet.'

'It could be a posse of armed men-at-arms after some rogue in a hue and cry,' Richard said thoughtfully. 'Why should anyone seek to detain us? No one knew of our stay in Blackheath.'

'True,' Sir Adam agreed, 'but it's likely we are being sought and enquiries could have been made in Blackheath.'

'I hope to God not,' Richard said between his teeth. 'I dread to think what might have happened to Jake and the others.'

'Our wagon was well hidden at the house,' Adam said, 'any news of our passing could merely have been told as we left even when we turned off the road. Josh has made preparations to have his family out of there fast in case of need. They should be safe enough.' He looked round uneasily for signs of cover but there was none. They appeared to be trapped on the narrow road and the pursuit, if it was so, could catch up with them in a matter of minutes if they attempted flight. 'The question is, what do we do if we are attacked? We can only stand and fight.'

'The women folk could make off into the field.' Richard

was descending from the driving seat. Wat had already jumped down and, with Simpkin, was attending to his weapons, easing his sword in its sheath and moving his arrow quiver forward, ready for action.

Sir Adam looked towards the hawthorn hedges which bordered both sides of the road and shook his head. 'They would make little progress through those, hampered by their skirts. Best if they remain in the wagon where we can guard them.'

Mary was drawing her two charges out of sound and range of any arrow fire. Anne felt deadly calm now she could hear for herself the sound of thundering hooves approaching and saw that Philippa was shaking a little but outwardly composed.

'It could be robbers,' she murmured, 'and if so I am sure our menfolk are capable of dealing with them.'

Anne nodded but she feared the worst. Bands of robbers were rarely so well mounted or so well equipped with weaponry as Simpkin had guessed at from his one glimpse from far off. She leaned back against the wagon's timber side supports and drew Philippa close to her. Mary looked white-faced and wide-eyed with alarm, opposite.

Richard had instructed them to remain under cover of the canvas so Anne did not see the company burst into view around the final bend in the road behind them, but she could not fail to identify the authoritative voice which hailed them as that of John Hilyard. She caught her breath in a terrible gasp and Philippa silently touched her arm consolingly.

'Stand in the King's name.'

Anne, despite Richard's orders, leaned slightly forward to watch John Hilyard's approach. Her escort had all dismounted and stood clustered around the wagon, ready for action if threatened.

Sir Adam said courteously, 'We are merely escorting two

ladies with their attendants on a journey, sir. I fail to see why you should wish to detain us. We do not threaten the King's peace.'

Hilyard gave a harsh laugh. His men, five of them, had drawn up behind him and Anne could see they all wore the King's livery while John Hilyard himself was clad for once for action in leather jerkin under a gleaming mailed breast-plate and wore a metal salet. He remained mounted and his horse curvetted under him restlessly. The beast was sweat stained so Hilyard and his company had ridden hard since this morning.

He eyed Richard Allard and a sneer formed round his womanish mouth. 'I see you managed to crawl free despite my efforts. I can save you the trouble of further journeying and return you to custody in the Tower where you belong. Your fellow conspirators are all doomed. Warbeck paid the supreme penalty for his perfidy and the traitor Earl, Warwick, will mount the scaffold to the block on December the fourth.'

Anne spoke clearly from the inside of the wagon and half rose so he might see her.

'You mistake your purpose, Master Hilyard. Master Allsop is not your quarry. I hold a warrant for his release from the Tower sealed under the King's own hand.'

'You may do, Mistress Jarvis, but I'll warrant the King does not know that Master Allsop has added to his former crime by abducting Lady Philippa Telford, whom I am commanded to return to the Court where she will become a royal ward and resume her duties in attendance upon her Majesty.'

Sir Adam Westlake spoke quietly. 'Lady Philippa has expressed a wish to be returned to the care of her father, sir, with the Queen's leave, and we are merely escorting her home. Let us pass peaceably and there need be no bone of contention between us. Mistress Jarvis has informed you that you have no further business with Master Allsop, who is free to go whither he wishes.'

John Hilyard moved irritably in the saddle and his horse reared. The look he directed at Richard was full of venom. His men waited stolidly behind him for his commands.

Lady Philippa had come to the front of the wagon and whispered urgently to Sir Adam.

'There must be no trouble. Perhaps it would be better if I returned to Westminster with Master Hilyard.'

'Certainly you must not think of that,' Sir Adam returned sharply. 'Such a course would do your father inestimable harm and it is the Queen's express wish that you return to Burgundy. Leave this business to me, my lady.'

Philippa subsided on to the bench again but Anne could see she was deeply disturbed.

'I do not wish for anyone to be harmed while guarding me,' she said uncertainly.

Anne said with a little catch to her voice, 'Sir Adam knows what he is about; so does Richard. You must trust them implicitly, Philippa.'

'But your Richard is in no state to fight,' Philippa objected hotly.

Anne bit down savagely on her bottom lip. Well she knew that and her fear was rising by the moment.

She heard John Hilyard shout imperiously, 'Either surrender the lady or I will be forced to arrest all of you and carry you back to London.'

'Then you must fight us if you intend to do so,' Richard said very coolly and Anne's heart froze at the decisive note in his tone.

There was a pause and, peering forward again, Anne saw that John Hilyard had moved his mount back a little and was, apparently, conferring with his men. At last he called, 'So be it.'

Philippa gave a startled sob and Anne pulled her into a tight embrace as she heard the distinctive rasp of metal against leather as all the men of her escort pulled their swords from their sheaths. She stayed well under the canvas in obedience to instructions given earlier, knowing neither she nor Philippa could do any good by attempting to descend from the wagon or even leaving themselves in any way exposed which would tie the hands of the men set to guard them.

The worst of it was she could only sit in numb misery, unable to view the fight which began almost immediately. Mary was muttering prayers at her side as the two companies engaged with shouts, harsh cries and the clash of cold metal. Anne could just view Simpkin's solid back as he remained very close to the wagon to protect his female charges, thus allowing Sir Adam, Richard and Wat to engage the enemy.

Philippa was crying quietly and Anne impulsively hugged her yet closer. Her own fears were for Richard. He had seemed better today but he was, she knew, hampered by the hard treatment he had received at Hilyard's hands. How could he survive a fight to the death, outnumbered six to four, for this was what this combat was, in truth.

She knew also that, in honour, the men could have taken no other course. They could not surrender Philippa, nor, if they had done so, would any of their number been safe, for all would have been carted unceremoniously back to London to the tender mercy of the Tudor King.

It seemed to go on for hours, though Anne knew in truth the actual time was short. Simpkin shifted slightly and from time to time nocked an arrow to his bow and let fly. Each time that manoeuvre was followed by a startled gasp and a gurgling cry, proving how deadly formidable he was at his craft. She could just see beyond him now, over the top of Philippa's bent head. Three of the King's men were down, either dead or nursing wounds, she could not be sure. All had dismounted and were grimly fighting on foot, hand to hand.

As Sir Adam turned Anne saw that a bright stain was marring his jerkin but he was still grimly continuing the fight with John Hilyard. Wat and Richard were fighting off the remaining two of Hilyard's company who were grunting and doggedly battling hard for mastery. Another arrow found its mark in Wat's opponent's throat and he fell with a frothy, blood-streaked gurgle as his companions had.

Thus freed, Wat turned on Richard's attacker. Anne's heart was beating stridently as she saw her love beaten back. He was tiring, she recognised, that punishing ordeal of days back taking its effect. Philippa had sat up and, with Mary, was staring wide-eyed through the opening of the wagon canvas at the frantic struggles before her.

Richard's opponent turned with an oath to meet his fresh attacker and Simpkin's deadly feathered missive flew once more but missed its target. He, too, gave a muttered soldier's oath and, for the first time, left his post to join the fray. Sir Adam was steadily engaging Hilyard and, though a much older man, was clearly the master. Experience gained over long years of combat had held off his younger antagonist thus far but, now, he, too, was tiring.

Anne murmured a hasty prayer to the Virgin for his safe delivery. She turned fearfully to see with relief that Richard's attacker was now down but, as Richard sprang to assist Sir Adam, the knight gave a desperate cry as Hilyard's broadsword found its mark and he slipped and fell to one knee at the mercy of the younger man. Hilyard bent over his fallen foe and Anne saw the terrible glitter in those pale eyes as he showed his clear intent to finish the matter once and for all.

At that moment Anne saw Richard reveal the deadly skill she had glimpsed before in the wood near Northampton. There was a sudden streak of light as Richard's dagger flew from his hand and buried itself in Hilyard's back. He fell without so much as a sigh and Sir Adam staggered to his feet to recover himself and look down at the man dispassionately.

Richard strode up, seemingly unhurriedly calm, but Anne, jumping from the wagon now, understood that he could not have hastened if his life had depended upon it. He was staggering and she rushed to his side and helped him to stand upright. Sir Adam was feeling his side gingerly.

'He's dead as a stone, Dickon, praise the Lord. He almost had me. I'm bleeding like a stuck pig.'

Mary had descended more slowly and Simpkin was helping Lady Philippa down. Two of the wounded men-at-arms scrambled to their feet, one holding tightly to a gash in his arm and the other, clearly injured in the thigh. Both turned towards the victors as if expecting further repercussions, but Richard shrugged and the two stumbled off to lick their wounds down the road to the nearest cover.

Anne assisted Richard to the wagon and he heaved himself up into the driving seat, nodding and grunting approval as he saw Mary tearing up cloth from one of the saddle bags to tend Sir Adam.

'Is it bad?' he demanded.

'Not bad enough to deter me from riding until we reach the port.'

Wat and Simpkin were engaged in the grim business of pulling the remaining bodies beneath the hedgerows. Wat hacked a way through so that the two could dispose of their burdens well out of sight into the field beyond.

Simpkin emerged and came back to the wagon. 'There's a dry ditch on the far side, Master Richard. It may be some time before Master Hilyard is discovered.'

'Good.' Richard gently disengaged himself from Anne's clinging grasp. 'There, sweetheart, I'm cut and bruised and feel like death itself but I'll manage to reach the port, never fear, and we must not delay. Those two men-at-arms could raise a hue and cry at the nearest village though I doubt they will. Both of them have had enough trouble for one day and my guess is they'll lay up for a while, but we dare not risk it.' He glanced at Sir Adam for confirmation. 'I think, if you are well enough, we should abandon the wagon and take to horseback.'

'Aye, I agree.'

'It will mean sacrificing some of our valuables but that cannot be helped. Wat, take Mary pillion behind you, as I will your mistress. Lady Philippa can ride behind Simpkin.' He shook his head as Adam sought to protest. 'My friend, I think you'll have enough trouble staying in the saddle without a further burden.'

Reluctantly Sir Adam nodded agreement.

Anne watched bleakly as the exchanges were made, what could be taken removed from the wagon and put into saddle bags, and the tethered horses saddled. The men mounted and took up their pillion passengers, all of which, instantly recognising need, made no interruption nor objections to what was proposed, though Mary obviously was deeply concerned for Sir Adam's hurt, Anne could see.

She looked round at the site of the recent struggle, uttering a brief prayer for all who had died, especially for the over-ambitious John Hilyard whom she had, only weeks ago, thought she had admired, then she took Richard's hand as he reached down to draw her up and mounted behind him. Throughout the rest of the nightmare ride she kept both arms firmly linked round his waist, feeling the reassuring beat of his heart and thankful that he had been spared to her.

They rode across country to Sir Adam's direction until, at last, as night fell, they saw the roofs of Rye etched blackly across the greying skyline ahead of them.

Chapter Eleven

It was Richard who took complete charge once they reached the port for, by this time, Sir Adam was fainting in the saddle. An inn was found for the party near the quay and, once having established them and acquired a private chamber for the ladies, Richard set off directly to enquire about passage to Damme harbour, the port of Bruges.

Sir Adam was assisted upstairs by Wat, and Mary and Anne set about treating his wound. Blood was seeping through the improvised bandage Mary had fashioned and it was clear that the terrible gash in the left thigh must be cleansed and stitched. Anne would have liked to summon a surgeon, but Sir Adam was adamant that time could not be spared for it.

'We must embark as soon as possible,' he said weakly. 'Hilyard's body could be discovered if his men report and a hue and cry could follow. The King has spies in every main town and port so it is essential Richard obtains passage for us quickly.' He smiled bravely as Anne produced her hussif with its needle and thread.

The wound was cleansed with wine and water and probed for any scrap of fabric which could give rise to infection and Anne set about the task of stitching, Sir Adam having previously primed himself with good wine against the agony. Anne had seen her mother perform this service for workmen and labourers on the manor, but blanched at the task which she had never before attempted.

Philippa did not shirk her task of holding the stricken knight steady by the shoulders while Mary and Anne set about their work.

Anne carefully drew together the torn skin and, avoiding the eye of her patient, began. Sir Adam bucked once under Philippa's hold and Anne paused, uncertain whether she should summon Wat or Simpkin from below, but Sir Adam muttered thickly that he would prefer the women to manage alone and promised to hold still. At last, the grim task was accomplished and the wound padded and bandaged once more. Sir Adam appeared very white about the mouth and deathly tired, but professed he would do well now that the bleeding had stopped.

Richard returned within the hour as Anne was rising from her cramped position by the bed.

He nodded, satisfied, as Sir Adam complimented Anne upon her skilful handiwork.

'I found a captain willing to take a substantial bribe,' Richard announced, 'though he fears a storm by tomorrow and says we must sail on this evening's tide. Are you well enough, Adam?'

'Of course I am. It will be time to summon physicians if needed once we disembark at Damme.' He moved fretfully. 'I shall rest easy only when Lady Philippa is safely with her parents again.'

Richard signalled to Anne that he wished to speak to her alone and she followed, faintly mystified. She was still feeling shaky after having finished her frightening task.

The taproom was, for the moment, empty and Richard

drew Anne to a corner behind one of the larger casks of ale.

He hesitated for a moment, his hand still resting imperatively upon her shoulder and she knew he had something unpleasant to say to her. She waited anxiously until at last he cleared his throat and said hastily, 'I have decided that you should return to your father with Wat and Simpkin. There could be hazards ahead of us and I want no part of the difficulties and discomforts we will be forced to take for you.'

At first she could not believe what she was hearing. She stood, eyes wide, staring back at him.

'You cannot mean it.'

'Yes, Anne, I mean it. Who knows how long I shall be forced to remain in exile? True, I have the King's pardon, but since then I have killed his squire of the body and challenged his will once more over the matter of taking Lady Philippa Telford from his charge. You have said many times that you would not wish to wed a man with such an uncertain future.'

She swallowed the painful lump which was forming in her throat. Her own words, used to threaten her happiness: she realised the justice of it.

To goad him she said, desperately, 'You have used me and now wish to discard me.'

He took her by the shoulders and shook her hard. 'Do not dare say this to me. You know I love you with every drop of my blood and fibre of my being. Do you think it is simple for me to part from what has become the very centre of my life? Your father will understand my need. Wait for my word at Rushton and—if I cannot return before the year's end to claim you I will release you from any betrothal vows. There, you can wed one of those fine young country sprigs whose whole allegiance is to King Henry.'

She drew back from him, white about the mouth as Sir Adam had been following surgery and as pained by his words.

'If you sail without me, I shall jump into the sea and follow you.'

He stared back at her as if she were insane. 'And can you swim?'

She said grimly, 'That will be for you to discover. I went to the Nene often enough with Ned.'

He turned away and she heard him mutter something beneath his breath and then he turned round again, jerked her to him and crushed her so close that she feared she would not be able to breathe.

At last he said hoarsely, 'Dear God, how can I ever have done anything to deserve such a woman?' For a second he held her at arm's length again, gazing deeply into her eyes. 'Are you sure? Do you know what you face? We have little gold now that I have bribed the ship owner. Life could be hard—and dangerous.'

She said breathlessly, 'I discovered I wanted you and no other the day I saw you face the boar, perhaps even before that when you killed that spy in the wood. Dickon, my darling, I truly believe I could not live without you. I would rather hazard myself in the sea if you leave me.'

She was tight against his heart again and he was kissing her hair, pushing back the linen of her cap to glory in the silky tresses. 'Never, my sweet love, never,' he murmured throatily. 'Never, while I live. Then if it is truly your wish we will leave together. Simpkin can carry letters to your father and I will take you before a priest and wed you the moment we reach Malines.'

Her happiness was so great she could find no words to answer him.

* * *

An hour later, after they had taken an early supper, Wat came up to the chamber and assisted Sir Adam down to the taproom while Richard was overseeing with Simpkin the final preparations for departure. Philippa had gone down to be with Sir Adam and Mary was packing up and checking the medicaments they had used to treat Sir Adam's wound. Anne looked at her keenly and thought she detected signs of recent tears on her maid's cheeks. For some time she had become aware that there was a growing fondness between Mary Scroggins and Wat Glazier and she realised, with a faint sigh, that Mary was finding the coming parting decidedly distressing.

She said decisively, 'Mary, I know you are hardly looking forward to this voyage. Lady Philippa and I could manage, you know. Would it not be sensible for you to return to Rushton with Wat and Simpkin?'

Mary turned on her in a flash, her cheeks red with indignation.

'Mistress Anne, you were entrusted to my care. I shall not leave you and Lady Philippa until she is with her father and you are true wife to Master Richard. How could I answer to your father or his, if I left you unchaperoned?'

Anne put a gentle hand on Mary's shoulder. 'But I am right, aren't I? You would like to be with Wat?'

'Aye.' Mary blinked back angry tears. 'Well, he'll have to bide his time, won't he?'

Simpkin had come up to the chamber to carry down the final small chest and, obviously, had caught the gist of what had been said.

'Mistress Anne,' he said thoughtfully. 'I've been considering. Your two gentlemen are in no state to face any further attacks from robbers in the Burgundian countryside, at least not until Sir Adam's wound has healed. You could do with one sturdy man with you till you reach the Duchess's court. I think Wat should go, and stay while he's needed. I've already spoken of it to Master Richard and he's in agreement. I can deal with selling the surplus horses and ride back to Rushton with the messages for Sir Guy.'

Mary's face lit up as if illumined from within as she turned to see if Anne approved the suggestion.

'Oh, yes, Simpkin,' Anne agreed. 'Provided you feel safe to travel alone.'

'Aye, mistress, I can travel faster and safer that way.'

So it was decided and Wat was rowed out with the small party to the waiting cog which was to carry them to Damme.

As the night mist rose and hid Rye harbour from them as the cog moved out into the swell, Anne stood with Richard near the forecastle, attempting to catch her last glimpse of England.

She gave a faint sigh and he turned to her, his grey eyes glinting oddly in the uncertain light. 'You are not regretting your decision, my heart?'

'No, Richard, of course not. I look forward eagerly to new sights and adventures.'

He grimaced. 'Not too many of the latter, I hope. It seems I have had far too many of those of late.'

She was silent for moments then she asked, 'Richard?'

'Mmm?'

'When we took our leave of Josh and Bess he mentioned travelling north to Castle Barnard and both you and Sir Adam looked at each other in a—well, shifty manner. What is there at Castle Barnard?'

He hesitated for a moment. 'Did your father never tell you that he conducted Prince Edward there just after the late King's coronation?'

She looked up into his face, startled. 'No. The prince, the elder of King Edward's sons?'

'Yes. He was conveyed there for his own safety after threats to the life of him and his brother and to learn military prowess. He was there early in 1485, for I saw him myself when I attended Lord Lovell on a visit of inspection to the north.'

'And after Redmoor?' she breathed curiously, eyes very wide. 'What happened to him?'

'Who knows? The King might well have sent word north while he himself was at Nottingham preparing to ride south to Market Bosworth. He may have been conveyed to safety overseas as Prince Richard was. Of course...' He broke off, shrugging regretfully.

'You think he might have been put to death, like the Earl of Warwick is soon to be—by King Henry?'

He frowned. 'I do not think so. Henry's behaviour, since Redmoor, suggests that he is as unsure about the fates of the princes as the rest of us.'

'And you are beginning to believe that Perkin Warbeck was indeed, Richard of York?'

'I cannot be sure, but no one who saw him as close as I did to the Earl could doubt that they were related. Adam believed in his royal identity, but he was deeper always in the Duchess's confidence than I.' He sighed again heavily. 'Josh goes north to try to find a new leader for his cause. I wish him well.'

Fearfully she pressed, 'And you, will you seek a new leader?'

He drew her close again, 'No my love, I shall have a wife soon and, in the blessedness of time, a child, I hope. They must have all my love and loyalty now. And, too, you are right in what you once said. It is time the realm of England is allowed some measure of peace after all the storms of these many years. This coming alliance with

Spain may very well grant us that and continued prosperity.'

She leaned her head upon his shoulder again and gave a prayer of profound gratitude to the Virgin that her most earnest desire would be granted and that, despite all the hardships facing them, she would be enabled, at last, to live in total happiness and security with her Richard.

* * * * *